Decoding the Heart
Profiling the Heart 1
Stephanie R. Caffrey

Cover Art Design by: Kelly Moran/Rowan Prose Publishing
Photo Credit: Adobe Images/Deposit Photos
First Edition
ISBN: 978-1-961967-60-1
Rowan Prose Publishing, LLC
www.RowanProsePublishing.com
Published in the United States of America

OTHER BOOKS BY STEPHANIE R. CAFFREY:

Mistaken Identity
Be My Little Baby
London Detective Agency

To my parents, who have always supported and believed in me.

Acknowledgements

I can't believe this is my third novel. If you told me I would be writing the acknowledgements of a third novel five years ago, I would have laughed at you. This dream seemed almost impossible, and yet, here I am!

First and foremost, I want to thank Kelly and Katie at Rowan Prose Publishing. Thank you so much for believing in me and my writing. All of your support through the entire process has been invaluable. You have made me feel like I'm part of a family, and I'll be forever grateful for that. You have made this such a fun experience.

Thank you, Sydney, you have been an amazing friend and so supportive. You have read everything I've written for over a decade and offered your editing and critique expertise, and I cannot imagine doing this with anyone else by my side.

Laura, I don't even know what to say. You've been an immense help, with both reading and offering critiques, to allowing me to text you constantly with ideas. You're an amazing friend, and I love that book club brought you into my life.

Amanda, I'm so happy that you were willing to read this book for me! You're right in my target audience, and getting the opinion of someone who is not in my writing circle. Your honesty and enthusiasm was amazing, and I can't wait for you to read the next book!

To my SAHM Book Club, I love you ladies, and love your support over the years, especially showing up and reading my books! You guys rock!

Super Awesome Book Club – You guys also rock! You let me bounce ideas off of you, and you also showed up for me and supported my own books. I love you guys so much!

Sharon, Jamie, and Sarah. I don't know what I would do without you three. You're more than my friends, you're my sisters, and I know I wouldn't be where I am without you. I never would have had the confidence to pursue any of this without you guys by my side.

Nikki and Kate – God really blessed me with giving me you as sisters. Not a day goes by without us talking in some way, and our relationship has only grown deeper over the last few years.

Mom and Dad – Thank you for being so supportive of me and believing in me.

Arthur – it's been so fun watching you grow up, and I love that I wrote the first draft of this right alongside you as you did your own writing.

Bea – Thank you for letting mommy write in between helping you discover your independence.

And finally, to my Matthew. Thanks for loving me and constantly providing me inspiration for creating the heroes of my stories. Someday you'll read my books, and I hope you see yourself in each and every one of them.

Chapter One

MATTHEW

Friday, May 15

"You can't possibly be the only driver who works this early, Jorge." Matthew Grant opened the door to the car and slid his duffel bag onto the seat. "I'm starting to think you have an alert set up to tell you when I'm requesting an Uber."

The driver of the compact sedan turned back to look at him as he slid into the almost too small for his frame backseat. "You know me, Matty, I'm obsessed with the true crime. And you, my friend, are always a source to feed my addiction."

Matthew laughed, shaking his head. "And I always tell you I can't discuss my case."

Jorge turned back around and put the car in drive. Traffic wasn't heavy in Matthew's neighborhood this early in the morning, so he had no problem pulling away from the curb and into the right lane.

"I know, but you always end up giving me a little kernel to tide me over until you get home. So, what is it this time?"

"Serial killer." He shifted so his long legs didn't feel so cramped behind the passenger seat. He really needed to remember to remind Jorge to pull the seat as far forward as possible next time. "Three victims so far."

"Local? I haven't heard anything on the news, but I've been keeping strange hours."

"No, not local, hence the four thirty drive to the Bureau. Midwest somewhere, I think. I wasn't fully away when my director made the wake-up call."

Jorge let out a low whistle. "Midwest is not exactly the place that comes to mind when I think serial killer. My brain immediately goes somewhere big, like here in DC, or like New York, or something."

"BTK was in Kansas. John Wayne Gacy, Illinois. Jeffrey Dahmer, Wisconsin. The people who commit these crimes can be anywhere, and with the right triggers, will act on their nascent desires."

"Here I am claiming to be a true crime fan and forgot where those notorious serial killers hunted."

"Sometimes, it's easy to superimpose your beliefs into the narrative. You think serial killers only really exist in large coastal cities, so you've placed the narratives of these notorious killers in those locations."

Jorge chuckled. "You're doing your profiler thing on me."

"I'm sorry," Matthew apologized.

"No, man, I love it. I welcome it. Makes me feel part of the whole thing, you know?"

Matthew laughed. "I'll remember that for next time."

They pulled up in front of the FBI Academy building, the twelve minute drive from his home in Garrisonville having gone quickly, as it always does when he was in the car with Jorge.

"Thanks for the ride, as always."

Jorge reached into his cup holder and stretched back. Matthew took the card from his hands.

"That's my personal number. When you get back in town, call me and I'll give you a ride home. I won't have to stalk the app that way."

Matthew pocketed the card. "Thanks, I'll call you. I don't know what time or when—"

"Just call me. Don't matter the time or whatever. This is my side hustle, but I work from home, and it's very flexible. I want to hear whatever you can tell me about this new Midwest serial killer."

Matthew opened the door, grabbed his duffel, and threw the strap over his shoulder. "I will tell you everything I can. I promise."

"Hope you catch the asshole."

"I hope we do too."

Matthew walked through the glass doors of the small meeting room, completely bypassing a stop at his desk. If he stopped, he would get dragged into something else he was working on and be late for the debrief. He prided himself on being one of the first of his Behavioral Analysis Unit team to arrive at the debrief. It probably stemmed from being one of the youngest on the team. The need to always prove himself. Even after nearly a decade of him being on the team, he still couldn't let it go.

Sure enough, looking around the room, the only other person present was Thomas Flemming, the director and team leader, sitting at the head of the single table, watching the door for his team. He was in his early sixties, but nowhere near ready to retire. And of course, even with all the stresses of the job, his face didn't give a clue as to how old he was, the Black skin of his face as smooth as Matthew's.

"Matty, first, as always. I don't know how you do it."

"I could say the same to you. Do you live here?"

Thomas gave him a wry smile. "Well, honestly, Carla and I are not in the best place right now, so I've been spending a lot of time here. It's why I could get the call so quickly."

"I'm sorry, man, want to talk about it?" Matthew cringed. He didn't know why he asked that. Silently, he hoped Thomas would turn him down.

Thomas cocked his head to the side, looking at Matthew strangely. "You want to talk to me about my marriage problems?"

Matthew shrugged, forcing a smile on his face he was certain looked more like a grimace. "Yes?"

Thomas shook his head, eyebrow still raised. raised. "Advice from my co-worker, who is perpetually single and two decades younger than me? No, thank you."

Matthew held his hand over his heart, letting out the breath he was holding. "Ouch."

"What in that sentence wasn't true?"

"It was all true, but as they say, truth hurts."

"If I'm going to get advice from anyone, I'm going to get it from Logan. The only one of us in a stable, happy relationship."

"Great idea. Logan would give much better than advice than I ever could."

As if summoned by the mention of his name, Logan Hayes came waltzing in through the door to the conference room. The next senior member of the team didn't look as put together as he normally did, his sandy blond hair hadn't been shellacked into place yet. He must have spent much longer saying goodbye to his husband.

"What will I be better at than you?"

"Giving relationship advice."

Logan grinned widely, causing the crow's feet on either side of his blue eyes to deepen. "Hell, yes. Who needs advice? Thomas? Everything okay with you and Carla?"

Thomas opened his mouth to answer, but was saved when the door opened again, letting in Millie Driscoll and Trevor Ford, the last two members of the team.

Millie and Trevor had joined the team around the same time, shortly before Matthew had. It was a running joke that they came as a pair.

Millie, with her black curly hair and fair complexion, looked every bit the part of someone who had a goth phase growing up, was one of the nicest people Matthew had ever met, but don't let her being the only female on the team lure you into false presumptions. She was definitely the toughest member of the team. Willing to take steps others weren't.

They were lucky to have managed to snap Trevor up when they did. He was the best hacker around. His caramel skin and dark brown eyes were a definite contrast to Millie's paler complexion. The two were best friends, and always together.

"Alright, we're all here. Let's go over what we know," Thomas said.

Trevor moved to the front of the room and connected his laptop to the HDMI cable. Once he opened the screen, a map projected onto the TV screen behind him.

Everyone took their seats, Matthew settling in between Millie and Logan, Thomas taking his place next to Trevor in the front of the room.

"Here's what we know," Thomas began. "Cove Creek, Iowa is a city with a population of about twelve thousand. In the last three months, there have been three murders."

Trevor pressed a button, and three crime scene photos came up on the screen. He touched the first one, enlarging it.

"Victim number one, killed three months ago, on February 20th. His name was Mark Lovett, age thirty-five. Blunt force trauma to the head and strangled."

He changed the picture.

"Victim number two, killed two weeks ago. His name was John Davies, age thirty-five. Same MO as Lovett."

He queued the next image.

"Victim number three, killed yesterday. His name was David Crandall, age thirty-five. Same MO as the other two."

"He's escalating," Matthew spoke up. "His cool-down period was approximately a quarter of the time between vics two and three as it was between one and two."

"Which is why we were called in," Thomas explained. "The local authorities are concerned with how little time has passed between the last two victims. Cove Creek is not a large town, and the fact that someone is killing their men is becoming very concerning."

"Any connection between our victims?" Millie asked.

"Other than age, there doesn't seem to be anything obvious. Mark and John were married with young children but didn't really run in the same social circles. David was single, and again at the surface level didn't seem to hang out with either Mark or David. But these are things I'm planning to dig into further as we get fully into the case. I haven't had time yet," Trevor said.

"Are you staying at the office, or coming with us?" Matthew asked.

"Coming. I don't know what the cell phone coverage is like in small town Iowa, and I want to make sure I'm close so we can communicate."

"The more feet on the ground in Cove Creek, the better. We want to make sure there aren't any more victims than there are already. Take care of what you need to in order to be ready for a long-term stay. Wheels up in thirty." Thomas dismissed them, and they all stood to leave the room.

Matthew stretched as the plane landed. Three hours of sitting in one spot took a toll on his back. He wasn't as young as he used to be. He stood and gathered his things.

"Matthew and Logan will head out to take a look at the crime scene. Trevor, Millie, and I will head to the precinct and talk to the chief and get Trevor set up in a room there."

"Sounds good." Matthew preferred heading out to the crime scene over talking to the other officers. He wanted a clear head when he took everything in, without the influence of other people. Millie always joked the crime scene could speak to him, but he didn't think that was wrong. He didn't fully understand why his brain worked the way it did, but whenever he surveilled a crime scene, it was as if it were really talking to him. He could see things no one else could. Which is why nine times out of ten, Thomas would send him to the crime scene first.

He stepped onto the concrete ground in the hangar and spotted the Bureau vehicles parked about twelve feet away. He and Logan fell into step, heading toward the nearest of the black SUVs. Logan stepped into the driver's seat while Matthew climbed into the passenger seat. As soon as he had the belt clipped around him, Logan pulled out of the hangar.

As they drove, Matthew opened the folder he had been reading on the plane.

"What can we expect?" Logan asked.

"Well, we're heading to Murphy's Woods, a popular hiking and biking trail here. It's where all three bodies were found."

"Dumping ground or murder location?"

"From what I can tell, dumping ground."

Logan sighed. "I hate when they move the bodies."

"Well, maybe we'll luck out and he didn't move them very far."

It didn't take long to get to Murphy's Woods. The town was on the smaller side. Logan pulled the SUV into a parking lot that butted up against a wooded area. The local police officer was already there, waiting.

"You know, when I think woods, I like to think of them being a little bit more remote than this." Logan gestured toward the sidewalk where there was a bike fixing station, a water fountain, and a bathroom, all leading toward the paved trail that led into the copse of trees.

"Yeah, not exactly what I was picturing in my head when I read the name or saw the pictures of where the bodies were found," Matthew replied.

"Not remote. Seems like it could possibly be very populated. How did this guy get the bodies here without anyone seeing anything?"

"Good question."

The two men pushed open their doors and stepped out. It was mid-May, the sun was at its highest point, and the temperature was rising. At the cusp of summer in Iowa, it was warm. Too warm for all the layers Matthew wore to look professional.

He should have forgone the suit jacket once he learned he was going to the scene.

"Agents," the officer on scene greeted them. "I'm officer Smith." She reached out and offered her hand.

"I'm Special Agent Grant, and this is Special Agent Hayes," Matthew said, taking her hand, followed by Logan. "Are there any cameras or anything in this park?"

Officer Smith shook her head. "Unfortunately, no. If there were, our jobs would be a lot easier."

"Can you take us to where they found the bodies?"

"Right this way."

They started down the trail. As they entered the woods, the trees grew denser, causing everything to fall into shadows. On either side of the trail, native grasses grew uncontrolled, and Matthew was pretty sure he spotted some poison ivy in the mix. It was early in the season, but the grass was already about six inches high.

"Who found the bodies?" Matthew asked.

"A bicyclist found the first one. Since it was February, he was easy to spot. It was an unusually warm day, otherwise he wouldn't have been found as quickly. These trails are almost abandoned in the winter except for the rare dog walker or bicyclist. Joggers found the second one. Again, everything was still dormant, so it was easy to spot. A family out doing our county's annual geocache challenge found the most recent victim. Their five-year-old son tripped over the body. With the grasses so high, he was not as noticeable as the last two."

Matthew grimaced. That poor kid. He would be in therapy for a long time, processing the sort of trauma that comes with finding a dead body.

As they walked, Matthew glanced around at their surroundings. The trail, while it was in the "woods" wasn't really in an isolated area. In fact, he could see the backs of houses peeking through the trees.

"Do any of these houses have cameras pointed toward the trail? Or wildlife cameras?" Matthew asked.

"No," Officer Smith replied. "Unfortunately, if they have cameras on the backs of their houses, they are pointed at their own property. And since the only wildlife we tend to get are the white-tail deer, which are here in an abundance, there are no wildlife cameras."

"That's unfortunate, because this isn't exactly an isolated area," Logan said.

"It is not," Matthew agreed. "With these houses barely concealed by the trees? The traffic on this trail? Our UNSUB is bold. There's no privacy here."

"Narcissistic," Logan added.

"Yeah, definitely dealing with a narcissist."

"We're here," Officer Smith said, coming to a stop in front of a large copse of trees.

The ground was overgrown and the grass was pressed down to create a makeshift path from the trail to the tree just wide enough for a person to walk through. Lots of people walked off trail here, probably because of the county geocache. The tree was probably where it was hidden.

"The bodies..." Matthew started.

"Were found about five feet from the trail." Officer Smith gestured in the direction of the tree.

"All of them? In this specific area?" Logan asked.

"All of them. Right here. Same spot."

"So, this is the dumping ground." Matthew clarified.

"Yes."

Matthew looked at the long grass. It looked like it would come about mid-calf. "How much poison ivy will I get if I wade in there?"

"You're wearing long pants, so I wouldn't worry," Officer Smith said.

Matthew nodded as he looked down, his forehead wrinkling. He took a deep breath and let it out. He would trust the local that this wouldn't end with him getting an unbearable rash. He stepped into the grass and cringed as the thorns on one of the plants caught on his slacks.

"Remind me to dress in my jeans the next time we come out here," he called to Logan.

"Noted."

Matthew carefully moved toward the spot Officer Smith had pointed out. As he got closer, it became fairly obvious. There was a depression in the grass about the size of a body.

"Found the spot," he called out.

Matthew squatted down to get a better look. The spot didn't look any different from the rest of the area. He glanced back toward the trail. They weren't far apart. He looked beyond the trail, and it seemed the trees were thicker here, the houses were more concealed. Matthew turned his head. Same on this side. If there was any spot in the woods he would call isolated, this would be it.

"Officer Smith, are there any houses beyond these trees?" he gestured in both directions.

"One or two, but mostly farmland on either side," she answered. "The neighborhood to the left ends in a cul-de-sac, the other side hasn't sold out to the developers yet."

"Our UNSUB has to be really familiar with the trail to know exactly where the houses stop and the farmland begins," Logan said.

"Yeah, but he also dragged a body incredibly far down this trail in order to dump it somewhere without any homes. Any of the owners of the other houses could have seen him. Especially in February when the trees would be bare." Matthew made his way back to the trail. "We're looking at someone who can carry a grown man quite a distance."

"UNSUB? You have said that word twice now, and I have to admit, I'm not familiar with it," Officer Smith said.

"Unknown Subject," Logan explained.

"We should head to the hotel and catch up with the others." Matthew smacked a mosquito that had landed on his neck. "And we can come back out here when we're more prepared for the elements."

Matthew pulled the SUV to a stop in front of a red brick building. He checked the address on the GPS against the address on the property.

"You sure we have the right place?" Logan asked. "This doesn't look like any hotel we normally stay in.

The structure looked like it had been built in the late nineteenth or early twentieth century and had once been a large house originally before being taken over as a hotel. Two stories tall, and completely made of brick, it had white trim, and a beautiful flower garden out front, surrounding a covered porch. It was very quaint, as if it had been taken out of time.

"It's the right address. And it says Noble Hill Hotel on the sign, so I'm guessing, yes. We're in the right place," Matthew answered.

"Looks nicer than the roach motels we're usually put up in when we come to these small towns," Logan observed.

"It does. I don't think I'll need to worry about bed bugs here."

"Or our room looking like someone could have been murdered there."

"Or they use it to film porn."

"Or it's haunted."

Matthew laughed. "I wouldn't rule haunting out here. This place definitely looks like it could be haunted."

They laughed before opening the doors to the SUV, reaching behind their seats to grab their duffels.

Matthew clicked the key lock as they headed up the brick pathway to the front door. The covered porch had several cushioned chairs and tables spread out across it, creating an inviting space to spend a morning drinking coffee or an evening drinking wine.

He pushed the wooden door open and stepped into the inviting entry way. The hardwood floors glistened under the various throw rugs. The room was decorated period appropriately with antiques scattered around; the couches looking both inviting but also like you probably shouldn't sit on them.

The desk sat empty, with a sign telling them to ring the bell for service. Instead of a period appropriate brass push bell, it was a wireless doorbell. Matthew pushed it and waited.

A door opened from the back of the building and shut. The creaking floorboards indicating that someone was coming.

"I'm sorry to have kept you waiting," a female voice said before appearing around the corner. "I wasn't expecting anyone so early."

Matthew did a double take. He was expecting an elderly woman. Wasn't that who usually ran places like this? Instead, he was greeted by a woman in her thirties. She was wearing baggy olive overalls over a black t-shirt, her long dark hair was pulled up in a messy ponytail, and she was trying to flatten flyaway hair with her hands as she walked toward them.

"When you called to book the place, you implied you wouldn't be in until much later, so I laid down to take a quick nap. I'm so sorry."

Matthew shook his head, telling himself not to stare.

"We're in early," Logan spoke up. "Turns out we were not prepared to traipse around in the woods."

The woman looked them up and down as she took her place behind the desk. "I'll say. At least you're wearing long pants. Poison ivy is terrible this year." She opened the laptop on her desk and typed in the password. "Alright, which two are you?"

"Hayes and Grant," Logan answered.

Matthew couldn't seem to find his voice. And he couldn't stop staring at the woman. There was something wrong with him.

"Right. You two are neighbors. Rooms five and seven. Upstairs. Here are your keys," she pulled two keys off the cork board behind her. "Breakfast is in the dining room starting from seven, but you can have access to the kitchen for other meals if you would like. Let's see what else. I keep the door unlocked until around ten, but if you're staying out later, please let me know and I'll keep it unlocked a little longer. I live here on the premises, I'll be here through the weekend, but on weekdays I'm at my other job. I feel like I'm forgetting something..."

"Your name?" Matthew cringed at how loud he sounded. "You haven't told us your name."

She laughed, and Matthew was certain he had never heard a more beautiful sound. "Rebecca. My name is Rebecca."

She met his gaze and smiled widely at him. And he swore his heart skipped a beat when his brown eyes met her hazel eyes.

"We'll get out of your hair and let you get back to your nap." Logan swiped both keys off the counter and handed one to Matthew. "The others won't be here for a while. They aren't in the outdoors."

Rebecca laughed again. "Noted. Have a pleasant stay."

"Thanks," Matthew said, turning around, his cheeks burning.

He and Logan headed toward the stairs, but not before he looked over his shoulder at Rebecca again. Their eyes met, and he turned away quickly.

"Dude," Logan said as they walked up the stairs. "You're acting like you've never seen an attractive woman before."

"Pretty sure I haven't until now."

Chapter Two

REBECCA

Friday, May 15

Rebecca stared at the backs of the two men as they made their way to the stairs and their rooms. Her gaze focused on the one who asked her name. There was something about him...Shaking her head, she was about to turn around and head back to her apartment, when the door to the hotel opened again.

Three more people walked in, led by a tall Black man.

"Welcome to the Noble Hill," Rebecca greeted, plastering a smile on her face.

"Hello," the Black man greeted. "I'm Thomas Fleming. I'm the Unit Chief of the Behavioral Analysis Unit. I think you're expecting us?"

Rebecca nodded. "I am. Two of your agents just finished checking in."

"Matty and Logan," the other man in the group said. He had caramel skin and dark hair. She didn't want to make any assumptions, but he looked Latino.

"They must have finished up at the crime scene quickly," the lone woman answered.

"Yes," Thomas answered "Can we check in? I'll text Matty and Logan and tell them we need to meet up and talk."

"Meet up where? The police station is obviously out," The woman said.

"Is there a problem?" Rebecca cringed. She was caught out listening in on their conversation.

"Typically, we set ourselves up to work at the local police station, however, your local station is being less than welcoming to us," Thomas replied.

"Well, your group has booked all of our rooms, so we aren't expecting anyone else. You could set up in our dining room. We serve breakfast there every morning, otherwise it sits unused."

"Do you have a decent internet connection?" the man who wasn't Thomas asked.

"We do. We have fiber."

"Trevor," the man reached out in introduction. "I'm the tech guru, and you've just made my job a lot easier. You never know what you're going to get in small towns like this as far as internet goes."

"Rebecca." She took his hand giving it a firm shake.

"As long as we're doing introductions, I feel like I should introduce myself. "I'm Millie."

Rebecca shook her hand as well. "Nice to meet all of you. I'll tell you what I told the other agents. I'm the night manager here. I live in the apartment in the back. If I am not at the desk, there is a doorbell here that you can push, and it will notify me and I'll be out in a few minutes."

She handed them each a key. "Here are the keys to your rooms. And as I said, feel free to set yourself up in the dining room."

"Thank you so much," Thomas said.

"Enjoy your stay!"

Rebecca watched as the agents left and sighed with relief. She was so happy they all checked in early so she could potentially have an early night. She checked to make sure the doorbell was visible and headed to her apartment. She shut the door behind her, leaning against it, letting out a long sigh.

"You okay, mom?"

She turned her head toward the living area. Her eight-year-old son, Benji, was sitting on the couch holding his book, looking at her with concern in his eyes.

"I'm fine, exhausted, but fine."

"I can make us dinner, if you want."

Rebecca smiled. Ever since her husband died a little over a year ago, Benji had stepped up, trying to fill in the gaps where she needed help. While it was very sweet, it killed her that he had had to grow up so quickly.

"It's Friday. Since our usual Friday Fun Night plans are canceled, let's do our own thing! How about we order in a pizza and watch something on Netflix instead?"

Benji perked up. "Can I choose what we watch?"

"Absolutely."

He set aside his book and picked up the TV remote. "I'm going to look for something to watch. Where are you going to get pizza from?"

"I don't know. Casey's?"

"Yes! Casey's pizza is the best."

Rebecca smiled to herself as she picked up her phone and opened the Casey's app. It was rare these days for Benji to be excited about anything.

After his dad died, he became withdrawn, and even more serious than he already was. She and Jaime had always joked they were raising a miniature adult ever since Benji was old enough to express opinions, but over the last year, things had gotten worse.

She wanted to blame it on all the changes in their lives since Jaime's passing, but she knew it was simply because he lost his dad, and he felt he needed to step into his shoes and become the man of the family. No matter how many times she told him she needed him to be a kid.

She finished the pizza order and looked at the clock. "Benji, I'm going to walk to the Casey's. Want to come with me?"

"Sure!" he set the remote down and stood up from the couch. He walked over to the entryway of their suite to the little cubbies they stored their shoes.

As he put his shoes on, Rebecca reflected on all the differences in their lives in the last year.

A year ago, they had a house of their own in a little cul-de-sac neighborhood. A yard for Benji to play in, a basketball hoop in the driveway. After Jaime passed away, she couldn't pay the mortgage on her own with her teacher's salary. Her parents were very generous to offer her the live in manager suite in their bed-and-breakfast hotel. The catch was she had to be the nights and weekend manager. It was a win-win for her parents. Their daughter and grandson didn't have to be on the streets or move away, and they saved money on staff.

Rebecca grabbed her purse from the hook by the door and slipped on her own sandals. She took a deep breath. She double-checked she had everything she needed and then they opened the door and walked into the hallway.

The manager's suite was behind the kitchen, down the hall from the check-in desk. She had installed a ring doorbell on the front desk so she wouldn't have to spend all her time sitting there. After spending all day teaching, she didn't want to spend more time sitting at the desk waiting for people to show up. That time was better spent with her son. As much as he didn't want to admit it, he needed her.

They made their way down the hall toward the front door. The hotel was quiet for being completely full. She peeked inside the dining room as they passed. There was no one there, but she wouldn't describe it as empty. The FBI agents had brought in a whiteboard on wheels, and there were stacks of papers sitting on one of the tables.

She tried to repress the shudder that went down her spine. Cove Creek was traditionally a safe place to live. Nothing ever happened here. Until now. Three men murdered off the bike trail she and Benji frequented. She hadn't taken Benji to the trail since they discovered the last body.

Poor David. They taught together at the elementary school, she fifth grade, him PE.

He had asked her out a couple of days before they found him in the woods. Rebecca told him she would have to think about it. She wasn't sure if she was ready to date again, yet, even though she did like him. Now, because of some asshole, she would never know.

Rebecca shook those thoughts from her head, swallowing the lump that had formed in her throat, trying to bring herself back to the present as she and Benji stepped outside. The sun was still bright in the sky, summer creeping ever closer. With only two weeks left of school, the warm weather had definitely made the kids at school squirrely.

"Can we eat outside at the park instead of Netflix?" Benji asked.

"Sure, it's too nice a day to stay inside."

Benji cheered and took her hand as they walked down the sidewalk.

Her heart constricted as she gripped her son's hand. Right before Jaime died, he was becoming more independent. Since his father's death, he had regressed a little, wanting to hold her hand, panicking if she's ever out of his sight for long. As if he was making sure she, too, wouldn't be taken away from him.

It was late by the time Rebecca and Benji let themselves back into the hotel. She knew she wasn't supposed to leave the desk unattended for so long, but she had checked in all the guests, and she knew their rooms were stocked.

She told her parents when she took the deal that she was going to make Benji a priority. Hard stop. Her mom understood. Her dad? He was another story.

As she shut the door behind her, voices talking carried over from the dining room. The deep baritone leading the conversation made her heart rate increase and Benji grip her hand tighter.

As they approached the dining room, they relaxed. The deep voice wasn't her dad. It was the man who had identified himself as the leader of the FBI team, whose name had already left her brain.

The floorboard creaked, betraying their presence, causing everyone to turn and look at them.

Rebecca's cheeks warmed at the attention.

"I'm sorry. Please don't let us interrupt."

The tall Black man at the front of the room gave them a wide smile. She was *pretty* sure his name started with a T? "Don't be sorry. Please, come in. I don't think we've met your small companion there."

"Um, okay," Rebecca stepped further into the room, Benji moving with her as if they were one being. With as tightly as he was gripping her right now, she would believe they were one person. "This is my son Benji."

"It's really nice to meet you, Benji. I'm Thomas, the head of our team. And this is Trevor, Millie, Logan, and Matthew." He pointed to everyone around the room, one at a time, clockwise from his position. This time, Rebecca tried her hardest to commit their names to her memory.

Everyone gave her a little wave, but her eyes lingered on the man he introduced as Matthew.

He was part of the pair that had checked in first. His light brown hair was longer, curling up slightly around his collarbone and around his face, framing it. It was his eyes, though, that caused her heart to skip a beat, and butterflies to flutter in her belly. Deep brown, they shone with a kindness and curiosity she was not used to but longed for.

And at this moment, he had them trained on her, full of interest. Interest she found herself not opposed to.

She tore her gaze off Matthew and turned her attention back to Thomas. "I will try my best to remember everyone's names, but please give me grace if I have to ask again."

Lies. There would be one name she wouldn't be forgetting. Her gaze slipped back toward Matthew, whose own gaze was still locked on her.

"How old are you, Benji?" Millie asked, her kind eyes trained on Benji, drawing his attention to the room.

Rebecca looked over at the boards behind Thomas. They had put up pictures of the men, alive and dead. She shifted herself, placing her body between him and the boards. She didn't need him worried about people getting killed in town. He already had anxiety. He didn't need anything else to push him over the edge.

"I'm eight," Benji answered, his voice barely louder than a whisper.

"That's a great age," Millie replied, giving him a smile. "If you have any questions about what we do, please feel free to be curious."

Benji gave her a tentative smile. "Okay."

Rebecca put her hand on Benji's shoulder. "We should get back to our room. Leave you to your work."

"Have a good night, and let us know if we're disturbing you, we will probably work late," Thomas said.

"Don't worry about us. We're far enough back that you shouldn't disturb us. Stay up as late as you need." Rebecca gave them a small wave and maneuvered her and Benji out of the room so he couldn't see the crime board.

She turned her head to get one more look at the people in the room, and while everyone else had turned their attention back to Thomas and the front of the room, Matthew's gaze was still on her. She turned around, heat climbing up her face.

They got back to their room and took their shoes off, Benji running to the couch to turn on the TV and pull up the movie they were going to watch. And as she walked to join him, she tried not to think of the handsome man who couldn't keep his eyes off of her.

Chapter Three

MATTHEW

Saturday, May 16

Matthew jerked awake, sweat covering his body. He held his hand up to his heart, trying to calm the erratic rhythm.

It was just a dream.

A dream, he had to admit, he hadn't had in a long while. One he thought he had finally moved past.

He closed his eyes, and he was drawn back into that car, hanging upside down, trapped in place by his seatbelt, helpless as he saw his mom on the street feet from the car...

He shook his head, snapping his eyes open. Dwelling on it didn't help. It never did. It couldn't change anything.

He threw off the covers and turned so he was sitting on the edge of the bed. He leaned forward, resting his elbows on his thighs, holding his head in his hands, his long hair creating a curtain.

Seeing Benji tonight must have triggered something inside of him, causing the nightmares to resurface in full force. Benji was about the same age as he was when the accident happened. And he was the child of a single mom, like he was. Matthew's subconscious must have latched on to those similarities and ran.

Matthew lifted his head and looked at the clock.

Four in the morning.

At least the nightmare was kind and let him sleep most of the night before guaranteeing he wouldn't sleep anymore.

He stood and stretched, lifting his arms above his head and bending backward. If he wasn't going to be sleeping anymore, he might as well get some work done.

Matthew walked over to his bag and pulled out a pair of lounge pants and his house shoes. He always packed light, but he always brought casual clothes for when he was sitting around in whatever hotel they were staying in. He pulled on the pants and slipped on the shoes before grabbing an old Rolling Stones shirt and slipping it over his head.

Making sure he had the key to his room, he quietly slipped into the hallway, carefully shutting the door behind him.

The house was quiet, and almost too dark, the only light filtering in from the moon and streetlights outside through the high windows. Luckily, it was enough light he could see his way down the stairs with no issues.

He flinched when the floorboard creaked as he stepped off the stairs and turned toward the dining room. He paused, looking around. When everything remained still, he continued on his trek to the makeshift conference room. It was fortunate the layout of the house was pretty easy to navigate. It was even darker on the main level since the curtains were drawn.

Once in the dining room cum conference room, Matthew flipped on the light and made his way to the board. They had covered it with a blanket while they slept. It was an easy consensus once they learned of Benji's existence. No kid needed to see dead people.

He pulled the blanket off the board and stood in front of it, focusing on each victim in turn.

Three men. All in their mid-thirties. And that was where the similarities stopped. Different hair colors. Different builds. Different careers. Nothing tied them together except for the fact they were men of similar ages.

Was it as simple as that? The killer was targeting men in their mid-thirties? Matthew knew that serial killers often targeted their victims based on their age and sex, but it was unusual for all the victims to be all in the same town. Even more uncommon for them to be well-to-do men and not transients.

And the cooling down period between kills indicated this was definitely a serial killer and not a spree killer, so it didn't feel like the victims were completely random. They were targeted. But why?

They were missing something. Matthew pulled out the case files and looked at the information on the crime scene again.

Everything pointed to an organized offender. The crime scene was too neat. Too meticulous. It had been picked out specifically to dump the bodies of his victims. But why? Why this spot? What they needed was the original location. The place the victims were killed before they were transported to the bike trail.

"Oh!"

"Fuck!" His hand flew to his heart urging it to slow down. Matthew spun around to see who interrupted him and drew back in surprise.

Rebecca stood there, looking as if she had just rolled out of bed. Her dark hair, which had been worn up previously, was down in soft waves around her shoulders. She had traded her overalls for a well-worn men's shirt and plaid pajama bottoms. Her feet were bare.

"I'm sorry." Her voice was soft. "I didn't mean to scare you! I woke up to use the bathroom, and I saw a light filtering under my door, and I thought maybe someone had left it on by accident. I came out here to turn it off. My dad hates it when electricity is wasted. I didn't know anyone would be up."

"No, no, don't apologize. I wasn't expecting anyone else to be up, either. I hope I didn't wake you."

She shook her head. "Not at all. I am up nearly every night at this time for a bathroom visit. What they don't tell you when you have kids is how you'll never sleep through the night again, even after the kids aren't waking up anymore. Your bladder is never the same." She let out a nervous laugh before looking down, but not before he caught her eyes widening, and her cheeks coloring a deep red.

"I never knew that." Matthew rushed to reassure her. "I haven't had a lot of experience with moms."

It was his turn to cringe at what he said. *No experience with moms?!* What did that even mean? It made him sound like he was more prolific in the dating world that he really was. Like he was collecting women.

"I mean—"

Rebecca looked up. "I think I know what you mean." She smiled at him, but it still didn't quite reach her eyes.

"No, I don't think you do. There are not a lot of women in my life who are moms. Not a lot of women, in general, really. I have Millie, but she's Millie. I'm really busy with work, so I don't have a lot of time to socialize."

Matthew inwardly cringed. He was rambling. He always rambled when he was nervous, and apparently talking to a beautiful woman while she was in her pajamas made him nervous.

"I get it. I don't have a lot of time to socialize either. Between this, my other job and trying to be present for Benji."

Matthew pulled out one of the chairs, and took a seat, positioning himself so he was fully facing her. He crossed his legs and rested his elbow on his knee, resting his chin in his fist. "What's your other job?"

Taking his change of position as an invitation, Rebecca pulled out a chair sitting across from him. "I'm a teacher."

"Yeah? What grade?"

"Fifth."

"Wow. Good for you."

She laughed. "I get that reaction a lot. But I love the age. They finally understand sarcasm and can use it properly. They're wanting to be adults, but they're still kids. It's a nice sweet spot."

"Do you teach at the same school Benji attends?"

She nodded. "Yeah. It's the only elementary school in town."

Matthew sat up straighter, uncrossing his legs. "So, you taught with David Crandall?"

"I did. He was a friend, actually."

"I'm so sorry for your loss."

"Thanks. He taught PE, so every kid in that school knew and loved him. They're all devastated. We're bringing in some counselors on Monday to talk to the kids to help them process their grief."

"How's Benji doing?"

She shrugged. "It's really hard to tell, honestly. I told him, since we were going to be at school and everyone was talking about it, and he kind of shut down, but no real reaction. He was clingy today, but that's fairly normal for him. I scheduled an emergency session with his therapist for this afternoon, so hopefully she can get him to open up. I worry about him."

"Well, it's a good thing he has her to talk to, especially if he's not comfortable opening up to you. Not every kid is lucky to have someone like that."

"Yes, I'm really happy we found her for him."

"Are you doing okay?"

She shrugged. "I mean, I'm hanging in there. My friend just died. Two other people have been killed in my town. And I can't help but wonder, who's next?"

"If my team and I do our job, no one."

"What exactly do you do? I know you're from the FBI, but from the registration, it says you're from the behavioral analysis unit? What exactly is that?"

"We're criminal profilers. We can look at the evidence and the victims and use that information to create a profile of the killer. The profile will help us and local law enforcement catch the killer."

Rebecca leaned forward, resting her elbows on her knees. "You can really figure out who the killer is based on all of those things?"

"Well, I've simplified things a little, but yes."

"That's amazing."

"That's psychology."

"Still amazing. You always see things like CSI and they solve everything with fingerprints and blood splatters. You never really hear about them solving crimes with psychology."

"Don't get me wrong, we still need all the forensic evidence. We don't solve the crimes merely with psychology. We simply use it as a tool to guide the investigation. Narrow the field of suspects. We're looking for a needle in a haystack. We help get rid of most of the hay."

"That is a great analogy."

"Thanks."

Rebecca let out a big yawn.

"You should probably go back to bed."

She laughed. "I should. It's my one sleep in day of the week and I need to take advantage of it. And if my parents came in and saw me talking with a guest in my pajamas, I would never hear the end of it."

"Your parents own the place?"

"Yeah, and Benji and I are here until we can get back on our feet, so I do the night managing to save them a little money."

"That's really nice of you."

She shrugs. "I get to live here rent free and not worry about Benji and I living in our car, so it's the least I can do."

Before Matthew could dwell too much on that sentence, Rebecca stood and turned her chair back into the table.

"Are you going to try to get some more sleep?"

He shook his head. "No, I'm going to stay up and try to puzzle this out."

She nodded, giving him a small smile. "Good luck, then."

"Thanks. Good luck getting back to sleep."

"I won't have a problem with that. See you around."

"See you around."

Matthew watched as she left the room with a feeling there was more to her story. There was something behind her eyes. Like she wanted to say more, but was holding back. Like she was afraid to say too much. Or he could be reading too much into everything. Rebecca could simply be just as socially awkward as him, and it was coming across like she was hiding things. But he was rarely wrong about these things. He was great at reading people, and his read on her was she was only showing him her surface level.

Which shouldn't bother him. Most people only showed their surface level to people they just met. However, he wanted to get to know Rebecca on a deeper level. And he could only hope he could find time during this investigation to do just that.

Chapter Four

REBECCA

Saturday, May 16

A pounding on her front door jolted Rebecca from her deep sleep. She sprung up in bed, disoriented. She put a hand down next to her and felt a body. Benji must have joined her sometime in the night.

He had started sleeping with her again shortly after Jaime died. She didn't care if people told her he was too old to be sleeping in her bed. It comforted him, and that's all that mattered. He must have come in some time after five, which was when she made her way back to bed and to sleep after her late-night chat with Matthew.

The pounding on the door continued, so she swung her legs over the side of the bed and put her feet on the ground. Reluctantly, she stood, and glanced at the clock.

Seven o'clock.

So much for her only day to sleep in. She was going to be dragging later today. All the coffee would be needed.

Thankful it was finally warm enough to pad around barefoot, she walked out of her room and toward the door, rubbing the sleep out of her eyes as she walked.

She opened the door to find, unsurprisingly, her father standing there, fist raised to pound on her door again.

"*Papi*, what are you doing? You're going to wake our guests," her voice just above a whisper.

"*Mija*, why are you still asleep? The hotel is full, and you are supposed to be working."

"It's Saturday morning. I don't work on Saturday mornings. You know this. I'm the night clerk. I work at night."

"Don't sass your father," her dad replied. "I know it's Saturday morning. I thought we had agreed you would work as long as the FBI people were here."

Rebecca shook her head. "I don't remember ever having a conversation about this."

"We did. A couple days ago. I told you I expected all hands-on deck as long as they were here. I even suggested you using some of your personal days to miss school."

She sighed and put her hand to her forehead. "We never had this conversation, because if we had, I would have told you I can't be here, it's the end of the school year, and unless I'm dying, I can't take time off. Besides, we have an agreement that my weekends are for Benji, not the hotel."

"Your obligation is to this family, not to some fucking school," her father bellowed, jabbing his finger at her.

She almost instinctively took a step back, but held her ground. "That fucking school is feeding my family!"

There was some rustling in her room and cringed. Benji was awake, and he would have to hear yet another argument between her and her father.

"I've told you again and again, you don't need that job. You are living here rent free. And your mother and I can throw in food."

"And I've told you again and again, that I don't want to rely on you and mom for everything. I want to stand on my own two feet again."

Her father narrowed his eyes. His nostrils flared. "You bring shame on this family. Get your ass dressed and in the kitchen. You're working today."

"Benji has a therapy appointment this morning. I am not working today."

Her father let out a string of expletives in Spanish before storming off down the hallway toward the dining room area.

She stood in her open doorway, willing away the tears that were filling her eyes. Her heart was beating a mile a minute, and it took everything she had not to sink to the floor.

She never told her dad no.

Never.

And she was sure to pay for it later. Sure to.

She turned toward the movement behind her.

Benji.

She took a deep breath, preparing herself to turn around when Matthew come walking down the small corridor. He had dressed for the day since she had last seen him, wearing slacks and a button-down navy-blue dress shirt. His hair styled to accentuate the curls.

He moved quickly. Concern etched across his features.

"Are you okay?" he asked as he got closer. "I heard yelling and now who I think is your dad is now banging pans around in the kitchen."

"Oh yeah, everything is fine. My dad and I had a small disagreement. It's nothing." Her voice caught at the end of her words, and she brought her hand up to cover her mouth, fighting to keep her emotions at bay, at least until he left. "Please, don't let us ruin your breakfast. We're pretty famous for our spread."

Matthew opened his mouth to reply, but stopped short, leaning so he could see behind her. "Hey, buddy. What you got there?"

Rebecca whipped around and this time she couldn't hold back the sob that threatened to tear out of her throat.

Benji was there, his face white as a sheet, and he clutched a Nerf baseball bat as if he were prepared to take a swing at someone.

"Where is he?"

"Who?" Rebecca asked, swiping at her tears.

"*Abuelo*."

"He's gone." She paused, taking a second to swallow the lump in her throat. "What's with the bat?"

His lip trembled. He was just as bad at hiding his emotions as his mother. "He was yelling at you again."

Her heart shattered with that one word. Again. When she became a mom, she vowed she would do better, break the cycle, and here it was, proof of her failure with one word. Again.

"Again? Is this something that happens often?"

Rebecca spun around so quickly she almost lost her balance. She had forgotten about Matthew. An FBI agent. Who just witnessed something that should probably have her kid taken away from her. *Fuck*.

"You should go have breakfast we're fine here." The words came out a little harsher than intended, but at the moment she really didn't care.

"Are you sure? Because we can talk through what just happened. It might be good—"

"I said, we're fine. I hope you enjoy your breakfast, and you have a successful day doing what you came here to do."

She didn't even wait for a reply before shutting the door and turning to lean her back against it. She slid down until her butt was on the ground; her legs not able to hold up her weight anymore.

"Is the FBI agent going to arrest *Abuelo*?" Benji asked.

She looked up at him, still standing where he had been, still clutching at his baseball bat. "For yelling at us? No baby. He's not."

"Is *Abuelo* going to come back and yell at us? Because you aren't listening to him?"

And there was the punch to the gut to go with the stab to her heart. She couldn't find her voice, so she just shook her head.

Benji dropped the baseball bat and closed the gap between them. He sank down until he was sitting on the floor next to her. She opened her arms, pulling her son to her body, and he buried his face into her chest.

And there they sat, holding each other, crying.

"I'm a total failure as a mom, and the FBI is going to take my child away from me."

"Becky? Slow down, take a breath and try that again, with a little context."

Rebecca had dialed her best friend the second she stepped foot on the sidewalk outside of Benji's therapist's office. Andy Mathis was Jaime's oldest and closest friend, and consequently after nearly twenty years of friendship, he had become hers too. She was so thankful he had followed them to Cove Creek after college. And she desperately needed him to talk her down off this ledge she was standing on.

She found an old wooden bench a few feet from the door to the office and sank down on it, bracing herself for what was sure to be a long conversation. "My dad was being my dad again this morning, and Benji overheard, and he came out to protect me with a Nerf baseball bat. A baseball bat, Andy. My eight-year-old was so afraid of his grandfather, he felt the need to protect me with a foam bat. In what world is this a normal situation?"

"No world, Becks, no world. Benji shouldn't have to see any of this, which is why I keep telling you that you should pull from Jaime's insurance payout and get the fuck out of there."

She sighed. "You know why I won't. That's Benji's money, and I want it to be there for him to go to college, or travel the world, or get the fuck out of Cove Creek."

"He can get out of Cove Creek now, if you use the money. It will benefit him still. But earlier, when he's at his most vulnerable. He will thank you for it later."

"Getting out of Cove Creek was always a 'me and Jaime' plan, you know? Planning it without him just feels wrong."

"It was a 'you, me and Jaime' plan. And we were so close, before..." Andy trailed off.

"Yes, before," Rebecca said simply.

Silence spread between the two friends as they sat and remembered what they had lost.

Andy cleared his throat. "You're not a terrible mom. You know that right? In fact, I would say you're the best you can with the circumstances you currently find yourself in."

Rebecca sighed. "Yes, logically I know that. But you didn't see Benji this morning, Andy. It was bad."

"And that is not your fault. It's your father's. And his shitty personality."

"Again, you're right."

"Of course I'm right, because I'm amazing, and I'm always right. Now, that we have established you're not a terrible mom, and that we should still all runaway together and get out of this hellish town, why the hell are you talking about the FBI taking Benji away from you?"

Rebecca leaned back against the bench. "So, you know the FBI is in town investigating the murders?"

"Yes. I've seen them around."

"They're staying in the hotel. One of the agents heard my father and I yelling at each other this morning, and he saw Benji with the baseball bat. I sort of implied this was not the first time, and the agent started asking questions, so I sent him away. They will probably have to take Benji away for like child endangerment, right?"

Andy laughed. "Becks. They are not going to take your child away because your dad yelled. You're fine."

"You didn't see his face, Andy. He looked very concerned and worried. He tried to come in and —"

"Like come in and take Benji?"

"No, no. I think he was trying to come in and comfort us?"

"Rebecca Clarke, have you been holding out some key information here? Like, is he cute?"

"Andy!"

"What? It's important to the narrative."

"In what way is the fact he's probably one of the most attractive men I've met important to the narrative?" Rebecca flinched as soon as the words were out of her mouth. Sometimes, her mouth worked faster than her brain.

"Becks," Andy breathed.

"Look," she swallowed the lump in her throat. "Let's forget I said that."

"You know he would want you to move on, right?"

"I know."

"So, don't feel ashamed that you find someone else attractive, or that you're ready to take the step. Not that finding someone attractive means you're ready to date, but it's a fantastic first step."

Rebecca took a deep breath, steadying herself to tell Andy something she had yet to tell anyone yet. "David asked me out last week. And I was going to say yes."

"Fuuuuuck," Andy drawled out.

"I think I'm cursed," she whispered into the phone, her voice tight with emotion.

"Where are you?"

"On the bench outside of Benji's therapist's office. In the square."

"Don't move. I'm on my way. This conversation is one we need to have face to face."

"You don't need to do this."

"I do. And I am. Wait there. I'm literally putting my shoes on and leaving out the door. And you know how close I am, it won't take me long to get there. Don't move."

The call disconnected and Rebecca put the phone on the bench next to her. She leaned her head against the stucco of the building, bringing her hands to her face, covering her eyes. Her and her big mouth. She hadn't meant to share most of what she had with Andy. She had just meant to get reassurance she wasn't a terrible mother. But then she mentioned she thought Matthew was cute, and it all snowballed from there.

And really, she thought he was cute. Very cute. But he was in town temporarily. He could catch the person terrorizing their town, and then get out. It's not like there was any chance anything could truly happen.

She heard the slapping of feet against the pavement, and as she removed her hands from her face. Andy jogging down the sidewalk.

His muscular frame looking more in control than his face was definitely reading. His sandy blond hair which he usually wore neatly styled and gelled into submission, looked as if he hadn't even brushed it. He was also wearing pajama pants and a shirt that had definitely seen better days. Typically, he wouldn't be caught dead in town looking like this. He must have been very concerned.

"Stand up," he rasped out as he approached her.

She dutifully followed his demand and as he reached her, he wrapped his arms around her and pulled her into a tight hug. His much larger frame engulfed her more petite frame, but the second his arms were around her, she immediately felt safe.

She and Jaime had met in college and immediately fell in love. It was like out of the movies. Andy and Jaime had been best friends since they were in elementary school, so Andy came with the package. Which didn't bother Rebecca any. She and Andy became fast friends, and it was the three of them against the world. Andy was Benji's godparent, and then it was the four of them.

Now it's the three of them again.

"You are not cursed," Andy whispered fiercely in her ear, holding her even tighter. "You're not."

"Maybe I'm not meant to have a partner."

Andy unwrapped his arms from her body, and grabbed her by the shoulders, pushing her away from him, then brought his hands until they were cupping her cheeks.

"Look at me. You're not cursed, and you're meant to have the whole world. You're going to find a man, and he's going to love you just as fiercely as Jaime did, maybe even more, and he's going to be an amazing stepfather to Benji, and the four of us are going to live happily ever after. You hear me?"

Rebecca nodded, tears flowing freely down her cheeks.

Andy leaned forward and rested his forehead on hers. "Until then, it's you and me Becks. And together we will get through this, and we will be everything we can for Benji, and we'll get the hell out of this town. I promise."

Rebecca closed her eyes and let herself breathe in the familiar scent of her best friend, taking comfort in his words, and believing that really the two of them could do anything.

Chapter Five

MATTHEW

Saturday, May 16

"Hey, isn't that the desk clerk, Rebecca?" Thomas asked, stopping in the middle of the town square, pointing across the way.

Matthew looked across the square to where a man and a woman were standing, forehead to forehead. He lifted his hand to shield against the bright sun. It was difficult to tell. Their faces were so close together, but her side profile seemed to be correct.

"Yeah, I think so," Matthew shrugged.

"Wonder if that's the kid's dad?" Thomas asked.

"I got the impression the dad wasn't in the picture."

"Really? From the little interaction last night in the dining room?"

"No, from our conversation this morning."

"What conversation this morning?"

"We were both up and we chatted a little."

"And she told you the father wasn't in the picture?"

"Not so much, but I don't know, it was a little bit more of a —"

"You profiled her," Thomas accused him.

"I can't help it. It just happened."

Thomas shook his head. "If you keep profiling women you are interested in, they are not going to want to date you."

Matthew tore his gaze away from Rebecca and the mystery man to train it on Thomas. "I never said I was interested in her."

"You're not the only person who can't help reading people, kid. And last night you couldn't take your eyes off of her, just like you can't right now."

"Am I that obvious?"

"To the team? Yes. To her?" he gestured across the square. "Probably not."

"I don't like that 'probably'."

"I think that woman has so much going on in her life that she more than likely isn't noticing you making moon eyes at her."

Matthew spun his gaze back to Rebecca. "Yeah, this morning certainly was something."

Thomas started walking again, and Matthew followed him. They were on their way to the police station to talk with the detectives in charge of the murders. See their suspect lists and go from there.

"What happened this morning?"

Matthew shook his head. "I'm not sure? I was walking to the dining room this morning and I heard some raised voices. As I went to check it out, Rebecca's dad, the owner of the hotel, came storming past."

"Was everything okay?"

Matthew shrugged. "Rebecca said everything was fine, but the kid was standing there holding a foam bat behind her. So, I think there's more to the story."

Thomas clucked his tongue and shook his head. He was the oldest member of the team, and he had a habit of adopting the younger members, bringing them under his wing. The only thing betraying his age was the gray in his hair and his mustache, otherwise, his smooth Black skin made him look younger than his sixty years. He was the closest thing Matthew had to a father figure, and he cherished him.

"Well, Matty, while we're here, we'll just need to keep an eye on the situation."

"I agree, sir."

Thomas chuckled. "You haven't called me sir in almost a decade."

"I know. I don't know why that came out."

"Because you're flustered. You have found someone you are attracted to. It's thrown you for a loop and you don't know how to act. I think my little Matty is in love."

Matthew shook his head. "Love? I barely know her."

"It's not impossible. Love at first sight is a thing. When I first saw Carla," he let out a low whistle and sucked his teeth. "Love at first sight." He got a far-off look, biting his bottom lip.

Matthew knew things had been a little rough between Thomas and his wife, Carla, but he also knew his boss loved his wife more than anything.

Thomas shook his head. "You should talk to Logan about when he first met Josh. I bet he has a similar story."

"I'll make sure I do that."

"Don't get me wrong, I don't mean to be pressuring you or anything. All I'm doing is making sure you know what you're feeling is totally normal and within logic."

"So, say I'm in love. What does it matter since she lives here, and I live in DC?"

Thomas shrugged. "Those are things you figure out along the way. Typically, together."

"We're here on a case. Are you giving me permission to fraternize with the locals?"

Thomas shrugged again. "I guess I am. Based on what we know about the victims, it is very unlikely she's a suspect. So, unless we find something that points to a team, I think you're safe to flirt with the cute desk clerk."

Matthew shook his head. "I think I'm just going to focus on the case for now."

"That works too. Noticed you had been up a while pouring over the files. Talk to me."

"I think we can all agree we are working with an organized UNSUB. The victims appear to be random. He's doing his killing in a primary location and the bike trail is obviously a secondary dump site. We have no weapon, and the deaths appear to be caused in an aggressive manner."

"I agree. You went to the crime scene yesterday. Did anything stand out?"

Matthew sighed. "It's really weird, because when you hear the term 'woods', it's not what you would picture. It's a very public area, and the 'woods' back up to houses."

"So, he's a bold motherfucker."

"Yep."

"So, I think next, we need to focus on the victimology. We'll split into teams and go talk to the families and try to get a read on the last days and see if there is anything that can tell us where this UNSUB is hunting."

They reached the police station, and Matthew jogged ahead so he could grab the door for Thomas. The two walked in and Matthew let Thomas led him to the conference room, where the rest of the team waited. They had driven while Matthew and Thomas walked the short distance.

Matthew felt a pit in his stomach when he thought about the sight of Rebecca in the square, touching heads with that other man. *Was this what jealousy felt like? He had never felt that before.* He wasn't sure he liked it.

"Listen up," Thomas said, taking control of the room. "Three victims, three families. We're going to split up into teams and each take a victim and we're going to do full victimology. Background. Habits. Family Structure. And most importantly where were they last seen? I want a full timeline of their last days. Who were they with? What routes did they take? Did their routine change?

"Our UNSUB is an organized offender, which means he is predictable and will have a hunting ground which these men frequented. We need to find out where that is. That's what's going to lead us to the UNSUB."

"Trevor and I will take victim number one, Mark Lovett," Millie said.

"I'll team up with some of the local law enforcement and do victim number two, John Davies," Logan said.

"Looks like Matty and I will be on our most recent victim, David Crandall," Thomas concluded. "Remember, we want to find out everything about our victims. While on the surface it looks like they have nothing in common, there is something there, below the surface. It's our job to find it."

"So, what do we know about David Crandall?" Thomas asked as they walked across the square again.

"He was thirty-six years old, and the PE teacher at the local elementary school. He was single and lived alone."

"All pretty rudimentary things. When was he last seen?"

"Two days before his body was found," Matthew said. "He didn't show up at school, which they thought was pretty unusual. Then the kid found the body Thursday night."

"Mid-week."

"Mid-week."

"Let's start with the school and move out from there."

"It's Saturday."

They stopped short.

"So, I guess we can start with the family?" Thomas asked.

"Yeah, probably a good call."

They turned around to walk toward the hotel to grab the other SUV. David's family didn't live within walking distance. They stopped when they were met with two familiar faces in their path.

"Rebecca, and Mr. Benji. Fancy meeting you here."

"Thomas, Matthew," Rebecca greeted. "Out for a walk?"

"On our way back to the hotel to grab our car to go out and start talking to some families."

Rebeca frowned. "Be kind. Mark and John have young kids."

"We're actually going to David's."

"It's just his mom. His dad passed away last year. She's," she paused, taking a deep breath, "not doing well. Be patient. She may be standoffish. She was never the nicest lady in the best of times."

Thomas pulled out his phone and took some notes. "Thanks. This is some good information. Anything else you can tell us?"

The four of them started moving in the direction of the hotel, Thomas taking notes on his phone while Rebecca talked.

"He lived alone, with his dog. I'm pretty sure his mom took the dog in, to keep a little piece of him with her. He coached basketball for the school, and the season was just about to wrap up before..."

"Can you think of anyone who would want to hurt him?" Matthew asked.

Rebecca shook her head. "Not off the top of my head. He was pretty well liked. He was pretty involved in the city. Did a lot of volunteer work."

"When was the last time you saw him?"

"At work on Tuesday. We talked a little in the hallway after school, and then Benji and I went home. He didn't come in on Wednesday without calling in, which was unlike him. The principal called him a few times and then drove to his house. When he couldn't find him, he drove straight to the police because he knew something was wrong."

"Can you describe your relationship with David? Friendly?" Thomas asked.

"Yeah, he was one of my best friends at work. We got along really well."

"Did you ever see each other outside of work?" Matthew asked.

"Of course. We all did. We go out most Fridays."

"Friday Fun Day," Benji piped in, his voice a little melancholy.

"Friday Fun Day," Rebecca repeated.

"What is Friday Fun Day?" Matthew asked.

"All the teachers and the teachers' kids would go to Pizza Ranch. It has pizza and an arcade and it is so much fun!" Benji explained enthusiastically.

"That does sound like fun," Matthew said, smiling.

"We didn't go yesterday because..." he trailed off, but recovered quickly. "But if you're still here Friday, you should come with us."

Benji looked up at Matthew, his gaze catching with his own, the amount of hope in them tugged at Matthew's heart, and he knew he would do anything to make sure that kid didn't have any more hurt in his life. Starting with catching the fucker killing the people in his town.

"Yeah, if we're still here, I would love to go. You'll have to show me the best games, though. It's been a long time since I've been in an arcade."

A wide smile spread across Benji's face. "I know just the one."

"I'm looking forward to it."

Benji broke their stare and looked away.

Before Matthew could turn his head, he caught Rebecca's gaze, and he couldn't quite read her expression, but he could sense some sadness in her eyes. He ducked his head, and then chanced a glance at Thomas, and immediately regretted it.

Because the man who he considered a father figure was looking at him smugly.

He shook his head and turned away. He could look as smug as he wanted. It wouldn't change a thing. As much as he genuinely liked and enjoyed Rebecca and Benji, this was all temporary. He felt bad saying he would go to Friday Fun Day, because in all likelihood, they would be gone by then. At least he hoped they would be gone by then. A week was a long time.

But they had stayed in places that long before.

It was possible they would still be here then. Highly probable even.

And even if they wrapped up the case before then, he could stay and hit up Friday Fun Day with them. He would hate to disappoint Benji.

"So, what kind of pizza are we going to eat on Friday?" Matthew asked, having concluded Friday was a foregone conclusion. It was happening.

"Pineapple, obviously," Benji answered without hesitation.

"Pineapple? Really?"

"Mmm hmm. We always have pineapple pizza. It's my favorite."

"I don't know if I've ever had pineapple on pizza before. I'm usually just a plain cheese person."

Benji looked at him as if he had just said he ate underwear on his pizza. "That's kinda boring."

"I'm not a very exciting person."

"Yeah, you are. You work for the FBI. That's really cool."

Matthew smiled at that. "I'm glad you think so, a lot of people would think my job was boring."

"Those people are dumb."

Thomas chuckled next to him. "I like you, Benji. Don't let anyone change you."

"Okay."

Matthew smiled and shook his head.

They had arrived at the hotel.

"Well, Benji, this has been great, but we have to go do some FBI work."

"Will you be back at dinner?" Benji asked.

"I don't know, why?"

"If you are, do you want to eat with us?"

Matthew snapped his gaze back to Rebecca's. Again, he couldn't read her expression. And that was not usual for him. He prided himself on how well he could read people.

"If I am back, I would love to eat with you," he answered, keeping his gaze on Rebecca.

Rebecca smiled at him, and mouthed the word, 'Thank You,' to him, before saying out loud, "We usually eat around six. But if you are busy working, don't worry."

"He'll be there. We all have to eat. He can take some time to eat with you all," Thomas answered for him.

This time Rebecca's smile was wide, and her cheeks colored a little. "Well, then, I look forward to eating with you. Any allergies I need to be aware of?"

"None," Matthew said.

"Okay, see you at six."

"See you at six."

Rebecca and Benji walked toward the house, and before they entered, she turned around and smiled at him one more time.

Yeah. Thomas was right.

He had it bad.

"Thank you for meeting with us, Mrs. Crandall," Thomas shook her hand as the older woman let them into her house.

"Anything to help figure out who would do this to my boy." Mrs. Crandall led them into a small living room. She gestured for them to the small floral loveseat. She took a seat in the matching chair opposite.

Matthew pulled out his phone and pressed record in his voice recording app. "What can you tell us about his last days? Was there anything different?"

Mrs. Crandall shook her head. "Everything seemed to be fine. David lived on his own. He had a lovely apartment in the square. It was just him and his dog, Clementine." she gestured over to the chocolate lab curled up on a bed in the corner of the room. "I talked to him on Wednesday after school, and his plans were to sit home and read. He said he was really excited to go to school the next day, but he didn't clarify why."

"Did he usually spend his evenings alone?" Matthew asked.

Mrs. Crandall nodded. "Yes. Sometimes he would hang out with friends, but mostly it was him and Clementine. He was so exhausted after teaching elementary PE every day."

"Who were some of his friends he would hang out with regularly?" Thomas asked.

"Oh, some of the teachers at the school. They would go out on Friday nights to the Pizza Ranch. And then he had his friend, Frank, he would hang out with him on occasion. Nothing super regular otherwise."

"And nothing stood out those last couple days?" Matthew asked for a second time.

"Just that he was really looking forward to hearing from someone. I think he had started dating again, but I don't know much more than that. He was so full of life. Looking forward to the future. And in a second, someone stole his future away."

Chapter Six

REBECCA

Saturday, May 16

Rebecca paced her apartment, glancing at the clock.

5:57.

Three minutes and it would be six o'clock. Three minutes and Matthew would be here. Hopefully. She didn't know what she would do if he didn't show up.

Well, she would probably throttle him for letting her kid down. That's what she would do.

Benji was so looking forward to tonight. He spent the afternoon making brookies, a dessert that was half chocolate chip cookie and half brownie. And while they were not the prettiest, he was so damn proud of them she would also throttle Matthew if he was anything less than enthusiastic about them.

Benji hadn't been this excited about something since...

Yeah.

It's been a long time.

5:59.

Watching the clock was not doing anything for her nerves. She took a deep breath and glanced over at the couch. Benji was there playing Minecraft on his Switch as if there was nothing out of the ordinary going on. As if he hadn't just invited a man they had just met over to dinner with them.

Or to Friday Fun Day.

Which he agreed to go to.

What the hell was going on?

6:00.

There was a knock on their door.

Her heart skipped a beat, and there was a little whooshing feeling in her belly.

He came.

Rebecca smoothed her hair, which she had taken the time to style in soft curls around her shoulders and took a deep breath before walking over to the door.

She opened it to reveal Matthew standing there. He was still in his clothes from this morning, and he had his hands in his pockets. He gave her a small smile when he saw her.

"Are you ready for me? Because I can go and come back later if you're not."

"We're ready," she said, a little too quickly. She took a breath. "You're right on time," she added, a little slower. "Would you like to come in?"

She stepped aside, and Matthew walked into the apartment. She closed the door behind him and turned around. "Please, make yourself comfortable."

"Shoes," Benji piped up, not taking his eyes off the TV.

Matthew immediately slipped his loafers off and set them next to the door.

Rebecca couldn't stop the smile on her face when she caught sight of his socks. They were green with Creepers on them. When she moved her gaze up to his face, he just smiled at her and gave a shrug before moving over to the couch and sitting next to Benji.

"Survival mode or creative mode?" he asked.

"Survival. Although I usually play on creative. I'm scared the Creepers are going to kill me before I get my house built."

Matthew leaned forward on the couch, looking intently at the screen. "Do you want some tips?"

Benji tore his gaze from the TV and looked over at Matthew. He saw his socks, and he smiled. "Yes, please. All the tips."

Rebecca could feel tears welling up in her eyes, threatening to fall. "I'll just leave you two to it While I finish getting ready. I thought we could walk to the local Mexican restaurant? I wasn't expecting company, so I don't really have anything for supper here."

The two boys on her couch both lifted their right hands and gave her a thumbs up, without looking away from the television, and that's when she lost the battle against the tears.

She rushed out of the room and into the kitchen, and in the safety of the other room, she let herself go. Holding her hand over her mouth to stifle the sounds, she sobbed. Whatever she was expecting from tonight, It surely wasn't this. It wasn't her son bonding with another man, that's for sure. It wasn't the FBI agent wearing a pair of Minecraft socks and offering her child advice on his game.

She reached into the back pocket of her jeans and pulled out her phone.

Becks - He showed up. Wearing Minecraft socks.

Andy - Marry Him.

*Becks - *emoji giving the finger**

Andy - Seriously. This is a good thing. Let yourself enjoy it.

Rebecca put her phone away and looked back through the doorway at the boys on the couch before wiping away her tears and taking a deep breath.

As she stalled for time doing little tasks in the kitchen, she could pick up bits and pieces of what was being said in the other room. It was all Minecraft talk, but it didn't matter. It made her happy that Benji wasn't talking to someone who wasn't her or Andy. Or his therapist. He would talk to the kids at school, but he kept them at arm's distance.

He loved Friday Fun Day because he was surrounded by people he considered family. But other times, well, making new friends hadn't been easy for him lately.

She didn't know how to feel that the first new friend he made in over a year was a grown man, but she would take it. Every kid needed a mentor. Maybe hers needed a Minecraft playing FBI agent.

She dried her hands on the kitchen towel hung on the oven bar and took a deep breath. She looked around the kitchen to see if there was anything else she could possibly do to stall just a minute more.

She was so nervous. It had been a long time since she had a first date.

Not that this was a date.

It wasn't.

Was it?

She pulled out her phone again.

Becks - Fuck. Is this a date? Am I on a FUCKING DATE?!?!?!

Andy - .....

Becks - YOU ARE NOT HELPFUL

Andy - So, technically, Benji asked him over.

Becks - So...not a date?

Andy - Oh no, you're totally on a date.

Becks - How did this happen?! Am I ready to be dating?

Andy - You were going to say yes to David before he was murdered, so I would say yes.

Becks - But I've known David all my life. I've just met Matthew yesterday. Less than twenty-four hours.

Andy - You knew Jaime less than twenty-four hours before you went on your first date with him.

*Becks - *panicked emoji**

Andy - You're going to be fine. Just pretend you didn't figure out this is a date, and be yourself.

Becks - I don't even know who that is anymore. Who am I outside of Benji's mom?

Andy - You're bad ass Rebecca, Benji's mom!

Becks - I'm going now.

*Andy - Remember - keep things PG *winky face emoji**

*Becks - *tongues out emoji**

She tucked her phone back in her pocket and took a couple calming breaths. She could do this. Maybe she and Andy were reading things wrong, and this wasn't a date. He was probably just being polite. He couldn't say no to Benji. Because it is impossible to say no to Benji, he's too adorable.

But they were going to a restaurant...

Before she could talk herself into a frenzy, she squared her shoulders and stuck her head through the doorway between the kitchen and the living room.

Matthew and Benji were completely engrossed in whatever it was they were doing on Minecraft. She almost didn't want to interrupt them. Benji was holding the controller, and Matthew was half on/half off the couch, almost simultaneously leaning in toward Benji and the TV, as he very seriously explained where to put the blocks of what she assumed would end up being Benji's house. She nearly considered turning around and find-ing something to kill some time with, but in a normal situation she wouldn't postpone supper for video games, and she was determined to keep this as normal as possible.

This is not a date.

"It's time to get going, so pause your game. You can play more after we get back," she called out, moving through the room to put her shoes on.

They both turned their heads toward her, and in a move completely uncharacteristic, Benji immediately paused the game and moved into entry way to get his shoes on.

Apparently, everyone was on their best behavior tonight.

Matthew quickly followed and, as he passed her, he gave her a big smile before slipping his own shoes on.

Matthew, ever the gentleman, opened and held open the door for her and Benji. She exited the suite and shut the door, locking it behind them.

"It's just a short walk from here to the square." Rebecca flashed a smile at Matthew, butterflies making themselves known in her stomach.

Fuck. She should have gone to the grocery store. Eating at home would have felt less like a date.

The three of them walked in silence out the door of the Noble Hill and started toward the square.

"So," Rebecca started, filling the silence. "Do you like working for the FBI?"

"Yep," Matthew replied, silence falling between them again.

They continued the short walk to the restaurant, Rebecca wondering if maybe she had misread the chemistry they had felt earlier in the day. She and Matthew exchanged awkward glances, waiting for the other to fill the silence the entire way.

They both failed.

Rebecca wished she hadn't realized this was totally a date. She was doing just fine when it was just going to dinner with an incredibly attractive man.

Was it still considered a date if your eight-year-old child was with you?

She resisted the urge to pull out her phone and text that question to Andy. It would be rude to text him while she was on a date.

Not that this was a date...

Finally, after what seemed like too long, they arrived at the restaurant and Rebecca held back a sigh of relief. Matthew jogged ahead and opened the door for her and Benji. As she brushed past him, she caught a whiff of the soap they stocked in the rooms. Even though he was wearing the same outfit as earlier, she had to wonder if he had taken the time to freshen up before coming over.

The restaurant had the most authentic Mexican food in town, however it definitely catered to stereotypes. Upbeat Mariachi music played a little too loud, assaulting them as soon as they crossed the threshold, and the walls were decorated with a few too many sombreros. Luckily, though, it wasn't crowded, so almost immediately after they entered, they were seated and had menus in their hands.

"What's good here?" Matthew had the menu open, eyes scanning through the wide variety of options.

"Tacos," Benji piped up. "You have to get the tacos. They're the best."

"Honestly, there's not anything I would tell you to avoid. It's all rather good," Rebecca added.

"Well, Benji said tacos, so I should try the tacos." He flashed Benji a smile over his menu.

Benji beamed. Truly beamed.

Matthew's gaze drifted over to hers, and his cheeks turned a light shade of pink before he quickly diverted his attention back to his menu.

Rebecca lifted her menu higher to hide her grin. He was just as nervous as she was. *At what point did he realize he was on a date? Probably the second they left her place and started the walk to the restaurant.*

They ordered when the waitress returned. Tacos all around.

"So," Matthew said when the waitress left, "What's your favorite subject in school?"

"Science," Benji didn't even pause to think.

"Really? That was mine, too! What do you love about science?"

Benji began to rattle off all the reasons he loved science, and Matthew leaned forward on the table, giving him his full attention. He actively listened and never pulled his attention away.

Rebecca fell even harder.

The tacos were delivered quickly to the table, and Benji immediately reached for her hand, and held his other out to Matthew. "We pray before we eat," he explained.

"You don't have to, if you don't want to," Rebecca immediately cut in.

"It's fine." Matthew took Benji's proffered hand in his before offering his other hand to Rebecca.

She slipped her hand into his much larger one and there were those damn butterflies again.

She closed her eyes and bowed her head. "Bless us oh Lord for these thy gifts for which we're about to receive through thy bounty through Christ our Lord, Amen."

"Amen," Benji and Matthew echoed after her.

Benji immediately dropped her hand, but Matthew lingered. She drew her gaze to his, and she didn't have to be a Behavioral Analyst to see he was definitely feeling the same things she was at the touch of their hands. His wide, deer in the headlights expression told her everything. At least he was caught off guard like she was.

Reluctantly, she untangled her hand from his and turned her attention to the dinner table.

"This looks amazing," Matthew said. "I really appreciate the dinner invitation. Usually when I'm traveling for a job, it's a lot of fast food."

"Sorry again for not cooking."

Matthew shook his head. "Don't worry about it. Honestly. This is great."

"What about when you're home? Do you cook for yourself, or mostly take out?"

"I cook for myself, but nothing elaborate." He took a bite of his taco.

"Mom always makes elaborate meals," Benji said, taking a more than generous bite of his taco. "She's the best cook in the whole world. You should eat with us every night. She'll cook next time!"

Rebecca and Matthew both laughed.

"Benji. The agent is here to work. We can't manipulate his time."

"I would love to eat with you every night," Matthew answered. "But your mom's right. I'm here to work, but if I can find time, I could try. At the very least, I can stop in and help you with Minecraft." He swiveled his gaze from Benji to Rebecca. "That is, if it's okay with your mom."

"Bedtime is eight, so as long as it's before that, I'm okay with it."

Benji cheered, and Matthew held Rebecca's gaze, just a second longer, before ducking his head to focus on his plate and eating his tacos.

She followed his example and worked on eating her own meal.

The sounds of the restaurant surrounded them, everyone focused on eating their dinner. It wasn't an uncomfortable silence.

It was much more comfortable than their walk over. The three of them eating together felt almost…normal.

Things couldn't be this easy, could it? It had to take work and heartache and trial and error and—

"What are you working on in town?" Benji asked. "Why is the FBI here?"

Matthew froze, with his taco halfway up to his mouth. He carefully set the taco back on the plate before sitting up straighter in his chair, folding his hands in his lap. He glanced over at Rebecca.

She shrugged. She didn't know what to do. He knew something happened to his PE teacher.

Matthew cleared his throat. "Well, I'm sure you know something happened to your PE teacher, Mr. Crandall."

Benji nodded. "He died. Like my dad."

Matthew snapped his head to look at Rebecca.

Yeah, guess she had left an important detail out of their back story in all the times she talked to him. "Well, he's dead, like your dad, but they didn't die in the same way," Rebecca said. "Your dad died in a car crash, Mr. Crandall…"

"A dangerous man killed Mr. Crandall. And that is why I'm here, why we're here. We're here to catch the dangerous man so he doesn't hurt anyone else in your town."

Rebecca didn't know why she was surprised at the tact Matthew took explaining everything to Benji. In his line of work, he probably had to talk to several kids about horrors they experienced. At least her own kid was at the periphery.

"A dangerous man killed Mr. Crandall? Like a Creeper?" Benji asked.

"Yeah, the dangerous man is like a Creeper. But you don't need to worry. Because this dangerous man doesn't hurt kids. So, you're safe."

"Plus, you're here. So, I'm super-duper safe."

Matthew smiled. "Yes. You've got me and the rest of my team staying right in your hotel. So, you're super-duper-duper safe. Plus, you've got your mom. Moms have superpowers that keep kids extra safe. So, please don't worry."

"I'll try not to. But I worry a lot."

"You do?"

Benji nodded. "Yeah. I worry about a lot of things. Casey, my doctor, says it's okay to have some worries, but it's not healthy to have as many as I do. So, I try not to worry about too much. But do you want to know what my biggest worry is?"

Matthew leaned forward in his seat, moving his arms so they were folded across the table in front of him, pushing his plate back slightly as he leaned forward. "What's your biggest worry?"

"That someone will be babysitting me and my mom will never come home. Like my dad. He went to the store for a quick errand, and he never came home." Benji's voice wobbled at the end, his eyes welling up with tears.

Rebecca moved to get up, to comfort her son, but Matthew was faster. He was out of his seat and kneeling next to him. Using the legs of the chair, he turned him until they were facing each other.

"That's my biggest worry, too," Matthew said. "That someone I love will go out and never come back. My mom died in a car crash when I was about your age," he whispered. "I know exactly how you feel. And I want to tell you that your worry will go away, but it doesn't. What I will tell you is that your worry will shrink and shrink until it's so tiny it won't bother you all the time. Just some of the time."

"I'm sorry your mom died in a car crash."

"I'm sorry your dad died."

Benji leaned forward, wrapping his arms around Matthew's neck, and Matthew reciprocated the hug, wrapping his arms around Benji's tiny body.

And all Rebecca could do was watch as tears filled her eyes.

Chapter Seven

MATTHEW

Saturday, May 16

The rest of dinner went without a hitch after that. Although the mood was a bit melancholy. When they finished eating, Benji asked if they could order dessert. Probably because of everything going on, Rebecca readily agreed.

"If you need to get back to work, you don't need to hang out while he eats fried ice cream," Rebecca said.

Matthew shook his head. "I can stay. We're not meeting back up for another thirty minutes. I have plenty of time."

"Long dinners a perk of being an FBI agent?"

Matthew laughed. "It's a luxury we don't get often, honestly," he explained. "Usually, we are eating sandwiches over the case files. But since today was our first full day here, it's tradition we get to explore the local cuisine while things are slow. Starting tomorrow we're back at sandwiches over case files."

"Where did the rest of your team go?"

"Gianni's."

Rebecca smiled. "Local staple, been in business for nearly fifty years. Best Italian Grinders in the state, and I would put my money on that claim."

"I'm sorry I missed it." Of course, he only half meant it. He was pretty sure he had the better end of the deal. Great food and even better company were leagues better than diner food with his colleagues.

"They do take out. If you call and place the order, whoever is working the desk can bring it to you, and you can enjoy it while pouring over case files."

"When you say person who works the desk, I know you're talking about yourself. And I won't inconvenience you to pick our food up for us. We're perfectly capable."

"Don't let my dad hear you say that." Rebecca frowned. "He prides himself with the fact that we are full service, and we will do pretty much anything to keep the customer satisfied."

"Well, if it's your dad on duty at the desk, I'll inconvenience him with being a door dasher. But you have enough going on, you don't need to be getting us food on top of everything else."

"I appreciate your consideration."

"Who is this?" a large man standing at the side of the table asked.

"Toby?" Rebecca asked. "What are you doing here?"

"Becky! I was picking up a to go order and saw you and Benji sitting here with a man I had never seen before. Thought I would come over and make sure you were okay. See if you needed help."

This wasn't the same man he saw forehead to forehead with her in the square, but a different one. However, seeing Toby didn't leave him with a jealous feeling in the pit of his stomach, it left him with an uncomfortable one.

Toby didn't notice him glaring at him though, his eyes were one hundred percent for Rebecca.

Or Becky as it were.

Again, something about this man rubbed him the wrong way.

He didn't like Toby.

"Nope. Don't need any help. We're okay."

Toby didn't take his gaze off of Rebecca. He lifted his arm and pointed at Matthew.

Matthew glared.

"Who's this?" Toby asked.

"Matthew, he's a guest at the hotel," Rebecca answered.

"What is he doing at dinner with you and Benji?"

"Why is that any of your business?" Rebecca asked, folding her arms across her chest.

"A couple weeks ago you told me you weren't ready to date, and now you're having dinner with a complete stranger."

"Still not seeing the part where this is any of your business."

"Fuck, Becky, it's been over a year since Jaime, and I was good, I waited a respectable amount of time before asking you out, and you said you weren't ready. But apparently," he jabbed his finger at Matthew, "that was a lie."

"It wasn't a lie." Rebecca hunched over, folding in on herself. "I wasn't ready. I'm still not sure I'm ready." She said this last part looking at Matthew.

He tore his gaze away from Toby. "That's fine. There's no textbook on grief. You'll know when you're ready."

"What are you, some kind of psychologist?" Toby sneered.

Matthew snapped his gaze back to the man in front of him. "A behavior analyst with the FBI, actually."

"FBI, is this because of the murders?" Toby asked.

"Yes. Do you have any information about them you would like to share?"

"I plead the fifth," Toby said, turning back to talk to Rebecca. "Becky, you, me, next Friday."

"No, Toby."

"Wasn't a question."

"She said no." Matthew shifted, getting ready to stand from his chair.

"Nobody asked you, Fed. I'll be at Blaze of Glory Friday at six. See you there." Toby didn't even wait for a response before turning on his heel and walking away.

Matthew shifted, so he was fully back into his seat. "Who was that?"

Rebecca ran her hands down her face before re-crossing her arms, tucking her hands into her armpits. "He was my high school boyfriend. We broke up when I moved away for college, with the caveat that maybe we would get back together. But then I met Jaime..."

"And he's never let it go," Matthew filled in.

"Exactly. And things had been okay, but then Jaime died, and then he started coming around. At first it started off out of concern, but then he started showing up places he had no reason to be. Cornering my kid. Then two weeks ago he asked me out. And I said no. No hesitation. I had already thought I may be ready to date, but definitely not him. He was creeping me out."

"Has he ever been this aggressive before?"

She shook her head. "No. This is a first."

Matthew sighed, and ran his hand through his hair, pushing it back out of his face. "I don't know if I like the escalation."

"It's fine. He's harmless."

"It may seem fine to the outside, but he is clearly a narcissist. And that could mean for some pretty dangerous interactions, especially when you don't show up to the date he's set for the two of you."

Rebecca's face turned ashen, and her lips trembled. "What do you think he could do?"

"Most likely scenario, he'll bluster about more, or yell. Make a scene. Come back here and yell at you. Worst case, he could become violent."

"What do you suggest I do?"

"File a report with the police," he answered without hesitation. "Create a record. Describe everything you told me, and I can corroborate the events of tonight. They probably can't do much right now, but you can probably get a restraining order."

"Is that what you would suggest? A restraining order?"

"Yeah. If it were me, I would at least try for that."

"Then that's what I'll do tomorrow."

"If you want me to come with you, text me." He pulled out one of his business cards from his pocket. "I'll meet you there. We'll be around town, but never far."

"Thank you." She looked down at the card, before looking back up at him, locking her gaze with his. "For everything. Not just the advice about Toby. For coming to dinner. For bonding with Benji. If I had known you were a fan of Minecraft, I wouldn't have been so hesitant."

"Oh!" Matthew exclaimed, reaching for his card.

After Rebecca handed it back to him, he pulled a pen out of his pocket and scrawled numbers and letters on the back before handing it back to her.

"This is my Switch Friend Code. This way even after I go back to DC, Benji and I can connect and play Minecraft or whatever," he fought to get the words out around the ache in the back of his throat. His stomach roiled at the thought of leaving these two behind. Especially with Toby lurking around.

Toby.

"We'll still be able to play when you go home?" Benji spoke up. He had mostly been ignoring the adults, too focused on conquering an obscene amount of fried ice cream.

Matthew smiled. "Of course. I don't think I'll be able to give you all my tips and tricks before I leave. Plus, if we build a city, I'll need to help maintain it."

The wide grin on Benji's face would rival any other kid's. You would think he had just told him he was taking him to Disney World

"Do you have any other games?"

Matthew opened his mouth to answer when the waitress set the check down in front of him. Before he could pull his wallet out, Rebecca's hand shot across the table and pulled the check to her before slapping her credit card inside and holding it up for the server.

His mouth dropped open to protest, but Rebecca simply shook her head.

"We invited you. It's our treat. You can get the next one."

The next one.

The prospect of another date with Rebecca made his palms sweat.

Not that this was a date.

Was it?

Matthew looked across at Rebecca and Benji.

This was totally a date.

Fuck.

Had he done okay?

He must have if she was mentioning a second date.

Matthew cleared his throat. "Um, yea. The next one."

After the server returned Rebecca's card, the three of them stood and exited the building. The entire walk back was spent chatting with an excited Benji about all the games they would play together.

All too soon, they arrived back at the hotel. Rebecca handed Benji the key, who throwing Matthew a quick goodbye, dashed back to their apartment to squeeze in some more game play before bed.

Matthew and Rebecca stood near the front desk. Matthew placed his hands in his pockets and rocked back on his heels.

"So, I guess I should be going."

"Yeah."

"Thank you for dinner. It really was really nice to have the company of someone other than my colleagues."

"You're welcome."

Neither moved.

Rebecca cleared her throat. "Um, so that stuff I was telling Toby about not being ready to date, wasn't completely true."

"It wasn't?"

She shook her head. "No. I, um, I decided this week actually that I was probably maybe ready to date, after, um, after David asked me out."

Matthew stood straighter. "David? As in David Crandall, third victim of the UNSUB?"

She nodded. "Yeah. Is that important to the investigation?"

"That depends. When did he ask you out?"

"Monday. He asked me out before we left school. But I wasn't sure. So, I talked to my best friend, Andy, about it, and then I talked to my mom, and I decided maybe I was ready to try it, but he didn't come to school on Wednesday. And then, you know the rest."

He pulled out his phone and sent a text to Thomas telling him to gather the team in the dining room. He was pretty sure they had their first real lead. And a suspect.

He tucked his phone into his pocket and smiled down at Rebecca. "Thank you again. And I really meant what I said to

Benji. As long as I'm in town, I'll try to stop by in the evenings. I really enjoyed our time together."

Before he could talk himself out of it, or over think the situation, he leaned forward and planted a lingering kiss on Rebecca's cheek.

His heart beating a mile a minute, without looking back, he opened the door to the hotel, and let himself in.

"What do you have for us, Matthew?" Thomas asked once the entire team had gathered in the dining room.

"Tonight, I had dinner with Rebecca and Benji."

"Ooooohhh." Millie and Trevor interrupted him, as they burst into giggles.

Matthew's face grew hot, but he chose to ignore them and push on with his discovery. "While there, I found out our victim number three, David Crandall, had asked her out on a date just days before his disappearance and his murder."

Millie leaned forward in her chair. "Oh. That's new information, but how does that tie into everything?"

"Also, while we were at dinner, a man named Toby stopped at our table. Apparently the two dated in high school, and he decided he had waited long enough for her to be ready to date again and basically demanded she go on a date with her. He did not react well when he saw me eating with her."

"Jealousy. Great MO to kill a man. Did Rebecca have any ties to the other two men?" Logan asked.

"I don't know. But I think it's worth looking into."

"Did you learn anything about what happened to Benji's dad? Is he still in the picture?" Thomas asked.

"He died a little over a year ago. Car accident."

"Fuck," Logan muttered. "Poor kid."

"Yeah. Between his dad and his PE teacher, he's had a really shitty year." Matthew felt a pang in his chest when he thought about the tragedies the kid had experienced in the past year. Too many for a kid so young.

Thomas' phone dinged loud enough to echo in the room. He pulled it out of his pocket and frowned, his gray eyebrows drawing close together. Without replying, he slipped the phone back into his pocket, but his face failed to return to neutral.

"Everything okay there, boss?" Trevor asked.

"Yeah, everything is fine," Thomas replied, even though everything about him screamed that every wasn't in fact fine.

"Was that Carla checking in?"

"It was nothing." Thomas shook his head. "Let's move on." He turned toward the board and under David he wrote, *asked out Rebecca.* And over in a blank spot he wrote, *Toby*?

"Tomorrow we are going to figure out more about our victims. We're going to trace their lives and see if there is any overlap between them and Rebecca. Jealousy may be our UNSUB's trigger."

"The other two victims were married, and from what I could tell, at least through interviews with my victim's family, happily married," Logan pointed out.

"Jealousy is not always logical. It could be a perceived wrong. Our UNSUB may have seen Rebecca and the other two victims talking innocently, or they could have hugged. While to ordinary people it would have seemed innocent or platonic, our UNSUB may have seen it as more. As a threat to his perceived claim on Rebecca," Thomas explained.

"Should we look more into Toby?" Matthew asked. "There was something about him that really rubbed me the wrong way."

"Pretty sure that was just you being overprotective of someone you are viewing romantically," Millie said. "And while it seems like he would be a good suspect with this narrative, it's simply that: he fits this narrative. Until we have more evidence that this was a crime stemming out of jealousy, we need to come at this from the physical evidence and what it tells us."

"Millie is right," Thomas said. "We can't build our profile around a suspect. We need to build our profile around the evidence."

Matthew rubbed his hands on his face. "You're right. Of course you're right. It's such a rudimentary step. I'm letting my emotions cloud my judgement. Maybe I should try to distance myself from Rebecca since it's apparently clouding my ability to be objective about the case."

"How did dinner go?" Millie asked.

Matthew sighed. He actually sighed, like a lovesick teen. "Really well. We went to the Mexican restaurant in the square. Benji is such a great kid. We played Minecraft before we left, and we really bonded."

"I would think so, with those socks you always wear." Trevor laughed.

"Matty, keep seeing Rebecca." Millie leaned over and placed her hand on his arm. "I think it will be good for you. And if you're not completely objective, we're a team, and that's what we do. We check each other's work."

Matthew looked up and met her blue eyes with his and nodded. He always tried to keep his team at a distance, but apparently, they were terrible at getting the memo that he was emotionally unavailable.

"Thanks."

"Now, let's sit here and go over the autopsy reports and see if there is anything we missed."

Later, after they decided to call it a night and try to get some sleep, Matthew walked up to his room, bidding good night to Logan who was bunked next to him. As he reached his door, he stopped short.

Sitting outside his door was a plate of dessert. Taped to the plate was a note scrawled in a child's clumsy handwriting.

Thank you for the friend code. I made this dessert. They are brookies. Brownies and cookies combined! I hope you like it. Your friend, Benji.

Matthew picked up the plate, taking a bite of the brookie. Delicious. He made a note to thank Benji in the morning. Unlocking his door, he carried in his plate. These were for him, and he wasn't going to share.

Chapter Eight

REBECCA

Sunday, May 17

Walking out of the precinct, Rebecca resisted the urge to slam the door behind her on her way out.

They couldn't do anything about Toby because he wasn't a direct threat to her. She should have known they weren't going to do anything. He was one of them. A highly respected police officer in a small town...

She even told them there was an FBI agent who could corroborate her story, but it didn't matter. It just made them angrier when she mentioned Matthew.

So, she left.

She pulled out her phone and, for once, the first person she pulled up wasn't Andy.

Rebecca - They told me I couldn't file anything against Toby because they're assholes.

Matthew - Rebecca?

Rebecca - Oh yeah, sorry. Forgot we didn't exchange numbers. Yes, this is Rebecca.

Matthew - But he was a direct threat. I was there.

Rebecca - yeah, they don't like you. 'Encroaching' is a word that was bandied about.

Matthew - I'm sorry.

Rebecca - It's okay. I'm sure everything will be fine. I should have expected this. He's one of them. Don't they protect their own?

Matthew - He's a cop? Here in town?

Rebecca - Yeah.

Matthew - I've met with a lot of officers here, but last night was the first time I had seen Toby.

Rebecca - I don't know what he does, but he doesn't do homicide. It's his one thing he complains about. He mostly does things like traffic stops.

Matthew - That would explain why I didn't see him.

Rebecca - Is there anything I can do?

Matthew - Watch your back. Document all instances when he harasses you.

Rebecca - Will the cops ever do anything about it?

Matthew - Don't know.

Rebecca - That's not very helpful.

Matthew - Domestic violence is common among forty percent of police officers' families. Out of those, few even get charged or convicted. They protect their own.

Rebecca - Well, fuck a duck.

Matthew - Just remember, he's a narcissist. That doesn't necessarily mean he's violent.

Rebecca - That's better.

Matthew - I'm on my way to interview someone. I'll stop by your place tonight and we can talk more?

Rebecca - There are still brookies left, so come hungry.

Matthew – Remind me to compliment Benji. Those brookies were delicious. I brought one down to breakfast and made everyone jealous because I wouldn't share.
Rebecca - He would love to hear it.
Matthew - See you later tonight?
Rebecca - Looking forward to it.

Rebecca tucked her phone back into her pocket and felt a lot lighter than she had before texting Matthew. It was strange to talk to someone other than Andy about problems. She didn't know how to feel about depending on other people who were not her core group of people.

A week ago, she was uncertain she was ready to date. And now a stranger who was just a visitor to her city was here, and she was texting him for advice a mere forty-eight hours after meeting him. What was happening?

She thought back to meeting Jaime for the first time. They just clicked. It was practically immediate. Their friendship effortlessly developing into something more.

The last couple of days with Matthew reminded her of that. She had the same feeling she had in those early days of her relationship with Jaime. The swooping stomach. The anticipation of talking with him again. To see him again.

But this was all dangerous. Matthew was here temporarily. He wasn't sticking around. Once they caught the serial killer, he would be on a plane back east, to his home. Where he lived. And she would be here. In Iowa. Stuck living in her parents' hotel for the rest of her life because a teacher's salary was not enough to keep her and her kid completely afloat.

Use the money, take Benji, and leave. A little voice in the back of her mind, that sounded very much like Andy, whispered in the back of her mind.

She shook her head, banishing those thoughts. Two days, and she was already thinking about running away with him. This was terrible. She's so fucking clingy. She was going to become overbearing, and he was going to get sick of her. If he knew she was already thinking about how to make their relationship work long term, long distance, he would stop talking to her. Hard stop.

She needed to rein herself in.

Rebecca walked across the square and toward the hotel. Her parents had Benji. They all attended Mass together this morning, but when church was over, she went to the police station to report Toby, and her parents took Benji back to make sure the guests were having an okay breakfast. Sundays were always stressful for her parents. They had a local teen come in on Sunday mornings to make sure the continental breakfast was handled while they were at Mass, but her parents wanted everything to be perfect at all times, in order to get five-star reviews online, they stressed out when they couldn't be the ones in control.

She pushed open the door to the hotel and heard laughter coming from the dining room. She recognized her dad's laugh. He must be chatting with some of the FBI team. Her heart was in her throat at the thought of her dad interacting with Matthew. He would ruin everything for her.

Rebecca picked up her pace and turned into the dining room. She found her dad holding court in the center of the room. Only two members of the BAU were there, neither was Matthew. She knew he was on his way to an interview, but it was still a great fear of hers that Matthew and her father would interact. And since Matthew already had preconceived notions about her dad the results wouldn't be ideal.

Jaime never got along with her father. He didn't like the way he talked to her. It was one reason they had been going to be move away. The other part was Jaime got an amazing promotion that would change their lives.

Their lives changed, all right, but not in the ways they had expected.

Rebecca shook her head and brought herself back to the present.

Her dad was keeping court in the center of the room, entertaining Millie and Trevor with a story from his childhood.

"My mama, she was screaming at us and chasing us with her *chancla* in her hand, waving it above her head, and *mi hermano* and I, we were running as fast as our little legs could take us," he laughed. "We thought if we could get away, she would give us a reprieve from our punishment. But we were wrong. We hid for hours and when we finally came home, she still whooped our ass." He shook his head as if he couldn't believe his own story. "And that put me off of chocolate cake for a long time."

Rebecca knew this story. He told it over and over again. While he found it amusing, she found it telling. It explained so much about his personality and how he became the way he did.

"Wow," Millie said. "That was, something."

"Yeah, thanks for sharing that story with us, Mr. Hernandez. But we need to get to work. We have people to interview," Trevor said.

"Thanks for humoring an old man," her dad said. "I hope you all enjoyed your breakfast."

"It was delicious, thank you." Millie smiled.

"If you need anything when you get back tonight, Rebecca will help you."

Rebecca gave a tight smile and a nod.

"Yes. She's been an immense help. Matthew has been talking nonstop about what great company she and your grandson are," Millie said.

"Matthew?"

"One of the other agents. He had dinner with them last night."

Her dad turned his head in her direction and, while he smiled, his eyes told her she had fucked up and he was going to let her know. "That's my daughter, a great hostess."

"We'll see you around, Mr. Hernandez. Thank you again." Millie grabbed her bag and headed out of the room, Trevor following. "Bye Rebecca!"

Rebecca gave a small wave as they walked by.

When they were alone, her dad turned to her. "Going to dinner with the guests now?"

She shrugged. "Benji invited him. So, we went out. There's nothing wrong with that."

"We don't fraternize with the guests," he said, his voice firm.

"I know. But—"

"No buts. It's not good for business. Plus, having a man alone in your apartment—"

"Benji was there. We weren't alone. Plus, we weren't even there long."

"Scandal. That's what that is. I won't have my daughter putting on the appearance that she's a whore—"

"I'm thirty-six years old," Rebecca interrupted. "An adult. And you can't tell me what I can and cannot do."

"I can when you are living under *my* roof."

"Maybe Benji and I will have to move then, if you're going to pull that shit."

"You can't move. You can't afford it. So, my house. My rules. No more men in your apartment. It's bad enough you're gallivanting all over the city with that homosexual. I will not have people talking about us after church if word comes out you are entertaining men in your residence."

"Andy is not some 'homosexual.' He is my best friend and your son's godfather, and you will treat him with the respect he deserves."

"He is a sinner, and he is causing you to sin."

Rebecca threw her hands up, sighing. "It's always the same argument with you. You didn't like Jaime because he wasn't Catholic. You don't like Andy because he's gay. And you have already you don't like Matthew because...?"

"Because he is scandalizing this family. I do not want my grandson around him, or the homosexual anymore."

"Fuck you," Rebecca hissed out.

"What did you just say?" her father growled.

"Fuck. You."

Her father's arm shot out before she had a chance to react, his hand landing hard on her face. She reached a hand up, cupping her cheek, tears welling up in her eyes.

"You do not talk to your father that way. You will not see those men anymore." He didn't wait for a response. He simply turned on his heel and walked back into the kitchen.

Rebecca stood, stunned in the middle of the dining room, hand still clinging to her stinging cheek.

Her father hit her.

He had never hit her before.

Typically, everything had been verbal, never physical.

Of course, she had never stood up to her father before. Was that the difference? Had she triggered her dad to react the way he did? She thought back to interactions between her father and other people. She couldn't think of one instance where she saw anyone argue with her dad. Not once.

A sound from behind her caused her to turn around. Standing behind her was Millie.

"I'm sorry," the agent said. "I forgot a file on the table." She held up a manilla folder.

"Oh."

"Are you okay?"

"How much did you see?"

Millie leveled her gaze. "Enough. Are you okay?"

Rebecca shook her head in the negative. "But I have to be. Benji is waiting for me."

"Has he ever—"

"No. This is the first time, and he would never..."

Millie kept her blue eyes locked with hers. "You don't need to live like this. We could help, *Matthew* could help."

"I'm fine. We're fine. Don't tell Matthew, please."

Millie narrowed her eyes but nodded. She reached into her pocket and pulled out a card. "This has my number. Call me if you need anything. Anything. But don't keep this from Matthew. If he asks about your face, tell him the truth." Millie didn't give Rebecca a chance to reply. Gesturing with the manila folder she exited the room.

Rebecca rubbed her face once more watching where Millie exited before she walked back to her apartment. She opened the door, slipping off her shoes as she entered.

Benji and her mom, Charlotte, were sitting on the couch snuggled in together watching a movie. It looked to be something animated and Disney.

Her mom looked up as she came in. "Is everything okay?"

Rebecca forced a smile on her face.

"Yeah, yeah. Everything is fine. What are we watching?"

"Coco," Benji replied.

"I love Coco." She walked over to the couch, sat next to her mom, and laid her head down on her shoulder.

After they had been watching the movie for a little while, her mom whispered to her. "Your father?"

Rebecca swiped at the tears rolling down her face and nodded.

"He told me you've been mouthing off. Maybe now you've learned your lesson."

Rebecca stiffened, but didn't say anything.

She had learned her lesson.

"I'm going to punch him in his fucking face the next time I see him," Andy ranted while pacing the room.

It was late, and Benji was already in bed, having gone there reluctantly and sadly. Matthew had called and asked to speak to him. He was caught up reviewing forensic evidence at the crime lab and wasn't going to make it back before bedtime, and he wanted to be the one to tell Benji.

Points to Agent Grant.

Andy came over the second he got off work, and Rebecca filled him in on everything that had happened since the last time they had seen each other the previous morning.

"Toby or my dad?" Rebecca asked from where she was lying on the couch.

"Both!" Andy yelled, throwing his hands up in the air.

"You're terrified of both of them."

"I don't care. They're both getting one, pow, right in the kisser." He swung his right arm like he was landing a punch on someone much larger than him. "Homosexual," he muttered under his breath.

There was a knock on the door, and Rebecca stood to answer it. She opened it to reveal Matthew.

"Did Toby do that?" he asked, pointing to her cheek, as she moved out of the way to let him in.

He stepped inside, slipping his shoes off.

"No," Andy answered for her. "Her father did when she told him to fuck off."

Well, Millie would be happy Matthew knew.

Matthew leaned forward and touched her cheek. Her dad had left quite the mark. Benji stared at it all day, but didn't ask any questions. He was probably too scared to know the answer.

She closed her eyes at the feel of his soft fingers as they softly brushed her bruise.

"What set him off?" His voice was soft, but there was definitely malice in it.

"He found out you were here last night and demanded I stop seeing you and Andy. I told him to fuck off. He's never hit me before. This is new."

Matthew immediately wrapped his arms around her and pulled her to him, wrapping her in a warm hug. Given the awkward way they had ended the night before, the physical nature of his action caught her off guard.

He must have realized what he had done and started second guessing himself, because he stiffened.

She rested her cheek against his chest and wrapped her arms around his waist. He relaxed against her slightly.

He smelled of the bar soap they stock in the bathrooms of each room and of something uniquely him. His button-down shirt was soft against her cheek. And the comfort of his embrace caused her to break down completely.

"Shhh." He pressed his cheek against the crown of her head. "We can go down to the station, and I can help you press charges if you want."

She shook her head. "I have school tomorrow. And besides, I don't think I want to press charges against my father."

Matthew squeezed her tighter. "If you change your mind, say the word and we'll make it happen. We should take a picture and document it, just in case you change your mind."

"Already done," Andy spoke up from behind them.

Matthew let go of Rebecca, turning around to look at Andy.

"You're the guy I saw yesterday in the square with Rebecca. I assumed you two were dating."

Andy let out the largest laugh. "Thanks. I needed that." He walked forward with his hand extended. "I'm Andy. Best friend, Benji's godfather, the *homosexual*." His voice was dripping with so much sarcasm with the last word you could practically feel the eye-roll.

Matthew extended his hand, taking Andy's. "Nice to meet you. I'm Matthew. Behavior Analyst with the FBI, and apparently sinner?"

Without letting go of Matthew's hand, Andy leaned around him to look at Rebecca. "I like him. I stand by everything I've said about him to this point." He moved back to be in front of Matthew. "I like you, but if you hurt her in any way, I will kill you."

"Threatening an FBI agent?" Matthew said, amusement clear in his voice.

"Threatening the potential love interest in my best friend's story, who just happens to be an FBI agent. There is a difference."

It was Matthew's turn to laugh boisterously. "I like you too."

The two men stepped apart, Matthew stepping back next to Rebecca.

"What are you doing here?" she asked.

"I felt terrible I couldn't be here earlier, and the guilt was really gnawing away at me. I wanted to come and apologize in person. I was hoping Benji would still be awake, but I'm guessing he's not?"

She shook her head. "I'm sorry. He went to sleep pretty quickly tonight."

"What time do you leave for school in the morning?"

"Seven fifteen," she said.

"I'll try to catch you on your way out the door so I can apologize to him again in person."

"You really don't need to do that."

"But I feel like I do, and it will bother me all day if I know I upset him."

Rebecca looked up at him and smiled. "Who are you?"

He quirked his head to the side, his brow furrowed just slightly. "You know who I am."

"Oh my God, I ship it, now kiss!" Andy exclaimed, reminding them of his presence.

That broke the tension in the room, and they all laughed.

"Do you still need to work?"

Matthew shook his head. "We're done for the night. We plan on getting up early and heading to the school tomorrow and asking them about David. I think we're getting closer to being able to build a profile."

"Are there a lot of steps?" Andy asked.

"So many. We're still in step one. Which is when we are investigating all the victims and building their profiles. This also includes crime scene analysis, and combing over all the police reports. It's honestly the longest step. And since we have three victims to analyze, it's taking a while. But We're going to finish up tomorrow morning and then spend the afternoon here piecing it all together. And then we start looking at other factors."

"They make it look so easy and quick on TV," Andy said.

"Yeah. TV has actually made our jobs harder. They call it the CSI effect. It's made it harder to convict people, because juries expect so much more evidence than there realistically can be collected."

"I never even thought of TV shows being such a hindrance. I thought they would be more helpful, educating," Rebecca said.

Matthew shook his head. "I wish. We're already on a time crunch with our job, hoping we can catch the asshole before their cooling period is over, and then you get people who watch too many true crime documentaries or shows like CSI, and they feel like it's been two days, we should have caught the guy already."

Andy cracked a wry grin. "Well, have you caught the guy terrorizing Cove Creek yet?"

Matthew laughed. "Not even close. And unfortunately, this guy's cooling down period is getting shorter, and we don't know how long we have until he kills again."

Andy's face drained of color. "Well, fuck. I don't want to hear that, as someone currently in the demographic of the people getting killed."

"Except, they were not homosexuals, so you have that going in your favor," Rebecca said.

"Good point. Hooray for being the homosexual."

"Can we talk about something other than the case? It's all I've done since six this morning," Matthew said.

"Of course," Rebecca replied. "We were going to watch something, but we hadn't really decided on what yet, because Andy went on a rant. Would you like to stay?"

"Sure!"

The three of them moved into the main part of the living room, Andy taking the armchair, leaving the couch for Matthew and Rebecca.

Rebecca sat down on the right side of the couch and picked up the remotes, handing them to Andy. There was no point in trying to control the TV with him in the room. Nearly twenty years of friendship told her this.

Instead of sitting down on the opposite end of the couch, Matthew sat down right next to Rebecca.

Her heart rate increased, knowing he was close enough to touch. Without turning her head, she darted a quick look at him. He was also keeping his gaze trained on the TV. He was so close, she could feel the warmth radiating off of his body, and she could smell his unique aroma.

She felt him shift next to her, and then suddenly his hand was next to hers, his pinky barely touching her hand, asking for permission. She shifted her hand until it covered his. After a second, she felt him turn his hand until their palms were together, fingers entwined.

His palm was slightly sweaty.

This poor guy. So nervous about everything. It was cute and refreshing after a year of Toby.

"Is this okay?" he murmured.

"Yes," she whispered back, her voice trembling, as her warmth spread through her body.

He turned his attention back to the TV, and as much as she tried to pay attention to whatever it was Andy put on, all she could focus on was the contact between their bodies and how nice it was to hold hands with someone again.

Chapter Nine

MATTHEW

Monday, May 18

Matthew rubbed at his eyes again. He didn't regret the reason why he stayed up so late the night before, but he was regretting the act of staying up late.

He had stayed at Rebecca's until nearly eleven watching...he wasn't even sure. Some show Andy put on. There was absolutely no focusing on the television as he held Rebecca's hand on the couch. He honestly didn't know where the confidence to hold her hand came from. But he was happy with the result. The hand holding evolved to her resting her head on his shoulder. He couldn't remember the last time he was that intimate with a woman. Which is sad, because nothing happened beyond snuggling on the couch. But, fuck, it excited him in ways he hadn't felt in a long time.

In his line of work, he's seen a lot of things. And he's met a lot of different people who have done a lot of horrible things to women, and he's met a lot of women who have had a lot of horrible things done to them. Consequently, dating had never really been a priority for him.

Something about meeting Rebecca flipped a switch in him, and he really didn't know what it was. All he knew was he wanted to get to know her better. And he wanted to do more. More than he had wanted to since probably college.

Of course, everything about their situation was complicated. They lived in different states. She was a single mom. A widow.

The last two nights, he had had his nightmare again. Each night more vivid than the last. And he knew it was the parallel between his and Benji's lives. Both were young when their parent was killed in a car crash. But the difference between the two was Benji had an amazing mother to take care of him and help him through the grief. The kid was already in therapy, which was huge. Matthew didn't have that. He had distant grandparents and an MIA dad. And it was the nineties, so no therapy for him. Just toxic masculinity platitudes to get him through the trauma.

No, Benji was going to be okay. Way better than he was, that was for sure.

He had caught Rebecca and Benji before they left for school this morning, since he was up anyway, and that kid...his face lit up when he saw him waiting for them by the door. When Matthew had apologized for missing him the night before, the kid had hugged him. Hugged him. Forget what the mom was making him feel. The kid had his heart. He knew whatever happened; he had to protect that kid from getting hurt.

Which meant he needed to figure out his fucking attachment issues, so he didn't destroy him.

Matthew and Thomas took a seat in the principal's office. It was barely large enough for the desk and the two chairs that sat in front of it. The overhead lights were off, the office lit by the sun coming in the window and a small lamp that sat on top of the desk. A whiteboard was on one wall with an ongoing game of tic tac toe.

"Thank you for taking the time to talk to us." Thomas adjusted his large frame in the small chair in an attempt to make himself comfortable.

"No problem. I don't know what sort of help I'll be, I only knew David in the context of school." Alan Baker, a middle-aged man with thinning blond hair and a protruding belly, shut the door to his office behind the men before moving toward his desk.

"Mr. Baker, you would be surprised how much help the most minute details can end up being," Matthew explained.

Mr. Baker settled himself further into his chair behind his desk and gestured toward them. "Then by all means, ask away."

Matthew set his phone on the desk in front of him. "Do you mind if I record this conversation?"

"Not at all."

Matthew pressed record on his phone. "What can you tell us about Mr. Crandall's life here at school?"

"The kids loved him. They enjoyed the games he planned for them in class, and he would often be found on the playground playing a football game with the older kids at recess."

"How were his relationships with the staff?" Thomas asked.

"He mostly kept to himself. Often, he took his lunch on his own in his office. And if he wasn't doing that, he was eating with

Rebecca. They were pretty close. I know he would go out on Friday nights with the staff for Friday Fun Night. Otherwise, all I have to say is he was a great employee, and I'm really sorry he's gone."

Matthew checked his watch again.

"Where the hell are they?" he asked.

Thomas looked up from the papers he was looking through as he sipped his coffee. "They ran down to the precinct to pick up the files we left there. They should be here any minute."

And as if he spoke them into existence, the rest of their team came spilling into the dining room lugging evidence boxes full of paperwork.

"Sorry it took so long." Trevor carried a box. "They insisted on printing everything out rather than just giving us a fucking digital copy."

"Couldn't you just access their files from here, regardless?" Matthew asked.

Trevor was their tech guy, and he could always get them in where they needed to go.

"Yes, but we don't want to tip them off in case they start deleting things. We'll start with this, and then I will go in through their back door and find whatever they decided to omit."

"Also, Toby was there." Millie set her box down. "And let me tell you, Matty, he fucking hates you."

Matthew sat up straighter. "Really?"

"He went on this huge rant about how unfair it was that you could just come from out of town and 'encroach on his territory'." Millie made air quotes around the last part of the sentence, quirking the left side of her mouth up and rolling her eyes.

"He actually said that. His territory?" Matthew said.

"He did. I was standing right there," Logan said. "And as someone who only knows Rebecca vaguely and likes what I know of her... I wanted to fucking punch him in his smug face. I can't even imagine how you didn't the other night. He sat next to Matthew.

"It took a lot of effort, especially when he basically told her she was going on a date with him on Friday."

"He said the whole thing completely straight faced and unironically. And he kept looking at me for validation, like I would agree with whatever it was he was saying. And I felt like saying, my friend, I am not the straight white dude you are looking for." Logan shook his head. "Fucker."

"I'm not going to lie, even if he's not our UNSUB, I'm hoping we can find something we can pin him for *just* so we can wipe that shit-eating grin off his face," Trevor said. "I'm going to make a note that I should sweep his online history."

"We can't just run sweeps on people. It is an abuse of power," Thomas chastised. "However, he is a person of interest, so it wouldn't hurt."

Matthew rubbed his eyes and failed to stifle a yawn.

"Keeping you awake there, Matty?" Millie teased.

"He came back to his room pretty late last night," Logan said. "Heard him enter his room around eleven thirty."

All heads swiveled to him, and he felt his face grow warm.

"Were you in a certain woman's room last night?" Thomas asked.

"Yes, but not in the way you are insinuating. We watched a show together with her best friend, Andy." He turned to look at Thomas. "That's who we saw her with in the square yesterday."

"Hmm." Thomas frowned. "Looked like they were a little more than friends. I hope you're not going to get hurt, Matty."

"He's gay, so don't have to worry about getting hurt. At least not in that way."

Millie looked at Matthew and frowned, her eyes looking at him as if whatever she was about to say was going to be something he didn't want to hear. "Matty, I'm thrilled that you've found someone you're clicking with. In all the years we've worked together, I don't know if I've ever seen you date."

"But..." Matthew encouraged.

"But," Millie continued. "This isn't some woman you've picked up at the bar or wherever it is you normally meet women. She's a mom. There's a kid involved. And from what I've seen, you've interacted with the kid. A lot. Plus, things seem complicated with her dad."

"And she's a widow. The kid lost his dad," Trevor added.

"What are you trying to say?" Matthew folded his arms across his chest, his voice hard. He had the distinct feeling they had talked about this together the night before, and this was some sort of intervention.

"We're saying, be careful," Thomas said. "This is unfamiliar territory for everyone and we don't want to see anyone get hurt."

"Why is it you think *I'm* the one who is going to do the hurting? Why don't you think maybe *she'll* be the one to hurt *me*?"

It was silent for a minute before Logan spoke up. "Honestly? You're not the most open person. We've worked with you for about a decade and while we consider you a friend, we don't know you that well. Which is fine. You're allowed to not share and have an in-depth relationship with us. However, that's not how it would work in a relationship. Especially with a kid."

Matthew bit his lip and looked down. Unexpected emotions welling up in his chest, tears prickling his eyes. "Well fuck," he said, his voice raw with suppressed emotions.

"Matty," Millie said, "we're not saying—"

"Just please, stop.," Matthew looked up at them, his eyes shining with unshed tears. "Just stop. You're right, I do keep you all at arm's length. And did you ever think I did that for a reason? That maybe I was preventing something exactly like this from happening?"

Logan shook his head. "Something like what? Us confronting you?"

"Ending our friendship."

"We're not ending our friendship. If anything, we want to have a deeper friendship with you. We want to know you better, Matty," Millie implored. "Let us in."

Matthew shook his head. "I need to go for a walk."

"We have evidence to go through," Thomas said.

"I'll be back. I need to get some air."

Millie sighed. "Matty. I'm sorry, please—"

Matthew just shook his head before turning around and walking out the door.

Once the door was shut behind him, he took a deep breath, trying to get control of his emotions. He shouldn't be angry at his friends. They were right. He didn't let them in. They didn't know anything about his life. He didn't feel he could open up and talk to them about it.

Besides, how do you even bring that up? Hi, I watched my mom die when I was a kid, and I've never been the same?

He rubbed his hands down his face, starting toward the square. He would do a lap and then go back and start helping with the evidence. They needed to get a profile before the UNSUB struck again.

He walked down one side of the square, looking inside the store windows. This town really was lovely. He walked past a shop that sold unique Iowa items. The next shop sold spices and teas. The one next to that was a bakery. This town had a lot of charm that was missing from living in the Washington, DC area.

He thought about what his friends said about him being the one to hurt Rebecca and Benji, and he knew they were right. They were right. He was going to be the one to hurt them. He didn't let anyone get close to him. And what made him think he would be any different with Rebecca and Benji?

He was fucked up. Completely and utterly fucked up. And bringing in other people to this mess he called his life. He would need to stop leading Rebecca on. He was not relationship material.

He finished his circuit around the square and headed back to the hotel.

He opened the door and let himself back in feeling lighter. Like he had made the right decision. It would be better this way. It would.

Instead of finding the rest of the agents sitting and combing through the files, he walked in and found everyone gathering their stuff.

"What's going on?"

"A man fitting the victimology was reported missing this morning," Trevor explained.

"Fuck. Already? But it hasn't even been a week."

"Yeah, the cooling down period is continuing to shrink," Thomas said.

"How long has he been missing?" Matthew asked, grabbing his jacket off the chair he had been sitting in, throwing it on. He checked his pocket, making sure he had his badge, and double checked he had his gun at his hip in its holster.

"He didn't show up to work this morning, which is apparently very unusual. And when one of his coworkers went to go check on him, his apartment looked as if a struggle occurred," Thomas explained as they moved toward the door and the SUVs.

"When was he last seen?"

"Yesterday."

"So, at most, we have twenty-four hours to find him before the UNSUB kills him."

"We do."

"Do we have a name?"

"Andy Mathis."

Matthew stopped in his tracks.

"What is it?" Thomas asked. "What's wrong?"

"I think," he swallowed. "I think I'm one of the last people to have seen him alive."

Chapter Ten

REBECCA

Monday, May 17

"Did you have a good day?" Rebecca asked Benji as they walked out of the school to her car.

Benji nodded. "Yeah. We had a lot of fun. We did a science experiment."

"Really?"

"Yeah, we had these hand-held scales, and we had to go around and weigh different things in the classroom. It was a lot of fun. I wish we had done more science experiments all year, and we didn't save them up for the end of the year."

"I'm sure you'll do more experiments in fourth grade."

Beni's face lit up. "Really? Do you do experiments with your fifth graders?"

Rebecca nodded. "Yes."

"School is the best."

"I'm glad you think so."

Her laughter was cut short when she saw Matthew leaning against a black SUV parked next to her car in the school parking lot. He was in his full suit, his gun strapped to his hip, and if it weren't for the grim look he wore, she would be swooning over how amazing he looked.

But she had seen that look before.

"What's wrong?" Her heart was in her throat, and a pit grew in her stomach. Thank God Benji was with her. She didn't think she could stand if he weren't with her right now when Matthew was looking at her the way he was.

Matthew opened his mouth but shut it again. He let out a sigh, averting his gaze skyward before bringing it back to hers.

"I wanted to be the one to tell you. I didn't want you to hear it from somewhere else."

"Matthew, please," her voice broke. "Tell me what's wrong."

He took a deep breath. "Andy is missing."

She put her hand on Benji's shoulder, steadying herself. "What do you mean, missing?"

Matthew swallowed. "I mean, he didn't show up to work this morning. And when they went to look for him, it looked as if there was a struggle in his apartment."

She shook her head. "Maybe he just hasn't cleaned in a while. Maybe he met a guy and—"

"Rebecca," Matthew whispered. "We went to the apartment, and it looked like he made it in the door last night but was stopped at the entrance. He didn't leave the apartment willingly or of his own accord."

A sob escaped Rebecca's throat. "No."

Next to her, Benji shook under her hand. She turned and looked down at him. He was crying.

Before she could react, Matthew closed the distance between them and wrapped Benji in his arms.

"I didn't want you to hear from somewhere else, and I didn't know what else to do other than meet you here." He talked over Benji's head to her. "We have spent all morning retracing his steps from your place to his. And the police are tearing apart the city trying to find him."

"Do you think…"

He nodded.

She brought her hands to cover her mouth. "But he's gay. The others…"

"We're taking that into consideration."

"When do you need to go back to work?"

"Immediately. Believe me, I don't want to leave you two alone after breaking this news to you, but…"

She shook her head. "No, it's more important that you're out there. Is there a chance…"

Matthew nodded his head quickly. "Yeah, yeah, the window between disappearance and finding the body is usually about twenty-four hours. So…"

"Oh my god. Go. Go and do whatever it is you have to do to find him."

Matthew unwrapped his arms from Benji and took a step back. The front of his shirt was wet from Benji's tears. But he didn't look bothered by it. He reached out and placed a hand on her cheek.

"Do you have somewhere to go so you're not alone?"

"My parents. They won't be happy we didn't go straight to the hotel, but…"

"It's empty right now. We're all out. Go to your parents. Don't be alone right now. I'll try to keep you posted on anything we know, if I can."

"Tell me the second you find him. The second. I want to give him shit for getting kidnapped," she tried to joke, but it fell flat since her voice cracked as she said it.

"I will. I promise." He turned to Benji. "I need you to try to be brave."

"Are you going to catch the dangerous man?"

"I'm going to try. That's what we're doing right now."

"I wish you could stay and protect us. I'm scared."

Matthew dropped to his knees in front of Benji, not even caring that his dress pants were on the asphalt. "I wish I could stay with you, too. But there are only five of us, and every single one of us is needed. But," he reached into his pocket and pulled out a shiny gold coin and handed it to Benji. "Keep this with you at all times. It's a lucky coin, and it will protect you when I can't be with you."

Benji held up the coin and looked at it. "Really?"

Matthew nodded. "Really. Promise me you'll keep it with you always."

Benji nodded solemnly and slipped it into his pocket.

Matthew stood and turned to Rebecca. He hesitated for a brief second before he closed the gap between them and wrapped her in a hug. "The coin is a tracking device. Make sure he keeps it around all the time."

Rebecca hugged him tighter, nodding into his shoulder, not trusting her voice.

He placed a light kiss on the top of her head before pulling back. He wrapped his hands around her face, his gaze meeting hers. "I'll do everything I can. I hope you know that."

She nodded. "I know."

"I need to get back. I'll call you the second I have any updates."

She blinked away tears, nodding.

He leaned in slightly, and Rebecca was sure he was going to kiss her. She *wanted* him to kiss her. But instead, he pulled back, clearing his throat. He gave her a small smile and walked to his car.

He climbed into the SUV and pulled away, giving them a quick wave as he pulled out of the parking lot before kicking into gear. She led Benji to their car and helped him in. As soon as he was settled, she threw her bag into the passenger seat and climbed in herself.

As she drove to her parents, she tried really hard to stay within the speed limit, and to not cry. She needed to keep them safe.

The ten-minute drive seemed to take forever. When she pulled into her parents' driveway, the car had barely stopped before Benji was throwing the door open and jumping out. He ran to the door and threw it open. Rebecca quickly grabbed her bag and followed him in.

Her dad greeted her at the door.

"What's wrong? Did something happen?"

"Not that you would care, since you hated him, but Andy is missing."

"Missing? What do you mean, missing?" her dad paused and then it dawned on him. "Oh, *mija. Lo siento. Lo siento mucho.*" He opened his arms, and she immediately crumpled and went into his embrace. He wrapped his big, muscular arms around her and held her tightly.

This was the dad she loved and wanted. The one who fixed things, not the one who berated her and smacked her in the face. This was her *papi.*

"Where did Benji run off to?" she asked, still pressed against her dad.

"He went in search of his *abuela.*" He pulled back from her and shut the door. "We should pray the rosary tonight for Andy. I know I said a lot of terrible things yesterday, but you know I don't mean them. I've been under a lot of stress with what is happening in the town, and with having the hotel full until further notice. I do like him. He's family."

She narrowed her eyes briefly at her father's change of opinion of Andy, but not wanting to fight with him tonight, she gave him a watery smile instead. "I know. I know. And yes. Let's pray the rosary. It will make me feel like I'm doing something useful."

"Okay, let's do that. After dinner. I was getting ready to make your *mami* and I some mole. Would you like to help?"

She smiled the first genuine smile she had since hearing the news of Andy. "Yes, I would."

It was after eleven when Rebecca and Benji walked through the door of their apartment. They had spent the whole night eating and praying and finally watching Benji's favorite show on the couch before Benji fell asleep between her and her mom.

That was when she called it. Rebecca had emailed her principal and Benji's teacher and told them they weren't coming in the next day. There was no way either of them would be able to focus on school with Andy missing. At least, she knew she wouldn't.

She helped Benji into his pajamas and into bed, where he promptly fell back to sleep, since he was never truly awake, anyway. *Oh, to be a kid again.* She changed into her pajamas and went into her room, checking her phone once more for any messages from Andy or Matthew or anyone, really. Nothing. It felt weird not having fifty texts from Andy on her phone. Her phone had been quiet all evening.

She got in her bed and pulled out her rosary, saying another decade before setting it aside and turning out her light. Laying in the quiet dark, she let herself fall apart for her best friend.

It had been twenty-four hours since Andy had last been seen, and Matthew hadn't messaged her with any miraculous news. In all likelihood, her best friend was dead. There was no way around it. He was dead. Just like her husband. Like the man who asked her out on a date.

She was cursed.

There was no way around it.

She had done something to piss off God, and he was punishing her.

Maybe her dad was right. She was a sinner, and she needed to repent, or more people around her were going to die.

What if Benji was next?

The person she loved most in the world had to be the most unsafe, right?

She grabbed her phone and checked when the next time her church was offering confession. She would go, repent her sins, and then God would forgive her and stop killing everyone she loved. This would fix everything.

She set her phone down and rolled over to try to go to sleep.

Sleep eventually found her.

A gentle knocking stirred her from her restless sleep. Glancing at the clock told her it was three in the morning and she had barely slept.

It could only be one person at this hour, and her stomach fell.

He had bad news. She just knew it.

Not bothering to cover up with anything, she made her way to the door. Her hand paused on the doorknob, and she couldn't bring herself to open it.

If she didn't open the door, the bad news wouldn't ever come in. She could just pretend Andy was on vacation. That he found a handsome man, and they ran off together.

Gathering her courage, she turned the lock and opened the door. It was Matthew. He was no longer as put together as he had been when she had seen him this afternoon. The jacket was gone, along with the gun harness. The top three buttons were undone on his shirt, and it was untucked from his slacks. His hair was untamed, curling in a wild mane around his head. He had bags under his eyes, and his stubble was thicker.

And in his eyes, he held sadness and regret.

Looking at him confirmed everything she knew. He didn't even have to say anything. Simply looking the way he did, looking at her the way he was, it was enough to confirm everything.

Her face crumpled, and she let out a loud wail. "No!"

Rebecca's legs gave out from under her, and Matthew rushed forward to catch her before she could hit the ground.

He gathered her into his arms, holding her tightly as she sobbed into his chest, as he rubbed her back, and said nothing.

It wasn't until she could feel the moisture on the top of her head that she realized he was crying right along with her.

Chapter Eleven

MATTHEW

Tuesday, May 19

Matthew woke when the sun hit his face. He opened his eyes, taking a minute to orient himself. He was not in his room in the B&B, and he was not alone.

Glancing next to him, he saw Rebecca curled up, asleep. Even in sleep, she didn't look relaxed. Her face was tense, and she was frowning, her eyes puffy from crying.

He held her as she wailed the night before, soothing her as she calmed down enough to move to her bed. He had helped her in with the intention of leaving her, but she held onto his hand, tugging him into the bed with her. Laying there, holding her, and listening to her breathing settle into a sleeping pattern, he had full intentions to leave.

But, several days of not sleeping well, and the exhaustion of rushing to find Andy, he caved and fell asleep. He didn't typically sleep with anyone. He never slept over, or let anyone sleep over, on the rare occasion he was with a woman because of the nightmares.

But he didn't have any nightmares last night. He had slept straight through without the recurring dream jolting him from his sleep. While he had little sleep, it was more than he had been getting in a while, and he felt refreshed.

Matthew slowly peeled back the covers, trying not to wake Rebecca as he stood from the bed. He had slept in his slacks and his dress shirt, and looked decidedly rumpled.

Standing from the bed, he stretched before buttoning his shirt back up and tucking it into his slacks. He was going to need to find a dry cleaner soon; he was running out of clean slacks, and now that the killer's cooling down period had basically cut in half, he foresaw many more days of looking rumpled and feeling like shit ahead of him.

"What time is it?" Rebecca mumbled from the bed, startling him from his thoughts.

"About seven. You should get more sleep," he whispered.

She shook her head. "I don't think I can sleep anymore."

"You didn't sleep very much in the first place. You're going to feel like shit if you don't try to sleep more."

"I am going to feel like shit regardless of how much sleep I get. There is a huge hole where my heart used to be. In the last year, I've lost the two most important people in my life. Two of the most important people in Benji's life. I don't know what I'm going to do." Her voice broke, and she brought up a hand to swipe at the tears falling down her cheeks.

Matthew moved back to the bed, sitting, so he was close to her. He lifted his arm, as if to put it around her, but it felt too forward. He lowered his arm and brough it to his front, clasping his other hand, placing them between his knees. "You keep doing what you're doing for Benji. Loving him. Being there for him. Sending him to therapy. You keep doing those things, and he will be fine. Having supports in place will help him process these traumas in a healthy way."

"Fuck, I'm so glad you're basically a psychologist," Rebecca muttered through her tears.

Matthew smiled. "I'm glad I can use my knowledge for something other than figuring out which type of psychopath is terrorizing a city."

"Where did you find him?" Rebecca asked quietly.

Matthew swallowed. He knew she was going to ask it, eventually. "Murphy's Woods. Like the rest."

"Same spot?"

Matthew shook his head. "No. Right at the entrance to the trail. We're thinking he did a quick dump because he knew we would start watching the spot. He didn't want to get caught."

"Did you see anything? Anyone?"

Again, Matthew shook his head. "We were all out looking still. The previous timeline meant we still had time. We weren't expecting..." he swallowed the lump in his throat. "We weren't expecting a body so soon, so we didn't have anyone watching the woods. The UNSUB is accelerating his timeline."

"I know TV isn't a reflection of reality, but I'm pretty sure accelerating a timeline is a bad thing."

"It is. It means he's becoming more unstable. Which means he's becoming more dangerous."

"Andy wasn't like the other victims. Does that mean he's changed?"

Matthew shook his head. "No. Andy was exactly like the other victims in that he was a white male in his mid-thirties. Andy, as a victim, just eliminates the fact that the UNSUB is targeting only heterosexual men. It means sexuality doesn't factor in."

"I can't help but feel like I'm responsible for all of these deaths."

Matthew froze. "Why would you say that?"

"Andy was my best friend. David and I were probably maybe going to start dating. Before he died, John and I had reconnected. We were in band together in high school. We ran into each other at the grocery store and got talking. Our sons are the same age, and he thought his wife and I would get along, which we did. He brought his son over for a play date a couple of days before he died. Mark and I were on a planning committee for our high school reunion, we were assigned the same thing to be in charge of. I'm cursed."

"You're the link."

"What?"

"We couldn't figure out what linked all the men together other than their demographics. Of course, it could all be a coincidence."

Matthew looked at Rebecca in the brightening room. Her face was ashen. She believed what she was saying. She truly believed she was cursed.

He reached out and cupped her face, making sure their eyes were locked. "You are not cursed. There is no such thing as curses. The logical explanation is someone is acting out of jealousy. They view you as an object they covet, and they are destroying all of their competition. The period between killings shows these are fantasy killings done by an organized killer. He has everything planned out and is not erratic. The shortening of the cooling down period indicates he is becoming frenzied and desperate, and that may be because of our presence in town. You. Are. Not. Cursed."

Rebecca closed the gap between them, pressing her lips against his. Stunned, it took him a minute to respond to the kiss, but once his brain caught up, he quickly reacted, returning the kiss. She wrapped her arms around his shoulders, and since she was still halfway laying in the bed, she pulled him down so he was lying next to her on the bed.

Once they were lying next to each other on the bed, Matthew wrapped his arms around her back, pulling their bodies tightly together. She moaned as their bodies met. The sound went straight to his cock, causing it to stiffen against her hip. He prayed she couldn't feel it. He prayed she could.

Rebecca brought her hands up to run through his hair, and it was his turn to moan. *Who knew he liked his hair played with? Certainly not him.*

Matthew rolled them so he was on top, never breaking the kiss. Never separating their bodies. He maneuvered them so his leg was between hers. He broke their kiss and began kissing down the side of her neck.

Rebecca's breathing was heavy in his ear as she moved herself against his thigh, rubbing her center against him, creating friction.

Matthew pressed against her hip, trying to relieve the pressure building inside of him.

He shifted his right hand from around her back until it was resting on her hip. He ran his hand up under the thin material of her night shirt, smoothing his hand across the soft skin of her stomach.

She bucked against his leg, her moans getting louder as her breathing grew more and more erratic. He began moving against her in earnest. He couldn't control himself. They were in their thirties, but they were acting like teenagers.

He drifted his hand down to the waistband of her sleep shorts. As soon as his fingers pressed under, she froze against him. Immediately, he pulled his hand back and rolled off of her.

"Are you okay?"

She shook her head. "I don't know. Like, I was enjoying what we were doing. A lot. But I don't know if I'm ready to…"

Matthew laid his hand on her cheek. "Hey. No, it's fine. If you're not ready, it's okay. We'll stop."

"Really? You're not mad?"

"Why would I be mad?"

"Because I could feel you," she whispered.

He shrugged. "So what? If you want to stop, we stop. And whenever, *if* ever, you're ready to do more, we'll do more. Simple as that."

"Simple as that." Rebecca looked at him as if he was an anomaly.

The look on her face, her eyes slightly narrowed as if she was trying to solve a difficult riddle, made his heart ache. He knew she had been married, but did her late husband never stop when she asked to stop? Was this a new experience for her?

Suddenly feeling as if maybe he had misread all the signals, he pulled back even more, diverting his gaze. All confidence he had moments ago dissolving. He cleared his throat. "We can, um, even take a bigger step back. We don't know if…"

Rebecca silenced him with a finger on his lips. "I don't want to take any more steps back than we already have. I really like you, which sounds bananas, right? We barely know each other, but I really like you."

Matthew smiled against her finger, relief flooding him. "I really like you too." His words jumbled against the finger pressed against him.

Rebecca laughed, removing her finger.

Matthew's smile widened even more. "I really like you, too," he repeated. "And you're right, we don't know each other very well, but isn't that how all relationships work? Friendship or otherwise?"

"You're right. And I know that, but I feel like everything is moving so fast between us, and with Andy..." she broke off, her voice cracking.

"We'll slow down, but not stop. We'll continue to get to know each other and see where this goes."

Rebecca nodded, a tear escaping down her cheek. Matthew brought his hand up and wiped the tear away with his thumb.

"Thank you, Matthew," she whispered.

"Matty," he whispered back. "My friends call me Matty."

"Becks," she said. "My friends call me Becks."

After taking some time to cool down, and just cuddle with Rebecca in bed for a little bit, Matthew left the Clarke's apartment and headed straight to the dining room. As expected, the entire team was already there, eating breakfast.

"Rebecca is the key."

Every head turned toward him.

"The key to what?" Thomas asked.

"The connection we've been trying to make between all the victims. It's Rebecca."

Trevor pulled out his iPad. "Explain."

Matthew took a deep breath and began enumerating the links on his fingers. "She and Mark were on a planning committee together and were working closely to plan the event. John's kid is the same age as hers, and they were having a play date together the day before he disappeared. David asked her out. Andy was her best friend."

"Fuck," Millie muttered. "Acts of jealousy. That has to be the motive, right?"

"The UNSUB is obviously narcissistic. We already established that. The killings, as an act of jealousy, make sense. Whoever this is has created a narrative that any man seen with Rebecca is someone who is standing in the way of him," Thomas said.

"How did you say the husband died?" Millie asked.

"Car accident," Matthew said. "A little over a year ago."

"The killings have been happening over the last three months, but I'm wondering if the death of her husband wasn't the triggering event?" Millie asked.

Matthew walked over to the board and pointed to Toby's name written on the board. "I know we're not supposed to zero in on a suspect yet, but something he said comes to mind. He told Rebecca that he had waited an appropriate amount of time before asking her out, but she still turned him down. I'm not saying it's him, but what if it's someone *like* him?"

Logan stood up, nodding. "Someone who feels entitled to becoming Rebecca's next significant other. They perceive any man who is close to Rebecca as competition."

"That doesn't explain Andy, who was gay, and obviously not someone's competition, romantically," Trevor pointed out, as he continued to type on his iPad.

"No, but he was the person closest to Rebecca, her gatekeeper, so to speak," Millie said.

"Get him out of the way, clear the path to Rebecca," Matthew said.

"But what is our UNSUB's goal when he gets her?" Thomas asked.

"If she rejects him, he could become violent. He's probably constructed an elaborate fantasy of the three of them becoming a family," Millie said.

"Or he's already completely entrenched in this fantasy and can't even imagine a world where she would even reject him, to the point where he's already created a wedding registry online," Trevor spoke up.

"That is very specific," Thomas drawled.

"So, as we were talking, I started an online deep dive into Toby, since the profile is leaning a little bit toward him. And low and behold, I found a big fucking red flag for Toby. I've stumbled upon a wedding registry for him and Rebecca created around the time of the first murder."

"You're joking," Matthew said. "Are you sure it's them? And not two people with similar names?"

"Toby Lee and Rebecca Clarke of Cove Creek, Iowa. Wedding date TBD. Registered for a lot of typical shit a man would register for if he were the one solely in charge of a wedding registry."

"Okay, so, new plan for today." Thomas wiped his mouth with a napkin and stood from his chair. "We're going down to the station to deliver our profile. When we are finished, I want Matthew and Logan with the crime scene team at Mathis's drop site. The dump was sloppy and quick. We need to gather whatever intel we can find. Millie, Trevor, and I will be on Toby. We are going to dig up whatever we can, but we cannot tip the police off on what we are doing. They will close rank and defend him at all costs. Everyone understand their assignment?"

Everyone in the room nodded.

"Good. Let's nail this son of a bitch before he kills again."

Thomas stood at the front of the conference room with every available officer in the room. Matthew stood to the side with hands clasped behind his back. His gaze locked on Toby.

"Ladies and gentlemen, we are ready to deliver the profile. Our UNSUB is a narcissistic organized killer. He not only specifically targets his victims; he has everything meticulously planned out. The shortening of the cooling down period between killings shows he's becoming a little more erratic and his desperation is rising." Thomas delivered the profile, his gaze roaming freely around the room.

Not Matthew, his was still locked on Toby, because he wasn't going to miss his reaction to the next part of the profile.

"We believe the main motivator for the UNSUB is jealousy, specifically around Rebecca Clarke. The men who were targeted are ones he perceives as romantic rivals. He views Rebecca as his, and that he is entitled to her. We are looking for a male in his mid to late thirties who has grown up in this town and has stuck around."

Thomas finished delivering the profile and the officers began talking amongst themselves. The town was not very large, and the profile was very specific.

Everyone began to stand up and leave the room, except for Toby. Toby remained in his seat, frowning. He pulled out his phone and began typing something on it, before he stood up to leave.

As he stood up, his gaze found Matthew's. The two men stood there staring at each other, neither one wanting to move. Matthew twisted his mouth into a smirk, Toby's twisted into a snarl, before he tore his gaze away and exited the room.

They'd hit a nerve.

Good.

Chapter Twelve

REBECCA

Tuesday, May 19

"I'll keep you posted, Mrs. Mathis. When I know more, I'll call you."

Rebecca held her breath as she listened to the woman on the other end of the phone. Andy didn't get along with his parents, and he had no contact with them since they all moved to Cove Creek after graduation. But Rebecca was Andy's executor. He made sure to get all his ducks in a row after Jaime died, and it fell on her to tell the family. And as much as he disliked his family, they would probably want to know what happened.

"I don't know when the funeral will be. We have to wait for the police and the FBI to release the," she swallowed, "the body."

It killed her to refer to her friend, who was always full of life as 'the body.' It was so unfair. While the other murders in town made her sad, they were men who she knew, and they were brutally murdered, this one made her angry.

This one felt personal.

As she listened to Mrs. Mathis rant on the phone, she looked over at Benji. He wasn't playing video games today. After she explained what happened to Andy, he had laid on the couch and turned some show he had already watched a dozen times on Netflix and that's where he stayed. His hand was clutched around the coin Matty had given him the day before. The one he said would give him special protection.

Rebecca's heart skipped a beat thinking about the fore-thought he had giving Benji a tracking device. She didn't like what it insinuated. The FBI felt her son was in danger, but she was so happy they cared enough to do something in case the worst happened.

But that was Matty, wasn't it?

Since this morning, if she wasn't thinking about Andy, she was thinking about Matty. Which made her feel terrible. She should be grieving. She should be sad. But instead, she was crushing on the man in charge of solving the murder of her best friend.

She rolled her eyes one more time at the over-dramatics of Mrs. Mathis. She never cared about him before, but now that he was dead, he was her *precious baby*.

"Hey, Mrs. Mathis, I need to go. I should probably keep this line open in case someone tries to call about the case."

She said her goodbyes and hung up her phone. She looked over at Benji sitting on the couch. Spacing out.

"Hey. Let's go out to the park."

He shook his head. "I'm too sad to go to the park."

"We can't just sit here and be sad. We should go out for a walk or something."

"Is God mad at me?"

Rebecca was taken aback by the question. "What? Why would you ask that?"

"He took dad away. And now Uncle Andy. Did I do something bad?"

Rebecca's heart plummeted. "Oh no, baby. You didn't do anything bad. Sometimes bad things just happen, and it's not because we're being punished for doing something wrong. Your dad was in an accident and a dangerous man hurt Uncle Andy. Those things had nothing to do with you."

"Will Agent Matty catch the dangerous man who hurt Uncle Andy and Mr. Crandall?"

"Yes." Rebecca didn't even hesitate at the answer. She didn't want to sow any doubts in Benji's mind. She didn't want him to think for even a moment the dangerous man was going to win. That this new person in his life wasn't the hero he thought he was.

"Good." Benji looked back down at the coin in his hand. "I like Agent Matty."

"Me too."

"I'm going to be sad when he has to go home."

"Me too."

"Do you think we could go with him?"

Rebecca walked over to the couch, sitting next to him. "I don't know. It's pretty early to make that kind of decision. We've only just met him. Would you even want to move?"

Benji nodded. "Being here makes me sad. It makes me think about how dad isn't here anymore all the time. If we lived somewhere else, I don't think I would be sad all the time anymore."

A tear rolled down Rebecca's face. "We can move." She moved closer, wrapping an arm around Benji. "But we don't need to move where Agent Matty is."

"But I want to. I really like him. He plays Minecraft, and he knows everything. *Everything*. And! He's so nice. And I think he likes me too."

Rebecca rested her head on his. "Yeah, I think he does, too. He's pretty great."

"He's the best. And I would be okay if you wanted to be more than friends with him. If you wanted to date him."

"You would?"

"Yeah. I think he would be a good stepdad."

Rebecca didn't know what to say to that. She was honestly shocked. She didn't know Benji thought about things like this. "Really?"

"Yeah. He would be fun. And he could protect us from the dangerous men. I can also tell he really likes you. A lot."

"I'll keep that in mind. I'm not going to promise anything, since it's still early, but I feel the same way. I think he's a really great guy. And I'm glad to know you like him and are okay with me dating him. Or dating in general."

Benji shook his head. "Not in general. Only him."

"Only him. Got it."

"Mom?"

"Yeah?"

"Where does he live?"

"Near Washington, D.C."

"Where is that?"

Rebecca smiled to herself. This is what they needed. A distraction. "C'mon. Let's get on the computer and look at some Google Maps."

The sun had set, and they had just finished up dinner when there was a knock on the door. Rebecca wiped her hands on a kitchen towel before heading to the door. There was a bit of a spring in her step. She knew who it would be, and she was eager to see him. She had been a little sad when he didn't make it to dinner again, but she knew he would try to make it before Benji went to sleep.

Throwing open the door, the smile faded from her face when she noticed who it was.

"Toby," she said, trying to mask the disappointment in her voice. "What are you doing here?"

"I heard about Mathis and figured I should come and offer my condolences. I wanted to come sooner, but I was on duty all day. Did you know there's a crazy bastard going around killing the men my age around here?"

Rebecca folded her arms across her chest. "I'm aware."

Toby looped his fingers through his belt loops. He was still in his full uniform, minus his gun belt. It made him look like even more of an asshole. "Can I come in?"

She shook her head. "No, I don't think you should."

He sighed. "I'm trying here, Becky. I care about you. You know I do. I always have."

"I know. And I have told you several times I don't feel that way for you. Not anymore. I've moved on. It's been twenty years. You should, too."

He shook his head. "I can't believe I agreed to that shit about a temporary break up back when we were in high school. I should have fought harder and made you—"

"You couldn't make me do anything, Toby. I'm my own person. And I never said the breakup was temporary. It wasn't. We were over."

"We were not. I never agreed—"

"You didn't need to. I'm sorry you were hurt. But you need to move on and find someone else. I did."

"That boy needs a father," Toby said, pivoting the subject. "And I would make a damn fine one if you gave me a chance. Let me show you. He hasn't had the influence of a real man in life before, especially during the last year."

"He's had plenty of 'real male' influences in his life. He has my father, and he had his dad and Andy. He's going to be fine."

"Stop rejecting me!" Toby screamed. He removed his thumbs from his belt loops and took a menacing step forward. "You *belong* with me. The three of us *will* be a family."

"*Maltido bastardo*, step away from my daughter." His hand came forward and grabbed Toby by the shoulder and pulled him back.

Rebecca breathed a sigh of relief at the sight of her dad.

"You."

"Hello, Senor Hernandez."

"I thought we were rid of you after Rebecca went to college. What are you doing here?"

Toby tried to puff out his chest. "I'm here to ask Becky out on a date. I think we should give it another shot."

"I don't want you near my daughter or my grandson," her dad threatened. "And from what I can see, she doesn't want you near her either."

"Senor Hernandez—"

"I want you off of my property."

"Sir—"

"Do not come back. I don't care if you are the police. I will call them and have them escort you off my property the next time I see you here. Do not bother my family again."

"But—"

"Get. Out."

Toby turned and looked at her one more time, but was sensible, and left the hotel.

Her dad walked the few steps to her and put his hands on her shoulders, meeting her eyes with his. "Are you okay?"

Rebecca nodded. "Yeah, I'm fine."

"Are you sure?"

"Yeah," she swallowed. "Yeah. Thank you."

"Of course. I never liked that boy. And now that he's wearing a police badge, he feels like he can do anything he wants. *El cabron*. Has he been bothering you?"

"Ever since Jaime died. He thinks we should get back together."

"He's been bothering you for a year? Has he always been yelling like this?"

"No. This is new."

"Have you told the police?"

"*Papi*. He is the police. I went and tried to file a report, and they brushed me off. I talked to Matthew, and he said the police are notorious for covering for their own."

"Can the FBI do something, then?"

"I think this is a little below their pay grade."

Her dad growled. "I will contact the police, and I will tell them he is no longer welcome on our premises. This is private property, and if he comes back, we will have him arrested."

Rebecca gave him a watery smile. "Thank you, Dad."

"Anything for you, *mija*. You and Benji are everything to me."

Rebecca smiled at him. "I needed this. It's been such a hard year."

"I know. And you know your mother and I are here for you. Whatever you need."

"I know. And you don't know how much I have appreciated everything you have done for us over the last several months. We could not have done it without you."

"That's what family is for. Family is the most important thing in the entire world. Never forget that."

Rebecca gave him a smile that she knew didn't reach her eyes. "I won't"

Chapter Thirteen

MATTHEW

Wednesday, May 20

Matthew rubbed his face and then looked at the clock. Well after midnight. It was now tomorrow. He looked around the room. Everyone looked as exhausted as he felt. The team had been at it all day. At one point, they had ordered food and had it delivered, but they never stopped. The cooling down period had dropped significantly. Which meant they were on a time crunch. They needed to find the son of a bitch before he killed again.

They had focused on investigating Andy's murder, and it was harder on him than he expected. This case was slowly becoming closer to him than any case before. Matthew honestly didn't know what to do. His gut was saying he needed to follow through with this to the end. His head said there was now a conflict of interest, and he needed to bow out.

He shouldn't have done anything with his feelings for Rebecca. It was going to compromise the case.

Thomas' phone pinged for the fifth time in the last hour. And just like every other time it pinged, he picked it up, glanced at it, and then set it aside.

"If you need to talk to Carla, you can take a few minutes to call her," Matthew said.

"It's not Carla." His voice was clipped and didn't invite any more comments.

"Okay." Matthew drew the word out, but Thomas' dismissal only raised more questions. But now wasn't the time to be asking them.

"Any luck on the background for Toby?" Thomas asked.

"He's lived here his whole life, and he has been single for most of his adult life. Doesn't look like he's dated anyone seriously since he broke up with Rebecca in high school. He frequents a lot of men's rights areas on the web. And the stuff he posts about women. Well, it's not worth repeating, but just know it's bad. He joined the police force right out of high school, and hasn't really risen in the ranks," Trevor read from his iPad.

"I think we need to question him," Millie said. "He's our best lead, and he fits the profile."

"I think you're right. Let's get some sleep, and first thing in the morning, we'll bring him in for questioning. See if he has an alibi for any of the murders," Thomas agreed.

"They're going to close ranks," Logan warned.

"Yeah, but we won't let them. We outrank them. He can't get away with murder if he is the one who did it," Thomas said.

They stood up from the table and threw the sheet over the board. Benji definitely didn't need to see the board now that his godfather was up on it. They split off, heading to their respective rooms, and Matthew held back.

He looked down the hallway toward Rebecca's room. He checked his watch and frowned at the time. She was definitely asleep. He shouldn't go down and check.

His feet didn't get the message, and they started on their way to her apartment. There was a light shining through the crack at the bottom of the door.

Matthew rapped lightly on the door and minutes later it swung open. Rebecca stood in the opening wearing her pajamas and holding a book in her hand. Her eyes were red-rimmed, as if she had been doing more crying than reading.

"I was hoping you would stop by."

"It's late."

"Will you stay here tonight?"

He nodded. "Of course."

"Just sleeping?"

"Of course," he repeated.

She grabbed hold of his hand, and pulled him in. He closed the door while slipping his shoes from his feet. He wordlessly followed her into the bedroom.

She walked over to a drawer and pulled it open, pulling out some sweats and an old shirt. "These were Jaime's. You can wear them to sleep, if you want."

"I'll go change."

Matthew gathered the clothes in his arms and made his way to the bathroom. As he walked past Benji's room, he peeked inside. The boy was curled up on his bed sound asleep, cuddling with a Creeper stuffie. Matthew smiled. At least he was sleeping okay.

He walked the rest of the way to the bathroom and quickly ducked inside, changing into the borrowed clothes. He made his way back to Rebecca's room to find her already lying in bed.

Tucking his clothes on a chair sitting in the corner of the room, he moved to the bed and climbed in.

Before he could talk himself out of it, he curled himself around Rebecca, pulling her close to his body. The big spoon to her little spoon.

"Thank you," Rebecca whispered in the dark of the room.

"You're welcome." He pressed a kiss to her head, just above her ear.

He closed his eyes and listened to the sound of her breathing, and the quiet breathing of Benji down the hallway and slipped into a dreamless sleep.

Matthew woke with the feeling he was being watched. He opened his eyes and startled. Standing right next to him, watching him sleep, was Benji.

"Hey, buddy." He sat up, wiping the sleep from his eyes. "What are you doing?"

"It's morning, and we have to go to school."

"Oh." Matthew rolled over and nudged Rebecca.

She opened her eyes slowly, and when she saw Matthew, she smiled. "Good morning."

"Good morning. Benji would like to remind you it's morning and you have to go to school."

"Benji—" Rebecca sat up and looked around Matthew at her son, who was still just standing next to the bed as if he were some child from a horror movie. "What time is it?"

"Six," Benji replied.

Rebecca let out a breath. "Okay, not late. Thank you Benji. Why don't you get dressed and get some breakfast? We have plenty of time. Thank you for waking me."

Benji didn't say anything. He simply continued to stare at Matthew.

"Is there something I can do for you?" Matthew asked.

"Do you like us?"

Matthew smiled. "Yeah. I do."

Benji broke out into a smile. "I thought so. We like you too."

Matthew returned his smile. "I'm really glad to hear that."

"We looked up where Washington, DC was on the map last night. You live very far away from us."

"Yeah, I do. But, we're friends on our Switches now, and we'll still be able to play Minecraft together."

"It wouldn't be the same."

"I could come visit when I have some time off."

"We could move to be with you."

Matthew's heart skipped a beat and his stomach did a weird loop. "Well, I guess you could. But that's a big change. Maybe it's something that could happen someday, but probably not right away."

"But someday?"

"Yeah. Like you and your mom would live here, and I would live there. And we can visit each other and continue to get to know one another. In the in between times, we could play video games together or talk on the phone or Zoom or whatever. And if we all still like each other and want to be together, *then* we can talk about you moving."

Benji leaned forward and climbed on the bed. He wrapped his arms around Matthew, pulling him into a hug. Matthew automatically wrapped his arms around him.

"I hope we still like each other, because I want you to be my dad."

Before Matthew could react, Benji let go of him, hopped off the bed, and skipped out of the room.

"Sorry about that," Rebecca said.

"Don't be. The honesty is refreshing. But, wow, the pressure to not fuck everything up is now even higher."

"I should have warned you that dating, or whatever it is we're doing, would be even more complicated because I'm a mom."

"I knew it would be more complicated. What I didn't expect was to fall so hard for your kid so quickly. He's already wormed his way into my heart, and regardless of what happens between us, I don't think I can ever get him out. So, how about we make a deal right now? If either of us starts to feel like the relationship is not going the way we want or expect it to go, we talk it out, and if we can't fix it, we end things amicably, while we still like each other, so we can still be friends and I can hopefully still be in Benji's life in some way."

Matthew held his breath. He didn't know if what he said was good or bad, but he spoke from the heart. And it terrified him. He was always one to shy away from commitment. Cut off all ties to people. Never wanted to get close, because if he got close, it would hurt more when they were inevitably taken from him. And here he was, putting everything out there, and saying he wanted to be in Rebecca and Benji's lives for the long haul in one way or another.

Is this what getting good sleep did? Made you rational?

"I like that," Rebecca said. "It takes some of the pressure off of us to make things work for Benji. He'll always have you in his life, no matter what."

Matthew turned, so he was fully facing Rebecca, his heart hammering in his chest. "I really want to try to make this work. Whatever it is. But you should know, I haven't had very much experience in relationships. I'm kinda fucked up emotionally, but I'm going to try my damndest to not fuck this up."

"I'm a widow who is also a single mom, and you've met my dad. So, I'm also kinda fucked up emotionally, and I come with a lot of baggage."

"Quite the pair we make."

"Quite."

Matthew smiled down at her. "As much as I love having this heart-to-heart discovery, pretty sure if you don't get up and start getting ready soon, Benji will be back in here yelling at you."

"Fuck, school, right." Rebecca threw back the covers and got out of bed.

"There's a spare key in the right most drawer in the kitchen. It's yours. Please take it before you leave today. I think I would feel better knowing you had a key. And if you wanted to stop here and just sleep...you could."

Matthew swallowed and nodded. "Sure. Yeah. I could do that."

After Benji and Rebecca left for school, Matthew went to his room to shower and change, tucking Rebecca's key into his pocket. Then he met with the rest of the team for breakfast.

"Are you doing okay, Matty?" Millie asked, sipping her coffee.

"Yeah, why?"

Millie looked down at her coffee before looking back up at him. "I watched you leave Rebecca's room this morning. I know that's a big step for you."

"It's not like that. I'm just comforting her." When the words came out of his mouth, the argument sounded weak even to him.

"Matty. I've known you for a decade. In that time, I have never been to your house. I barely know anything about you. You're notorious for keeping everyone at arm's length. So, seeing you with Rebecca the last few days has been really nice. I've seen you open up like you've never opened up before. But, at the same time, this is a lot for you."

Matthew looked at his lap. "I'm sorry."

"Why on earth are you apologizing to me?"

"Because I've been a shit friend. I'm going to do better from now on."

"You don't need to change, Matty. We love you and your stoic ways."

He shook his head. "I want to be a better friend. Let people in more. I didn't realize how lonely I was, how much I kept people at arm's length until now. I'll do better. I *want* to do better."

He looked up to see Millie smiling at him. "Well, maybe it's not bad to have more Matty in our lives. Are things getting serious between you and Rebecca?"

Matthew shrugged. "We like each other, and Benji likes me. Benji wants to move to Washington to live near me."

"Wow. Won the kid over. That's big."

"It is."

"Are you—"

"I'm not going to let this compromise the case. But I probably shouldn't be in the room when we interview Toby. I won't be able to control myself."

"And there's the Matty we all know and love. Logical. We had already decided Logan and Thomas will be in. The rest of us will be out, observing."

"Good call. They're the best to be in there."

Millie set her coffee mug on the table. "For what it's worth, I like Rebecca. Her life is pretty complicated at the moment, but I think you're a good stabilizing force for her right now."

Matthew listened to her, his heart pounding. This was a lot of pressure for something he kind of sucked at and had no experience doing.

Millie stood up, interrupting his min-existential crisis. "Should we get going?"

Matthew wiped his hands on a napkin and stood. "Yeah, let's see if this is our bastard."

The drive to the police station was short. They could have walked, but they wanted the trucks there, just in case they needed to go out further into the town.

The interrogation room was small, and the observation room was even smaller. Trevor, Millie, and Matthew were crammed in front of the window so they could watch Toby for tics. They were wired into comms that Thomas and Logan were wearing so they could pipe in and help lead the interrogation based on their observations.

Toby sat across from Thomas and Logan. He was wearing his full uniform, including gun belt. He was slouched back in the chair, his arms folded across his chest.

"Why am I here?" Toby asked.

"We just need to ask you a few questions about the murders that have been happening around here." Thomas folded his hands on the table in front of him, sitting up straight behind the table. He didn't smile. Logan, on the other hand, had a more relaxed posture, and his face wasn't as hard. They were playing Toby.

"I don't understand. What do I have to do with the murders? I'm a cop."

"The fact that you're an officer of the law doesn't exempt you from being a murder suspect. Look at the Golden State Killer. He was an officer of the law," Thomas pointed out.

Toby sat up, a little taller. "Do you have evidence against me?"

"Where were you two nights ago?" Logan asked.

"Home."

"Alone?"

"I live alone, so yes."

"That's not a good look, Toby." Logan sat up a little straighter in his seat.

Thomas never moved. He remained sitting up straight, watching.

Matthew was also watching. He was specifically watching the movement of Toby's eyes and the level of his fidgeting. He was also listening for the moment his speech altered. All signs of someone covering up a lie.

Toby was nervous. That was obvious. His breathing had increased, and he kept eying the exit. He sat up even straighter and unfolded his arms. "I don't know what to tell you, man. I live alone."

"Tell me about your relationship with Mark Lovett." Thomas didn't even miss a beat.

"I don't know. We went to high school together. We saw each other around town sometimes. We were on the planning committee for our high school reunion before he died. Otherwise, we ran in completely different circles."

Matthew leaned toward Millie. "That's the same committee Mark was on with Rebecca."

"So, he would have seen them together." Millie activated her comm. "Ask him what subcommittee he was on. If he and Mark were on the same subcommittee."

"Were you and Mark on the same subcommittee?" Logan asked.

"No. We weren't a large planning committee, so subcommittees were partnerships. I was partnered with Lisa something or another, and Mark was put with Rebecca."

"How did you feel when he was put on a subcommittee with Rebecca?" Thomas asked.

Toby shrugged. "Fine, I guess. I didn't want to do what they were doing, anyway. Sounded boring."

Matthew frowned. He was telling the truth.

Logan picked up a piece of paper laying on the desk and looked at it. "What about your relationship with John Davies?"

"Again, went to high school together, but we ran in different circles. Saw him around town, but didn't say much to each other." Toby's leg bounced frantically under the table.

"Really?" Thomas said, leaning in a bit closer to Toby, almost resting his chest on the table.

"Fine. We played poker together. John was a shitty person. He was cheating on his wife, pretty openly. I didn't shed many tears for him when the lunatic offed him."

"He was cheating on his wife?" Logan made a note of this new information on his piece of paper.

"Yeah, and rumors were going around that he was cheating with Becky, but everyone who mattered knew it wasn't her. She would never do that."

"Did you think they were having an affair?" Logan didn't even look up from the paper.

"I just said everyone who mattered knew it wasn't her."

Thomas leaned back a little. "Getting a little testy there, Toby. Were you jealous of their friendship?"

"Me? Jealous of fucking John Davies? Fuck no. Becky would never go for a married guy, and she wouldn't go for a nerd like John," Toby scoffed. "She married that asshole from out of town, and pretty sure she got that out of her system."

"Did you know David Crandall asked Rebecca out on a date the day before he was murdered?" Logan continued writing on the paper. Matthew was pretty sure he was just doodling.

Toby's leg began bouncing even faster. "Yeah. I heard that. But she never would have said yes."

"She told us she was planning to say yes." Logan again with the jabs.

Matthew watched as Toby's face grew red. "She wouldn't."

"And her best friend, Andy, who is also now deceased, was encouraging it."

Matthew leaned in until his nose was practically touching the glass, never taking his eyes off of Toby.

"Andy was an asshole who didn't belong in this town. He should have left when Jaime fucking died," Toby said through clenched teeth.

Still doodling on the paper, Logan went in for the kill. "It probably all worked out for the best, anyway. I just watched Agent Grant leave her apartment this morning. Seems like things are getting pretty serious between him and Rebecca."

With a roar, Toby flew up from his seat, the chair flying to the ground behind him. "Where is he? I'm going to fucking kill him!"

Matthew pulled away from the glass with a smirk on his face. And there it was. Probable cause. Time to go get a warrant to search his residence.

Chapter Fourteen

REBECCA

Wednesday, May 20

Matty - Waiting for the judge to issue a warrant. Don't worry about dinner. Bringing takeout from Gianni's, my treat.

Rebecca smiled down at her phone. She was sitting behind the desk, catching up on hotel emails. Her parents left them to her because, for some reason, computer technology stressed them out. The emails were mostly people who couldn't figure out their online reservation system, something Rebecca also managed, and so she had to reply and either confirm the dates or gently tell them their date was booked.

She couldn't wait until she didn't need to do this anymore.

But the text from Matty definitely brightened her day. It was a struggle to get through school. Not because of her grief, but because the kids knew there weren't very many days left of school. They. Were. Antsy.

Knowing she wouldn't have to cook dinner tonight, complete bright spot.

She shut down the computer and gathered her phone and her book. She placed her little sign informing guests to ring her doorbell for service and walked back to her apartment, where she had left Benji to zone out after school.

She opened her door and shook her head. He was exactly where she left him. On the couch playing Minecraft.

"Agent Matty is bringing us supper, so I hope you didn't eat too many snacks while I was at the front desk."

Benji turned away from the TV, a wide grin on his face. "Agent Matty is coming? Do you think he'll have time to play with me?"

Rebecca shrugged. "Maybe? I don't know how long he'll have. Let's eat first, and then if there's time, I'm sure he'll play with you."

Benji turned back to his game, practically vibrating with excitement.

Rebecca pulled out her phone and stopped short. She was about to scroll to Andy's name and tell him everything that had happened today. About giving the hot FBI guy a key to her place, about him bringing them dinner, and Benji's obvious love for him. But she couldn't. She would never be able to text him again. Because he was gone. Some bastard took him away from her.

She tossed her phone on the table and plopped herself down in a chair, covering her face with her hands. She let the grief run over her. Being in school all day, she had to hold it in. Crying in front of the kids would have been bad. But now, all the pent-up emotions she had been holding in all day were leaking out of her body as tears. So many tears.

The door opened, and she heard the rustling of bags.

"Hey, Benji," Matty greeted, coming into the apartment. "Getting a head start?"

"Agent Matty!" Benji threw down his controllers and sprinted across the small space. Matthew could barely set the food down on the ground before his arms were full of Benji.

Seeing her son enthusiastically greet Matty and watching Matty happily embrace him was enough to lift some of the grief hanging over her.

Matthew let Benji down and turned to smile at Rebecca. Man, she loved his crooked smile.

"I hope you two are hungry." He picked up the bags and moved toward the table. "I didn't know what to order, so I ordered a variety, and I figured we could pile it all in the middle of the table and eat it family style."

Rebecca eyed the bags of food. There was so much of it. "Wow."

"Yeah, I know. But hopefully it will reheat well, and we can have lunch tomorrow."

We.

How was it that one word could do so much to her heart?

"Definitely. The word you were looking for there was definitely."

Matthew laughed as he continued to unpack containers of food. Rebecca went into the kitchen to grab plates and utensils to serve the food and eat.

"How was your day at school?" Matthew asked.

Rebecca hid a smile. The awkwardness that was between them a couple days ago had almost vanished, but she could still hear some hesitation in Matthew's voice as he started a conversation, as if he was still learning. She loved it. It was sweet and refreshing, but she also loved that his confidence was slowly growing.

"It was fine. The kids know summer break is literally days away, so they were pretty rowdy. But I got through it."

"We did more science experiments." Benji didn't even bother looking away from the TV while he shared the excitement of the day.

"Oh yeah? Science was always my favorite. What was your experiment?"

"We each got a bottle of diet coke and a package of Mentos. And when the teacher counted backwards from five, we dropped all the Mentos into the pop and it exploded like a volcano!"

Matthew let out a low whistle. "Man. That sounds pretty exciting. Was it?"

Benji paused his game and turned to face them. "It was super exciting. It was probably the coolest thing I've ever seen. I don't know how my teacher is going to top it tomorrow."

Matthew laughed. "I don't think your teacher is in the business of entertaining you. Pretty sure she's there to make sure you're learning something."

"Psh," Benji said. "My teacher is the best in the entire world, and I'm going to be super sad when school is over."

"Is science your favorite?"

"Yep! I want to be a scientist when I grow up and make lots of discoveries."

"That sounds like a fantastic goal."

Rebecca finished setting the table. "Benji, come on over, it's time to eat."

The three of them settled in at the table and began passing the food around. There were mashed potatoes, pot roast, three different vegetables, rolls, and some kind of seasonal cobbler for dessert. Matthew had gone all out. And there would definitely be leftovers for tomorrow.

As they ate, they talked about mundane things. There was more discussion about science and school. About the food. And what they were watching on Netflix.

Eventually, the food was finished, and the boys kept glancing at the couch.

"Go." She laughed. "I'll clean up."

Benji cheered and ran to the couch. Matthew hung back for a second. "Are you sure? I can help."

"Go," she repeated. "He's been looking forward to playing with you for days. I've got this."

Matthew walked over to her and gave her a soft kiss on her lips. It was the type of kiss that, even though it was quick, almost a peck, it lingered. "Want to know a secret?" he whispered, as their faces were still close together.

"Sure," she whispered back.

"So have I."

About an hour after dinner finished, Matthew had gotten a text that the warrant had gone through and had to say his goodbyes, well, at least to Benji. He didn't know how long he would be gone, and he knew Benji would be in bed already when he got back.

Rebecca hoped she would still be awake when he got back, but she also knew she should probably get some sleep. Tomorrow was a school day, and she was dragging today after being up so late the night before.

She checked in with Benji who was laying in his bed reading a book. He looked like he wasn't going to make it to the time his light went off for the night. It had been a long week. A long, emotional week.

Rebecca walked down to her room and turned on the light. She walked over to her dresser and picked up the picture she had sitting there of her and Jaime on their wedding day. She carried it over to her bed, sitting on the edge.

They were so young on their wedding day. So, so young. But they were in love, and they made it work. He was the love of her life. Her best friend. They were supposed to have forever. But forever wasn't even twenty years.

"Hey, babe," she whispered. "So, I'm sure Andy has already caught you up on everything after you two were reunited up there. How pissed was he that he was taken in his prime? Doesn't matter, I bet he was super excited to be reunited with you. You guys were always inseparable in life. I'm glad you two have each other now."

She took a deep breath and wiped the tears making their way down her cheeks. "I guess I wanted to talk to you about the huge development in my life." She took another deep breath. "I met someone. And things are moving super-fast. Like, I gave him a key to my place fast. I really, really like him, and so does Benji. He's amazing with Benji, Jaime, like amazing. He reminds me a lot of you in that respect. So caring, and focused on what Benji has to say. Doesn't talk down to him. Plays Minecraft with him, of all things. How is that for fate? Finding a guy who likes Minecraft just as much as our kid?"

She laughed a little. "He brought us dinner tonight and made sure there was enough to have extras for lunch tomorrow. He's checking in with us even though he's a super busy FBI agent. And, I am falling hard. So hard."

She ran her fingers along the outline of Jaime's face. "I'm also scared. I'm scared everything is moving too fast. That I'm letting go of you too quickly. It's barely been a year since I lost you. I always told you that if you died before me, you were it. I would never be in another relationship. I would just become an old cat lady. And then I met Matty. I promise, I wasn't looking for it. I was content with my life. And now I'm second guessing everything. How can I feel this way about another man when I was sure you were it for me?"

She pulled the picture frame to her chest, hugging it as she cried in earnest. "I wish I could talk to you for real. Ask you if I'm making the right choice. If this is okay. Am I allowed to move on? If only you could give me some sort of sign you approved of my choices."

A soft music filled the quiet room. Rebecca glanced over to her bedside table where a music box Jaime had given her for one of their anniversaries sat. It was a custom-made music box with ice skating penguins on the top, and the song that played was their song, but instrumental. As the notes of Cat Power's "Sea of Love" played through the room, the sobs she was holding back escaped from her. She couldn't remember the last time she wound the music box. There was no logical explanation for why it would be playing.

Except for one.

Jaime was giving her a sign.

He was listening.

He was there in the room with her, giving her a thumbs up.

He wanted her to move on. To find happiness with someone else.

It felt as if a weight had been lifted from her shoulders. As if a burden she was carrying had been relieved.

Everything was going to be okay.

Chapter Fifteen

MATTHEW

Thursday, May 21

Reaching for the cup of coffee, Matthew glanced out the window. The sun was coming up. He groaned as he took a sip. The coffee had already grown cold.

The team was still combing through Toby's apartment. The warrant had come in around seven the night before and by the time they got there, and had the place fingerprinted, it was well after midnight. But they didn't want to leave and come back. They didn't have enough evidence to arrest Toby. Waiting risked Toby coming in and destroying any evidence there could be.

And so far, there was no evidence.

None.

There was nothing tying him to any of the murders. They still needed to run the fingerprints, but they were probably going to come up as just Toby.

Plus, this apartment was not very large nor built well. If this were the primary location of the murders, neighbors would have called in complaints. They would have heard everything.

Trevor was combing the internet looking for other locations owned by Toby but was coming up empty so far.

The murders were happening somewhere in town, just not here.

He had sent a text to Rebecca around midnight telling her he was not coming over and to apologize to Benji. He hated disappointing him, but he also had to do his job.

Which was feeling incredibly fucking tedious right now.

"Fuck. Yeah." Trevor's shout echoed through the small apartment.

"What'd you find?" Thomas asked.

"Guess whose parents signed their house over to him last year when they retired and moved to Florida?"

"Are you fucking kidding me? He owns a fucking house?! Why the hell is he living in this bread box then?" Matthew slammed the papers he had been rifling through down.

"No clue. But we should probably head over there and check it out."

"Where is it?" Thomas was already standing, grabbing his jacket off the chair.

"You'll never believe it. It's one of the houses that backs up to Murphy's Woods."

Every member of the team leaped up from their chairs and headed for the door almost at once. On the way out, they nabbed a few of the crime scene people.

Matthew jumped behind the wheel of one of the SUVs and immediately started it. Logan hopped into the seat next to him, and two crime scene people climbed into the back. Peeling out, Logan grabbed the light, rolled down the window, and stuck it to the roof of the car. With the flashing light in place, Matthew flipped the switch and then pressed on the gas.

Toby had had full access to his secret house ever since the warrant had been issued. Who knew what sort of evidence he could be destroying right now?

The beauty of a small city was it didn't take long to get to where they were going. They were screeching to a halt in front of the house in under ten minutes.

Before he could even turn the car off, Logan and the crime scene people were leaping from the car and running for the door. Matthew jumped out as soon as he could and went into the house.

Toby wasn't there. But who knew what damage he caused while they were at the apartment? He probably destroyed everything.

Moving through the first floor, though, Matthew noticed the house didn't look very lived in. Most of the rooms were completely empty.

"If you didn't want to look like you kept a house for secret serial killing, you should probably furnish it," Matthew muttered to himself.

Weaving his way through the rooms, he found himself at a door that probably led down to the basement. Matthew steeled himself before turning the knob and opening the door. He found the switch to the light and flipped it on.

Descending the steps, he moved cautiously, keeping on hand on the butt of the pistol at his hip. The house had seemed empty, but Toby could be hiding down here.

As he stepped into the basement, he found it just as empty as the rest of the house. It wasn't finished, so the walls were mostly open, and he could see through the entire basement. The only thing visible, really, was an old washer and dryer. There was one wall that had been dry walled, but not much else. There was a door. Matthew assumed it was the bathroom, but he made his way over to check it out.

He pushed open the door and instead of finding a bathroom, he found a small room with photos pinned up on three of the walls.

He walked closer to the pictures, and anger immediately rose in him.

All the pictures were of Rebecca and Benji.

Pictures of them walking around the square. Shopping. Eating. Playing in the park. At the school. Hundreds of pictures of them together. Apart.

Matthew saw red when he noticed how many pictures were just of Benji by himself, playing on the playground at school.

He pulled out his cell phone.

"Where are you?" Thomas answered.

"Basement."

"Find anything?"

"We need to bring him in, and this time, I want to do the interrogation."

"What did you find?"

"He's stalking them."

"Who?"

"Benji and Rebecca."

"What did you find?"

"Come down here." He hung up the phone and continued to stare at the pictures, bile rising in the back of his throat. There were footsteps behind him, but he didn't need to turn around to know it was Thomas.

"Fuck."

"I want to do the talking."

"This doesn't prove he's the killer."

"No, but it proves he's been stalking Rebecca and Benji." He walked over to one of the pictures of Benji at school. "This one was obviously taken while Benji was at school. He's a danger to them. Rebecca tried to get a restraining order the other day and they wouldn't let her. At the very least, I can get her that restraining order. At best, we get him confessing to the murders. But I want to be the one to confront him about stalking an eight-year-old kid at school."

"Fine. But you're not allowed to hit him."

"I'm not making any promises."

Matthew glared at the man at the table in the interrogation room. He was sitting there with a smug look on his face. As if he knew he had gotten away with everything.

He may not be the murderer. Or he very well could be. They still hadn't found any evidence of the victims being in the empty house, but they had him for something else.

At the very least, Matthew could get this man off the streets and away from Rebecca and Benji. Thinking back on the pictures of Benji in that basement, Matthew's hands formed into fists.

"Hey." Thomas' voice caused him to bring his gaze away from the man in the chair and back into the room. "No hitting. But feel free to do anything else. Any tactic you can think of. After about ten, we'll send Logan in to play good cop."

Matthew nodded. They had already discussed all of this already. They were letting him have Toby to himself for ten minutes. And then all bets were off.

He squared his shoulders and straightened out his jacket. After running a hand over his hair to make everything was in place, he hoped he didn't look like a man who hadn't slept for over twenty-four hours. Steeling his nerves, he walked to the door and opened it, stepping inside the small room.

The only thing in there was a table, three chairs, and fucking Toby.

"No." Toby sat up straighter in his chair. "I don't want you. I'll talk to anyone but you."

"Too bad. You get me."

"You're a fucking bastard."

"Wow. I am pretty sure I haven't said more than two words to you, and this is the welcome I get?"

Toby leaned forward, resting his hands on the table, palms flat against the cool surface. "You know why I'm less than welcoming to you."

Matthew sat back in his chair, folding his arms across his chest. "Please, remind me."

"You stole my girl." Toby's voice was low, his words coming out practically as a growl.

"Last I checked, she's her own person and can do whatever or see whoever she wants. Also, she's not an object to be stolen."

"She belongs to me. No one else."

"So, you're killing off the competition?"

Toby froze. "I didn't say that."

"Should I worry I'm next?"

"I haven't killed anyone."

"You keep saying that, but I'm still not believing you."

"You don't need to believe me. It doesn't change the fact that it's true. Hook me up to a lie detector. It'll prove I'm telling the truth. Just watch."

Matthew tilted his head to the right. "You want me to hook a police officer, who probably learned back in the academy how to game them, to a lie detector?"

Toby narrowed his eyes. "Fuck. You."

The side of Matthew's mouth quirked up a little. "Touched a nerve I see."

"Did you find anything in my apartment?"

"We did not."

Toby scoffed. "So, I'm guessing I'm free to go? No evidence. You can't hold me."

Leaning forward in his chair, Matthew rested his arms on the table. "Oh, we didn't find anything at the apartment, but we sure as hell found something at your house."

The smile melted off his face. "What house?"

"You know, the house your parents gifted you last year before they moved to Florida."

"I don't know what you're talking about."

"You're a terrible liar. You have all the tells. It's very text-book." Matthew leaned forward even more. "You see, I think you've forgotten that this is my job. I read people. And I'm reading you like a book."

It was Toby's turn to lean forward and rest his arms on the table.

"I think you're bluffing."

"That we found your house? Oh, we found your house. Your incredibly empty house. How come you live in that shitty apartment instead of the house?"

"None of your fucking business, that's why."

Matthew was taken aback by the brute force of his response. He touched a nerve. Now to poke at it even more. "Is it because you only use it for illicit activities?"

"I haven't killed anyone there."

"Are you implying you've killed someone somewhere else?"

"No. I haven't killed anyone at all. I've said that over and over again. You mentioned illicit activities, and I know that was code for murder. The house has been empty since my parents left. There's nothing there."

"Nothing? Pretty sure there's *something* there."

Toby froze. "Lawyer."

Matthew opened the folder in front of him and pulled out the spy shots of Rebecca and Benji. "I'm pretty sure there were hundreds of things there." He placed the photos one by one in front of Toby.

"Lawyer."

"This looks like some heavy-duty stalking, Toby. Of a child, no less. A child."

"Law-yer."

"He's eight years old. Eight. Years. Old. And you're following him to school? Sitting outside his school snapping photographs of him? This is fucked. Up. Not a good look, grown man, sitting outside the elementary school taking pictures of kids. People might get the wrong idea. Or maybe the right one?"

"Fuck. You. Also, lawyer."

"We've got you." Matthew stood from the table, gathering all the pictures. "We've got you on stalking. We've got you on stalking a minor. And pretty soon we're going to get you for murder. It's just a matter of time."

Matthew walked out the door and back into the observation room.

"He sure went to lawyer pretty quick after he learned we found those pictures in his house," Millie said when he shut the door behind him.

"Yep."

"Makes someone wonder what else there is to find in that house."

"Do you think he's our UNSUB, or are we latching onto him because we *want* him to be our UNSUB?" Matthew set the folder down on the piles of folders they brought with them. They were moving back to the hotel after this. They needed sleep and they'd worn out their welcome in the precinct, questioning one of their own twice now.

Millie picked up her jacket and put it on. "Honestly? At this point, I don't know. Before that performance in there, I would have said we're trying to fit him in a box that's not a good fit because we needed him to. But after that…"

"He's hiding something," Logan finished. "I don't know if it's more stuff to do with the stalking, or if it's something else, but he's definitely hiding something."

"I've already contacted the judge about filing protective orders against him for Rebecca and Benji," Millie said. "Just so you know. The precinct can't block it. There is enough evidence to get one without her filing a report."

"Thank you," Matthew said, his shoulders sagging in relief. "That's one thing I can cross off the list to do. She tried to file a report a couple days ago after he yelled at her in the restaurant, but they refused. Tomorrow's the day he ordered her to go on a date with him…"

"I put a rush on it, and we'll make sure it's in place before then. Can't go on a date with someone you're not legally allowed to be around. If he tries to see her tomorrow, he'll be in violation of the order, and then we can finally arrest the bastard." Millie was calm and reassuring, everything he was not.

"As much as I would hate for him to confront Rebecca again, it would be really nice to be able to arrest the asshole." Matthew led the trio out the door.

The team opted to not drive the SUV back to the hotel. They hadn't slept in over twenty-four hours and the walk wasn't far. They didn't want to chance driving while impaired.

"So, we know he is hiding something, but what?" Logan said once they were outside. The sun was bright and making its way overhead. It was nearly midday, and traffic around the square was a little busier than normal as people made their way to eat lunch.

"It has something to do with that house. And I have a feeling it's not because he's killing people," Matthew said. "Did you find anything upstairs?"

"Everything was empty," Logan said.

Matthew sighed. "We're missing something."

"We are. Once we all get some sleep, we can go back to the house and look around again," Millie said. "We're all exhausted. Everyone else has already gone back to get some sleep. It's our turn. We'll try again this evening."

Matthew nodded in agreement. She was right. They were all exhausted, and if they continued on this path in this state, they were going to make mistakes, and they couldn't afford to make any of those.

They walked up to the hotel and let themselves in. He said goodbye to Logan and Millie as they made their ways up to their rooms.

Matthew hesitated for a minute at the base of the stairs, he could head up to his room and get some sleep, or he could use his key to take a nap at Rebecca's and be there when she and Benji returned from school.

Deciding the second option was better, he headed to Rebecca's apartment. Pulling out the spare key, he let himself in.

Being in the apartment without Rebecca and Benji felt weird. But also, not really. Like he already belonged.

He slipped off his shoes and walked into the bedroom. Quickly, he shed his clothes, trading them for the pajamas Rebecca had lent him the day before. Changed, he walked over to the bed, passing the dresser.

A picture sitting on the surface caught his eye. It was Rebecca and her husband on their wedding day. They were very young, and very happy. Matthew smiled as he looked at Rebecca's bright smile. He hoped he would be able to see her smile like that again. She was too young to have experienced so much loss. She deserved to be happy.

Matthew turned from the picture and walked to the bed, climbing in. He pulled the covers up and settled into the bed. He rolled over so he could see the spot where Rebecca would normally be sleeping.

This was weird, right? He shouldn't be here. Maybe he should just grab his things and go back up to his assigned room. It was one thing to stay when she was here, but she wasn't. He was here alone. Things were moving really fast. They had only known each other for a couple days and here he was making himself at home. As if he lived here. The audacity.

He moved to pull the covers back and let himself out, when something stopped him.

The music box next to the bed started playing.

The room filled with Cat Power's "Sea of Love". Matthew stared at the box in wonder. He had never heard of a music box that played that song before. This must have been custom made for Rebecca. Probably by her husband.

Matthew was a man of science, not faith. He knew there should be a logical explanation for the music box to just start playing, but he also knew that there could be other nonscientific reasons as well.

And at this moment, as his anxiety threatened to ruin everything because he was pretty much incapable of letting someone get close to him.

He was going to choose to believe this was some sort of sign that he needed to calm the fuck down, tuck himself back in, and go to sleep. That he needed to stop overthinking things, and allow himself to be happy.

So, he did just that. He laid back down, pulling the covers up and over his head. As he fell asleep, he let the notes of "Sea of Love" wash over him and lull him to sleep.

Chapter Sixteen

REBECCA

Thursday, May 21

"Rebecca!"

Rebecca turned at the sound of her name coming from the dining room.

She had just come home from school, her backpack slung across her back. It had been a long day, and she couldn't wait to put her feet up.

"Did you need something?" she moved into the dining room to see Millie, and who she thought was Trevor, sitting at a table.

Millie shook her head. "No, just wanted to see how you're doing. I'm so sorry for your loss."

Trevor looked up from his tablet, his deep brown eyes meeting her own. "We're going to catch the bastard who did this."

Rebecca gave them a smile. "Thank you. I'm holding up. School and Benji have been a great distraction."

"If you ever need to talk, about anything…" Millie trailed off.

Rebecca was a bit caught off guard. She didn't have a lot of friends. Colleagues she was friendly with, but not friends. And now that Andy was gone… "Yes. Thank you. I would like that. I'll um, send you a text?"

Millie smiled at her. "I'll let you go. You look like you need a nap. I'll look forward to that text."

Rebecca gave them a wave and walked back toward her rooms. She pushed open the door to the apartment and immediately clocked Matthew's shoes and smiled.

Good.

He had to be tired. She had tried to stay up to wait for him the night before, but after he sent the text at nearly midnight saying they were finally getting in to start looking at stuff in Toby's apartment, she knew she wasn't going to see him and went to sleep.

Waking up alone in bed this morning had been disappointing. After two nights, she had grown used to him wrapping himself around her body as he slept. She enjoyed waking up in his warm embrace. The bed felt cold without him.

She would try to not get her hopes up about him being here tonight. It probably wasn't the best sign that he was home sleeping in the middle of the day. But she would take any time she could with him.

She slipped her shoes off and walked to the closet to put her backpack away. Benji had asked to stay at her parents' tonight, and they jumped at the chance to have him. They would take him to school in the morning.

Which meant either she and Matthew would have the apartment alone tonight. Or she would merely be alone.

She really hoped for option number one.

After her sign from Jaime the night before, giving her approval to move on, she had been more than ready to get Matthew alone.

And fate handed her a kid desperate to stay with grandma and grandpa.

Thank you, Fate.

She padded her way to the bedroom and quietly opened the door. Light snores filled the air as she took in a deeply sleeping Matty. He was facing the door, and had dark circles under his eyes. He needed this sleep, and hopefully, he could sleep even more. She hoped he didn't need to be back at work anytime soon.

She quietly closed the door behind her and moved into the kitchen. Looking through the cupboards and opening her fridge to see what she had, she quickly decided on what to make for dinner. It had been very kind of Matty to bring them dinner the night before, but she wanted to cook for him.

It was quite possible her love language was cooking for people because she loved to feed others. And since she had come to terms with how she was feeling about Matty, she had been itching to feed him properly.

With everything that had gone on this week, she desperately needed to go to the store, but not so desperately that she didn't have everything she needed to make a simple pasta meal. They always had pasta and sauce, her easy go to meal.

As she put the water on to boil, she began opening cans of tomato sauce and pouring them into a pot. She pulled out all her spices and sprinkled in whatever amount her heart told her to. You don't measure spices. The spices tell you how much you should put in that day.

Rebecca stirred the sauce and set it on to simmer. Next, she pulled out the frozen green beans she bought in order to convince Benji to eat something green and read the directions on the back of the package.

She glanced at the clock and back at the freezer. Did she have time to make the bread she had in there, or would that be too much? She already felt like she was being a bit extra with this meal, but, truly, would bread be a step too far? She shook her head. Of course it wouldn't be. She was making pasta; it was almost expected there would be bread. If she didn't make it, he would probably be disappointed.

"You're focusing *really* hard on that freezer. Is everything okay?"

Rebecca jumped and spun around, clutching a hand to her chest. "Holy shit."

Matthew chuckled. "Sorry I scared you."

"It's okay. I didn't think you would be awake."

"I heard you moving around out here and realized I better get up. We have a lot to do, and I am really hoping we're not up for another twenty-four hours to do it, and would like to hopefully sleep at a normal time."

"Makes sense. But still, sorry for waking you."

"It's okay." He stretched his arms above his head. The t-shirt she lent him riding up a little revealing his V-shape. Rebecca found herself mesmerized by it. "Where's Benji?"

"He's at my parents' house. He asked if he could stay there, and they said they would get him to school in the morning, so I let him go."

"So, we have the apartment to ourselves?"

Rebecca smiled. "We do."

Matthew smiled slowly. "Hmm. Interesting." He walked toward her, closing the gap between them. She saw him hesitate for a split second before he wrapped his arms around her body and pulled her flush against his body.

She looked up at him and grinned as she saw him smiling down at her. He lowered his head and took her lips in his. She returned the kiss as she wrapped her arms around his neck. Their kiss quickly went from sweet to frenzied as Matthew moved his hands lower on her back, resting at the top curve of her ass. Rebecca dropped the bag of green beans she was holding and brought her hands up, lacing her fingers through his hair. His hair was so soft, and she loved running her fingers through it. Jaime always kept his hair so short, but she loved Matthew kept his so long.

He moaned into the kiss as her nails scraped against his scalp and pushed her backward until her hips hit the counter. His hand moved over the curve of her ass until they grabbed her thighs, lifting her up onto the counter. She gasped as she was settled on the counter, the granite cold against her bare thighs. Matthew stepped between her open thighs, never breaking the kiss.

Matthew moved his hands down her thighs to the hemline of her dress. His fingers slipped under the dress and his hands began slowly moving back up her bare thigh.

Rebecca pulled away from Matthew's lips, gasping for air. His lips moved down her neck as his hands continued their trek up her thighs. Her breathing kept increasing as his fingers made their way to their destination. Finally, they touched the edge of her underwear.

His finger slipped under the elastic band of her panties, touching her slick heat.

"Yes," she whispered into his ear as he moved his fingers artfully against her.

She slid her hands down his back and around to his belt buckle, trying to fumble it open. He removed his hand that was merely resting on her thigh and batted her hands away.

He pulled away from her neck, pressing his lips against her ear. "Just feel. This is about you." His breath tickled her ear.

She let out a mewl of protest but obeyed, bringing her hands up to the back of his neck, lacing her fingers back into the hair at the nape of his neck. Matthew brought his lips back to the base of her neck, the place where it met with her shoulder, and she threw her head back as his fingers continued to do amazing things to her.

She allowed herself to become lost in the feelings, clearing her mind of anything else. The pleasure rushed through her. Matthew knew exactly what he was doing. His fingers were magical, combined with what his mouth was doing on her neck, plus it had been a while since she used anything other than her *own* fingers, it wasn't long before she was tumbling over the edge, feeling the euphoric pleasures of her orgasm wash over her.

When she calmed down, she rested her head on his head, forehead to forehead.

"Wow."

Matthew chuckled, his warm breath tickling her as he exhaled. "I'll take wow."

"How about we move this to the bedroom, and we can make sure you get your wow moment?" She moved her hand down his body, cupping him through his pants.

"We don't need to if you don't want to. I don't want you to feel obligated. I wanted to make you feel good. Plus, aren't you making dinner?"

She leaned forward, planting a small kiss on his lips before gently pushing him away. Once she had enough room, she hopped down from the counter and moved toward the stove, turning off both burners. She then took Matthew by the hand and dragged him toward the bedroom.

Later, they laid in bed, Rebecca's head resting on Matthew's chest, his arms wrapped tightly around her body. "That was..." Her mind went blank, unable to properly form words.

"Amazing?" Matthew suggested, his voice filled with mirth. "Mind blowing? Knocked your socks off?"

She laughed. "Well, technically, my socks were knocked off."

"Right off."

She placed a kiss on his chest.

"You don't have any...regrets about what we did, do you?" Matthew asked, his voice barely above a whisper in the room.

"No," she answered firmly. "I don't. Do you?"

She felt him shake his head. "No."

"Why do you ask then?"

"Because just a day ago you were asking to take things slow. That maybe you weren't ready to take things further. And then I sort of...got handsy in the kitchen."

"Oh yeah, you did."

They both laughed.

"Seriously, though, I have no regrets. It's going to sound *insane,* but last night, I sort of asked Jaime for a sign that it was okay to move on, and he...gave me one? I know I sound like I should be committed, but I really and truly feel he gave that sign to me."

"It doesn't sound crazy, because if you're crazy, I'm right there with you, because I'm pretty sure your husband gave me a sign earlier today that it was okay was here."

Rebecca sat up, propping herself up on her elbow to look at him. "Are you serious?"

Matthew nodded. "Yeah. I was in here earlier having a lot of anxiety about being here without you, and all of a sudden, the music—"

"...box started playing?" Rebecca finished.

"Yes. How did you know?"

"Last night when I asked Jaime for a sign that I was doing the right thing, that it was okay for me to move on, my music box began to play. He had that custom made for me for one of our anniversaries. Penguins are my favorite animal, and it plays our song. So, when it started playing, I knew it was him."

"I figured it was a custom made. It's a strange song to have in a music box. And when it started playing, this calm passed over me. And I knew I was getting the okay from Jaime to stay here."

"It feels so weird to be saying these things. We haven't even known each other for a week."

"It'll be a week tomorrow," Matthew pointed out.

"Are we moving too fast? Do you think?"

"I think that if we had met on a dating app, we wouldn't have thought twice about jumping into bed with one another on the first day we met each other."

"Yeah, but we aren't just having sex. You feel this right? Whatever this is between us?"

"I do."

"That's what I'm talking about. This is fast, right?"

Matthew looked down at her, his gaze tender as it met hers. She could read his feelings in his eyes. She felt as though she had his superpower. "People always talk about 'love at first sight.' I always thought they were full of shit. No way can anyone know the second they meet someone that they're going to spend the rest of their lives with them. People who claim they do must be projecting their current feelings back on their past selves."

He gave her his half smile that never failed to make her melt. "And then I met you."

Rebecca returned his smile. "And I smashed all your expectations?"

"And one conversation with you had my heart rate increasing. I couldn't take my eyes off of you. And each subsequent minute spent with you continued to smash my reality and what I believed to bits. I don't know if I'm completely ready to say the words but know that I am feeling a lot of powerful feelings toward you. And while they scare me, I don't think they've come too fast."

"I also am feeling a lot of powerful feelings toward you. And I'm also scared of them, because they don't just affect me. I have Benji to think about. Who is also feeling a lot of powerful feelings toward you. A lot. And I need to protect him. I don't want him hurt."

"We already talked about protecting his feelings yesterday, and I stand firm by that. He comes first. Always."

Rebecca shook her head in disbelief. "I can't believe I could be so lucky as to find the perfect man twice."

"I'm glad to hear you say you're lucky. It's much better than what you were saying yesterday. And I'm the lucky one. I've finally found someone who I'm willing to put my heart on the line for. I never thought this would happen to me."

Rebecca stretched her neck up, capturing his lips with hers. Matthew returned the kiss with fervor. He dragged her up his body, and she swung her leg over his hips.

Dinner was going to need to wait just a little bit longer.

Much later, dinner was finally finished and the two of them sat around the table eating pasta and green beans, they had decided the bread wasn't really needed.

"I feel like I need to update you on what is going on with the case, since what we discovered today does, in fact, affect you."

Rebecca paused, her fork halfway up to her mouth. "What do you mean, it affects me?"

Matthew took a deep breath. "You know we were waiting for a warrant to investigate Toby, right?"

"Right. You messaged me pretty late saying you were getting into his apartment."

"Well, turns out he has a house his parents gave him over near Murphy's Woods, so we went and investigated it."

She put the fork down, giving up eating. "You're being cryptic. What did you find at the house? Is he the killer? The person killing people around me?"

Matthew shook his head. "We don't know if he's the killer."

"Then what is it? You're making me nervous."

He took a deep breath. "We found evidence that Toby has been following you and Benji around for some time."

"Following us around? Like stalking?"

"Yeah."

"What sorts of evidence?"

"Pictures. Lots of pictures."

Bile rose in her throat. "Of Benji?"

He simply nodded.

Rebecca stood from her chair and rushed to the bathroom, throwing open the toilet, making it just in time to lose everything that was in her stomach. She felt Matthew as he entered the bathroom. He kneeled beside her and laid a hand on her back, rubbing it.

She waited a few minutes to make sure she was finished before she sat back on her heels. Matthew handed her a glass of water.

She didn't know he had brought it in with him. She gratefully took it, taking a sip. Matthew smoothed over her hair, pushing it out of her face.

"Are you okay?"

She shook her head. "How long do you think he's been following us?"

"We're not sure, but it's been a while. Probably a few months."

"Was he only taking pictures of Benji when we were together or…"

"He sat outside the school and took pictures of him on the playground."

"I think I'm going to be sick again."

Matthew leaned forward, wrapping his arms around her, pulling her tight against him in a hug. She sat the glass of water down on the bathroom floor and wrapped her arms around his body, clutching the back of his shirt in her hands.

"Millie contacted a judge and put in a protection order. If I check my phone, I'm guessing there will be confirmation that it went through. He can't come near you anymore. If he breaks the protection order, he *will* be arrested."

"Do I need to do anything?"

"No. We took care of it so you wouldn't have to. Plus, coming from us, it would be rushed. We could skip the police report."

"Thank you."

"You're welcome."

"I can't believe he was following me around town. Taking pictures of my kid. I want to punch him in the face for his audacity."

"I interrogated him this morning, and let me tell you, I had to hold back quite a bit, because I had the powerful urge to punch him myself, but I was under strict orders not to."

"If he shows up at my door again, am I allowed to punch him in the face?"

Matthew let out a laugh that ruffled her hair. "Well, usually I would say yes, but I would guess he's a petty asshole and he would press assault charges, so I would advise not to punch him in the face."

"Yeah, I won't be any good to Benji if I have a record. Think of the missed scholarship opportunities for him."

"You're going to be okay," Matthew whispered. "You both are."

"I know. But you know what would make everything even better? If he also turns out to be the killer. Then I would have even less to worry about."

"We're working on the killer. Don't worry."

A knock on the door interrupted them. Rebecca pulled back, rubbing at her eyes.

"That's probably someone from my team telling me it's time to get back to work. I'll go answer it."

Matthew stood from the floor and headed to the door, and Rebecca stood from the floor as well and looked at her reflection in the mirror. She's looked better. She turned on the water to splash her face with water but stopped halfway to the tap as a voice bellowed through the apartment.

"Where is my daughter?"

Chapter Seventeen

MATTHEW

Thursday, May 21

Matthew stared at the angry man in the door. His face was red and his eyes were narrowed. This man was not happy to see him.

"Hi, Mr. Hernandez. I'm not sure we formally met, I'm—"

"I don't care who you are. Where is my daughter?"

"Um, she's in the bathroom, she should be out in—"

The man shoved past him and marched into the apartment. Matthew stood there for a second, mouth agape, one hand still on the doorknob. The audacity...

He closed the door and turned to follow the man into the apartment.

"I think maybe you should—"

Mr. Hernandez whipped around and threw out a finger, pointing it at him. "You think? This is not your home. You have no say about what goes on in here. I am looking for my daughter."

"It isn't your home either."

"I own the Noble Hill Hotel, so this is my home."

"Just because you own the building, that doesn't give you any right to come marching in. There are tenant laws, and—"

"Does it make you feel important saying all these legal words and making me feel like an idiot?" Mr. Hernandez's face was growing redder by the minute, his accent growing thicker with each word.

"That wasn't my intent. I was merely pointing out—" Matthew stammered, his hands grew clammy.

"Stop. Just stop. I need to talk to my daughter."

Matthew's stomach dropped. "Is something wrong? Is Benji okay?"

"My grandson is none of your concern!"

"Dad!"

Both men stopped and turned toward the bathroom. Rebecca had taken a minute to refresh herself, brushing her hair and putting the dress she was wearing earlier back on. She was also pissed.

"Mija! What is this man doing here? I have told you—"

"Is Benji okay?"

"Benji is fine."

"Then what are you doing here, dad?"

"You told me to come and get his things. That you would pack him an overnight bag. I told you we would come after dinner before he goes to sleep."

"Fuck," Rebecca muttered. "That's right. I completely forgot."

"Because you were sinning with this man." He shoved a finger in Matthew's direction.

"Hey!" Matthew protested.

"I'll go get Benji's things," Rebecca ignored what her father said about sinning.

"Do you want help?" Matthew asked. He didn't really want to be left alone with her dad.

"I'm good. I'll go faster if I do this alone."

Matthew watched hopelessly as Rebecca disappeared into Benji's room. He turned back toward Mr. Hernandez. "I don't think we were properly introduced before. My name is Matthew Grant, and I'm a Behavior Analyst with the FBI." He held his hand out for Mr. Hernandez to shake, but the other man just stared down at it with his lips curled back.

"I know who you are. You think you can come here with your big city ways and corrupt my daughter? I'll tell you something, *senor*, I will not let another man from out-of-town influence my daughter. She has a son to think about."

"I'm not here to corrupt your daughter."

"Are you Catholic?"

"Um, I actually don't really subscribe to any religion." As soon as the words left his mouth, Matthew knew he had said the wrong thing.

Mr. Hernandez crossed his arms over his chest. "I rest my case."

Rebecca came back carrying a blue backpack and a stuffed bear. She thrust both of them into her father's arms. "There you go."

"*Gracias*. We will get him to school in the morning."

"Thank you. Send him my love."

"I will."

"And dad?"

"Yes?"

"I'm an adult, and I can make my own choices. I don't need or want you to interfere. Matty is a good person, and I really like him." She looked at him, giving him a small smile. "And he really likes me. He's doing a lot of good for this town, and you should give him a chance."

"I just don't want to see you damned to hell for the choices you make."

"I'll go to confession after he leaves."

He frowned. "I can't change your mind?"

"You can't."

Mr. Hernandez turned to face him. "Agent Grant, I apologize for my rash behavior. Sometimes I forget my daughter is an adult and can make her own choices. I only want what is good for her. And for my grandson. They are everything to me." He stuck his hand out. "You can call me Guillermo."

Matthew took the man's hand and tried not to flinch when the other man squeezed his hand firmly. When he let go, Matthew flexed his fingers a few times. "Thank you, sir. I can understand where you're coming from, especially right now with what is going on in your city."

"Yes. Are you any closer to catching the guy? It's very upsetting. I'm not too worried because I'm much older than the men getting killed, but these are all people I've watched grow up, or who have been very close to our family, like Andy, and my heart breaks with each murder."

"We have a few promising leads we're hoping will pan out."

Guillermo nodded. "Good. I will sleep better at night once this *pendejo* is caught." He turned back to Rebecca. "I need to get back. Your mother and Benji made cookies after school, and he has taste tested a lot. He's going to want these things before he passes out from a sugar coma."

Rebecca shook her head. "Tomorrow is going to be rough, isn't it?"

"I'm not making any promises, but I will try to get him to bed on time."

"Thanks, Dad."

Guillermo closed the gap between them and gave his daughter a hug. "*Te amo, mija.*"

"I love you too, dad."

Guillermo pulled away and turned back toward Matthew. "Agent Grant."

"Mr. Hernanadez."

And he didn't even try to correct him. He waltzed out the door without looking back.

Silence filled the room as Matthew and Rebecca kept their gazes on the closed door. It was as if they were waiting for it to reopen.

"Your dad certainly is—"

"A lot?" Rebecca finished. "Mean? Oblivious to the feelings of others?"

"I was going to say boisterous."

"He's that, too."

"Has he always been this way? Like flipping a switch to become a completely different person?"

"My entire life. I never know if I'm going to get 'doting dad' or 'I'm going to scream at you dad'. But, as long as he's the center of attention in a crowd? I get 'I'm indifferent toward you as long as you don't contradict me, dad'."

"Classic narcissistic behavior." The words were out of Matthew's mouth before he could stop them.

"My dad's a narcissist? You figured that out from this one interaction?"

"I'm sorry. Sometimes I can't help myself. But, yes. This one and a couple of other previous interactions. It's pretty textbook."

Rebecca moved to the couch and sat down. "Are there consequences to being raised by a narcissist?"

Matthew shrugged. "I guess? But nothing more than being raised by anyone else? Everyone is who they are because of or in spite of the way they were raised. Everyone has their traumas, and how they choose to let them define them is what really matters."

Rebecca drew up her legs under herself on the couch. "Have you let your traumas define you?"

Matthew moved to the spot next to her on the couch. "Yes. Unfortunately."

"In what ways?"

Matthew let out a breath. "Well, I should probably start with what I consider my defining trauma, right?"

"Oh, you don't need to. If it's painful. The way you look right now tells me it's something way worse than mine."

Matthew turned his body, so he was sitting sideways on the couch. He crossed his legs and leaned forward so his elbows rested on his knees, propping his chin on his hands. "I want to tell you. Because it will explain a lot about me, and it will give you some insight into why I may do some of the things I do and have anxiety about things normal people probably wouldn't."

Rebecca mirrored his pose on the couch. "Tell me."

He closed his eyes. "Growing up, it was always me and my mom. She raised me all by herself. I've never met my father. He never wanted anything to do with me. Which was fine. My mom was my superhero. She was my whole world. She worked really hard to make sure we could survive. Just the two of us. One of our favorite things to do every year was drive around and look at Christmas lights. We would drive town to town, and she knew all the best blocks. We would have hot chocolate, and she would tuck me in with a fluffy blanket in the back seat, and we would stay up past my bedtime just looking at these lights."

Matthew could feel his throat closing up. It was going to be a struggle to get through this without breaking down. But he would try. "The year I was eight, Benji's age, we were doing our normal circuit. Driving town to town. Seeing the lights. Except this time, it was a little slick out. It had snowed earlier in the day and the roads were refreezing. My mom was being so careful, driving slower. But then a deer leaped into the road. My mom tried to swerve to miss it, but she hit some ice and flipped the car. I don't know how many times the car flipped, but when it stopped, it was upside down. Kudos to early 1990s backseat seat belts because I was in tight, hanging upside down like a bat."

"And your mom?" Rebecca whispered.

"She didn't enjoy wearing her seat belt. Nine times out of ten, she'd have had it off."

"Matthew." Her voice was so quiet, filled with anguish for him. And he hadn't even told her the worst part.

"I could see her, in the road. She wasn't very far from the car. She was moving. Like her arms were trying to move. I could see it clearly. But I couldn't get to her. I was stuck in the car. Upside down. And so, I had to watch as she eventually stopped moving. I knew. I knew the second she stopped moving, she was gone. And I was alone in the world."

The couch moved under him, and the next thing he knew, Rebecca's arms were wrapping around his body, pulling him tightly to her. He settled his head in the crook of her neck and let himself go. He couldn't remember the last time he cried about his mom. It was something he learned to repress from a young age. His grandparents he was sent to live with didn't tolerate a boy who cried all the time.

"You're going to be okay," Rebecca murmured into his ear as she ran her hand soothingly on his head, smoothing his hair as if she were petting him. "You're not alone in the world. Not anymore. You have me and Benji. And your team. You're not alone."

Matthew knew it was true. He wasn't alone. But something inside of him refused to believe it. Even still. "That's my flaw. How I let my trauma define me. I push people away. I never let them close. Because the last person who got close to me died. What happens if the next person who gets close to me suffers the same fate? What if I'm destined to be alone forever?"

Rebecca let out a small laugh. "Funny. Pretty sure I was saying those same things yesterday. And it was *you* who told me that people dying around me had nothing to do with me. I wasn't cursed. So, pretty sure the same applies to you."

She pushed up on him gently until their faces were level. She cupped his face, running her thumbs under his eyes, drying his tears. "You can let people in. God is not going to strike them down because you care for them."

"Was Jaime Catholic?"

Rebecca froze. "No, why?"

"Something your dad said to me tonight. Asked me if I was Catholic. I want to be clear I'm more of an atheist than anything. My Faith died with my mother."

"That's okay," she said. "Being Catholic is not a prerequisite to be with me. I won't let your lack of religion define you, as long as you don't get in the way of me and Benji practicing ours."

"I would never do that."

"Then we're fine."

"I still have nightmares about being trapped in that car. Almost nightly."

"Wow. I never noticed the last couple—"

"Except for here. With you. I don't have any nightmares when I'm here with you."

Rebecca gave him a small smile. "I'm glad I can bring you comfort. Is that why you didn't argue when I gave you a key?"

He nodded. "Yeah. Even with all the anxiety I had about getting close to you, about things moving so fast, the benefits of being here outweighed all of that. And then Jaime gave me that sign..."

She leaned forward, planting a kiss on his lips. "Thank you for trusting me enough to let me in and share that with me."

"Thank you for creating a safe space I felt comfortable sharing with you."

His phone ringing broke the quiet reverie that had settled over the room as they had sat nearly nose to nose sharing their feelings. Matthew pulled back and reached into his pocket to pull out his phone.

Thomas.

"Grant."

"Break time is over. Come to the dining room. We're going to comb through everything we have again. We are missing something. And we need to find out what it is."

"Be right there."

Hanging up, he put his phone back in his pocket. "I have to get back to work. It's probably going to be another late one, so don't wait up for me."

Rebecca placed a kiss on his cheek before they both stood from the couch. "I won't. Good luck. I hope you find something."

Matthew moved to the door. "Me too."

Chapter Eighteen

REBECCA

Friday, May 22

Rebecca looked at the clock. It was noon, her lunch break was ending in about twenty minutes. She had time to send a quick text.

She hadn't seen, or talked to, Matthew since he had left to go back to work the night before. He had been right to tell her not to wait up for him. She hoped he would be able to find time sometime this morning to get some sleep. This going days between sleeps couldn't be good for his body. She couldn't help but wonder about things like what his schedule was like between cases. How long did he usually have between cases? Was he always traveling?

That was the thing that got her. If they were going to be serious about this relationship, she felt like she needed to know how much she would *actually* see him. If he was never home, was it worth uprooting her and Benji's lives to move to Washington, DC?

And now she was just as bad as Benji. Jumping way ahead of everything. They were not anywhere near the point of relocating.

But she couldn't help but think about it.

Especially after last night.

Which was amazing.

She looked at her phone again. She didn't want to bother Matthew if he was working, but she also wanted to let him know she was thinking of him.

Which she was.

Her brain felt like what she was sure her students' brains felt like. Spacey with a constant countdown to the end of the day. The end of the year.

Maybe she and Benji could take a trip to visit Matthew over the summer? She could probably swing some cheap flights.

That's if he wasn't working the week they chose.

Which brought her back to the question of how often he traveled for work.

She opened her messaging app and clicked on her second most used thread. She and Millie had been texting a lot. Turns out, they both enjoy a love for reading, and they had a lot to talk about when it came to the new romantasy trend.

Rebecca – How often does your team travel for work?

Millie – Pretty often. But not like all the time. It's hard to answer this question. Wait. Is this about Matty?

Rebecca – Maybe...

Millie – You should really be asking him this.

Rebecca – I don't want to bother him while he's working...

Millie – You do realize we're both working on the same case, right?

Rebecca - …

Millie – Text him. He will appreciate the break, and it will do you both good to talk about these logistical issues. I'm rooting for you kids.

Rebecca – We're the same age.

Millie – I'm slightly older, I stand by my statement. Text him.

Rebecca smiled down at her phone and switched over to her and Matty's thread. Millie was right. It would do them good to talk this out.

Becks - How often do you travel for work?

She closed her phone and set it aside.

Her phone buzzed almost immediately. She picked it up and looked at it.

Matty - This feels very random. But it varies. Sometimes a lot. Sometimes not at all. Why do you ask?

Becks - Just spiraling a bit during my lunch about the future. Don't worry about it.

Matty - Lots of agents have families. It can work out. I promise.

Rebecca looked at the last message and swooned. Swooned. She was thirty-six years old, and she was actually swooning at a message from a man.

Who was she?

The door to her classroom opened and her fellow fifth grade teacher, Julie, came in. Julie was a little older than her and was her teaching mentor. She loved her. "Hey, Becks, just checking in."

"You have checked in with me three times already today."

Julie shrugged. "What can I say other than I'm worried about you? You just crossed the one-year anniversary of Jaime, and then David and Andy were murdered within a week of each other. I'm worried."

"I'm fine."

"You don't sound fine. Fine is not fine."

Rebecca laughed. "No really, I'm fine, considering the circumstances."

Julie looked at her, cocking her head to the side. "What are you not telling me?"

"Nothing."

"Ah ha, you said that much too quickly!" Julie pointed her finger at her, grinning widely. "You are hiding something. What is it?"

Rebecca glanced down at her phone, her stomach doing another loop-de-loop. Her mouth formed into a smile before she knew what she was doing.

"Goofy grin," Julie began, enumerating on her fingers, "staring longingly at your phone. Oh my God, you're in love!"

Rebecca whipped her gaze up from her phone to Julie. "No, I'm not."

"Yes, you are. You're in love! This is amazing! Who is he? Someone local?"

She shook her head. "No."

Julie gasped. "One of those FBI guys staying at Noble Hill?"

Rebecca opened her mouth but closed it again.

"It is. This is amazing, Becks. I'm so happy for you!"

"Really?"

"Really. What made you think I would be anything but?"

Rebecca shrugged. "I don't know. Maybe because I met him one week ago, today? Because I've only lost my husband a year ago? I'm a single mom? I can keep listing reasons."

Julie walked over to where Rebecca was sitting, pulling out a small chair to sit in front of her. She took her hands in hers. "Rebecca. You're allowed to be happy. No one is going to judge you for finding happiness. In fact, people are going to *rejoice* at the fact you're happy. After everything you've gone through this past year, hell, this past *week*, no one deserves this more than you. So, stop feeling guilty, and tell me everything."

Rebecca laughed. "There isn't that much to tell. It's been a week."

"Yes, but there must be *something*. You're in love!"

"He's a behavior analyst for the FBI. He's incredibly smart. But he doesn't take himself completely seriously. Apparently, he's super into Minecraft, learned that early on. Completely won Benji over with that one. He's thoughtful, and selfless, and just as scared as I am about this whole thing. Which is refreshing."

"What does Benji think about him?"

"Benji is ready for us to move across the country to be with him."

"No greater judge of character than a kid. Especially a kid who has been hurt and doesn't trust easily. How is he with Benji?"

"Remember how Jaime was so hands on, and the two of them had their own secret language almost and their own interests that were just *theirs*?"

"Of course."

"It's that. But different. The two of them have meshed so easily. They clicked so quickly. Quicker than I could have ever hoped for. You read all these cautionary tales about dating as a single mom, and making sure the kid doesn't meet your romantic interest until you're *sure* he's the one. When I expressed my concerns for Benji, you know what Matthew said? He said that if either of us feels the relationship is going south, we need to talk about it and end things before we hate each other. That way we can still be friends, for Benji's sake."

"Marry him," Julie said. "Snatch him up. Lock him in. That man's a keeper."

"I mean, technically, he's a psychologist, and he's really good at reading people, so of course he would be good at expressing his own feelings better than most people."

"To get so lucky to meet two amazing guys in your life? You're truly blessed."

"Blessed, other than the fact that all these men around me keep dying."

Julie shook her head. "This serial killer business is really something else. I can't believe Cove Creek, Iowa, is home to a serial killer. I'm not going to lie, but I'm kinda okay he's targeting men."

"Why?"

"Because usually it's the women, you know? We're always the victims. These men taking out their sexual frustration or their mommy issues on unsuspecting girls. But this time, it's the men who need to watch out."

"Men have been victims of serial killers before."

"Yeah, I know. But I'm just saying if there had to be a serial killer in Cove Creek, I'm glad they're targeting men. I don't have to be wary of every shadow I encounter."

Rebecca had to give her that one. She had thought the same thing before.

"Oh!" Julie stood up, preparing to go back to her classroom. "Before I go back and get ready for the kiddos to come back, did you hear?"

"Hear what?"

"Toby Lee didn't show up for his shift today, so they went to his apartment. Completely trashed. And he's missing."

Rebecca felt the blood leave her face. "Missing? What do you mean, missing?"

"I mean exactly that. No one has seen or heard from him since he left the station yesterday morning. Apparently, the officers and those FBI people are in a tizzy trying to find him. I'm surprised your beau hasn't said anything."

Julie walked out of the room and left Rebecca sitting at her desk in a state of shock. She knew why Matthew hadn't told her. He knew it would only make her worry.

But there were only two reasons Toby would be missing.

He was the killer, and he had gone on the lam.

Or he was the killer's next victim.

Chapter Nineteen

MATTHEW

Friday, May 22

Matthew practically threw his phone to the side with a growl of frustration.

The dining room at Noble Hill was in complete chaos. Everyone's phones were pinging with activity.

They found out at ten o'clock this morning Toby Lee was missing. By noon they had made a statement about Toby being missing and delivered the killer's profile on screen. They provided a number for people to give tips.

Now, at three thirty in the afternoon, the phones were ringing off the hook and they were getting a lot of tips.

None of which were solid.

They should have found a way to hold him.

But he didn't present as a flight risk.

Of course, his apartment was also trashed.

Which meant he may be the next victim.

Or, he made it look like he was the victim.

The whole thing was a mess, and they were again facing down the clock. And a shorter cooling down period.

They lost a day.

Matthew pushed back his hair that was hanging on his forehead. He was exhausted, but he couldn't sleep until Toby was found.

He was last seen leaving the precinct after being handed the protection order to stay the hell away from Rebecca. Matthew was worried that with the new restraining order, Toby would be completely unhinged and target Rebecca. He would ignore the protection order and go after her and Benji. They had broken his fantasy, and he would want revenge.

These scenarios almost always ended in a murder/suicide, and he was desperate to prevent that from happening.

Rebecca had texted earlier, asking about how often he traveled for work. Which, coming in the middle of this debacle, had been refreshing. He reassured her that everything would be fine.

Which it would? He traveled a lot, but nothing that would even be considered weekly.

Matthew knew he should tell her about Toby being missing, but he didn't want her to worry while she was at school. Especially with the knowledge he had staked the school out in order to take pictures of her son. Of course, the school was the safest place for them right now.

"He's not going to hurt her."

Matthew looked up to see Logan standing above him, holding two mugs of coffee.

"You don't know that." Matthew took one of the coffees out of Logan's hands and nodded in thanks.

"I do. He's going to go to ground and wait for the heat to let up. And then he'll confront her. But he won't get to her, because we won't let him. We'll catch the bastard."

"I hope you're right."

"Of course I'm right. I'm always right. It's my superpower."

Matthew let out a tired laugh. "That's true. Hell of a superpower."

Logan pulled out the chair across from Matthew and sat down. "Everything okay? Other than your girlfriend's stalker is on the loose somewhere and he may be a serial killer?"

Matthew's heart skipped a beat at the term 'girlfriend' while at the same time his stomach clenched at the official title he and Rebecca had never discussed using. But he ignored both of those feelings. Here was someone who had experience, someone who could answer his questions and ease his anxieties.

"Logan, how do you and Josh make your relationship work with your job?" he blurted.

Logan let out a low whistle. "I have to admit, of all the things I thought you were going to ask me, that was not it."

"Rebecca sent me a message earlier asking me about how much I have to travel for work."

"Wow. Things must be getting pretty serious between you two, if you're discussing things like that."

"Yeah, they are. It's only been a week, but honestly, having her in my life feels right."

"Wow, Matty. Coming from you, those are some pretty strong words of commitment. I can't even get you to commit to coming to a weekly D&D game with me and Josh."

"I know. Every time I say something like that, I can almost feel myself break out into hives."

"It's good for you. I like it. Now, carry on."

"Anyway, I told her that lots of us have families, and everything would work out. Not to worry. But I feel like I lied a little, because you're the only one of us who has managed to keep a relationship."

"Fifteen years and counting."

"Thomas has Carla, but I think there is something up with their relationship."

"Have you noticed all the weird messages coming into his phone this week?" Logan asked.

"I have, and he just keeps ignoring them. Says they're not Carla. It's suspicious."

"Yes, but it's for another time. Let's get back to you and receptionist girl."

"Rebecca. And she's a teacher. Which is amazing all on its own. Anyway, you and Josh seem to make it work. How?"

Logan chuckled, crossing one leg over the other. "Communication and understanding. Josh knew from the start what this job was and what it entails. He knew I would be traveling a lot, and I would see a lot of terrible things I would need to decompress from. That I would need space to deal with the horrors we see every day. He also knew I would have some down time where I didn't travel at all, and we would cover mundane tasks, a cold case or two where there wasn't intense urgency. Interviews with criminals. Because he knows the nature of the job, we can keep our communication open."

"Do you think things could work out with me and Rebecca?"

"Absolutely. Especially if you're honest with her. Tell her when the job is bothering you. Text her at least once a day while you're gone. Calling once a day is better, but we all know that is impossible on days like today. Prioritize time as a family when you're home. She comes with a kid who is also going to want you to remember him while you're gone."

"I know."

"That's a lot, Matty. Do you think you're ready to be a dad?"

"Yes."

"Wow, didn't even have to think about it."

"If you had asked me a week ago, I would have told you I had no interest in a family. In any of this. But I don't know, something has changed."

"When you meet the right person, everything changes."

"Yeah, I just didn't realize how quickly it could change."

"It only takes the space of a single heartbeat for everything to change. You know this better than anyone."

Logan was the first one Matthew had ever opened up to about the loss of his mom. It was his first step in trying to bond with another person. It went well. But he never felt the need to push past it and continue to bring people closer. He had opened up with Logan, and then Logan and Josh began inviting him to hang out with them, and that scared Matthew. So, he did what he always did and backed off.

He really missed out on a lot of opportunities because he was too scared to get to know people. Get close to them.

"Hey, look," Matthew started. "I'm sorry about—"

"Don't apologize. We just move forward. Okay?"

Matthew nodded. "Okay."

"Good. And that's what you do with Rebecca and her boy. You take things one thing at a time, and don't dwell on things that go wrong, or you mess up. Just move on. You talk about it, and then move on from it. If you dwell too much on what happened or what could have been, you lose your focus on what is happening in the present. That's how you make things work. Always make sure you're present."

"That seems so easy."

"It's all about communication. It's key."

"Do you think that's where Thomas and Carla went wrong?"

Logan shook his head. "I don't know. He'll tell us when he's ready."

"Thanks, man. I really appreciate the advice."

"It's no problem. Don't hesitate to ask me again. And Matthew?"

"Yeah?"

"I'm going to expect you at the next D&D game."

"I'll be there. I promise."

Matthew had just hung up the phone on yet another tip when he saw her come rushing in, Benji trailing behind her.

"Is it true?" Rebecca was out of breath, like she had run in there from her car.

He didn't even need to ask for clarification about what she was talking about. He knew she was asking about Toby.

"It is."

She began breathing heavily, pressing her hand to her chest, her gaze flitting around the room, not really focusing on anything in particular. Her gaze kept coming back to Benji, who was looking around the dining room in awe.

Matthew moved himself into Benji's line of sight, blocking his view of the board. It had too many pictures on it, and he didn't want the kid to be scarred.

"It's going to be okay. We're not going to let anything happen to you or Benji. We're going to find him."

"But what if you don't find him in time? I Googled some statistics the other night after you explained police and domestic violence, and these situations almost never end well."

"It will for you. This story will have a happy ending."

"How do you know?"

"I just do."

"What should we do?" Rebecca brought her hand to her mouth, chewing on the nail of her thumb.

"Go home, lock your door. Don't answer it unless you know for sure who it is."

She nodded vigorously. "Okay, I'll do that. Benji, let's go to our apartment."

"Okay, mom. Are you coming, too, Agent Matty?"

Matthew kneeled down in front of him so they were eye to eye. "I'm sorry, buddy, but I have to work. But I'll be there as soon as I can."

Benji frowned. "Okay. You haven't been home in a long time."

Matthew's heart leapt at the implication that Benji considered his home Matthew's as well. "I was there last night, but you were at your grandma and grandpa's."

"Boo. Now I'm regretting going over there."

Matthew gave him a smile and patted him on the arm. "Don't regret that. I'm sure you had a wonderful time with your grandparents."

"Grandma and I made cookies and watched a movie, and then I had to go to bed because it was a school night. Tonight is Friday, and we usually have Friday fun night, but everyone is too sad still to have Friday Fun."

Fuck. That's right, he had promised to do Friday Fun Night with him this week if he was still here. But Toby was still on the loose out there somewhere.

"Yeah, it's Friday, isn't it? How about if things work out, we do a cinema Saturday tomorrow, and we'll order pizza and watch whatever movie you want?"

Benji's face lit up. "Yes! I want to do that!"

"Good. Start thinking about what movie we should watch, and your favorite pizza. We'll wear our pjs and snuggle on the couch. It will be amazing."

Benji leaned forward, closing the gap between them, wrapping Matthew's neck in a hug. "You're the best," Benji whispered.

Matthew immediately hugged him back. "You're pretty great yourself, kiddo."

Benji took a step back, giving Matthew a peck on the cheek before moving back and taking Rebecca's hand.

Rebecca's gaze met his as he stood to his full height. "Thank you," she said.

"You don't need to thank me."

"Yes, I do. Thank you. And please. Stay safe."

"I will."

Rebecca led Benji out of the dining room and toward their apartment. Matthew watched them the entire way.

"Motherfucker!" Thomas's voice carried over the voices in the room.

"What's that, boss?" Logan called back.

"Another asshole prankster wasting our time."

The phone in Matthew's hand rang. He sighed before answering it. It was probably another prank call.

"Hello, this is Agent Grant."

The voice that came through was distorted, as if the person were using some sort of voice changer. "Agent Grant, just the person I was hoping to talk to?"

"Who is this?"

"I think you would find a walk in Murphy's Woods to be quite the refreshing activity this afternoon."

"What?"

"Have a delightful walk."

The phone disconnected before Matthew could say anything else. He stood and stared at the phone for seconds before jumping into gear.

"We need to go to Murphy's Woods. Now."

Everyone in the room stopped, turning to look at him.

"Did you get a promising lead?" Thomas asked.

"The caller wanted to talk specifically to me and told me I should probably go for a walk in Murphy's Woods before hanging up. They were using a voice changer. It's the most promising lead we've had all afternoon."

"We've had people stake out at the beginning of that trail all day," Logan pointed out.

Trevor picked up his phone and sent a message. It immediately pinged back. "They haven't moved from their spot and have seen nothing."

"So, are we writing this off as another hoax?" Millie asked.

"It didn't feel like a hoax," Matthew said.

Thomas nodded. "That's good enough for me. Let's go. Now."

In less than five minutes, the team, along with several police officers, were speeding through town to Murphy's Woods.

Matthew slammed on the brakes, skidding the car to a halt, and jumped out. He and the rest of the team stopped at the entrance to the woods.

"Alright. We don't know what to expect going into the woods. Be vigilant. This could be a trap," Thomas instructed.

Matthew made sure his vest was on properly and drew his weapon before he started walking into the woods. He took the farthest right side of the line, keeping his gaze on the tree line several feet in front of him the whole time. He didn't want to miss anything.

The team slowly moved down the bike path. They were not covering a lot of ground quickly, but they were doing so efficiently. They were all spaced about three feet apart from each other, which meant Matthew was walking through the grass. He was glad he was wearing long pants, since the grass seemed even longer than it had a week ago when they came to check out the crime scene of the third victim.

Fuck. How was that only a week ago?

As they got deeper into the woods, Matthew's heart rate picked up, and his stomach turned itself into knots. They were getting closer to the dump site. That had to be significant. Right?

As they got closer, he noticed something on the ground. He signaled to Logan on his left to look at the ground, and he passed it down the line. They slowed down as they approached the lump.

Matthew raised his gun as he inched closer.

The lump appeared to be a body, wearing a Cove Creek police officer's uniform.

"Son of a bitch," he muttered as he kneeled next to the body.

The face was almost unrecognizable. He had been beaten so badly. The other victims had some brunt force trauma to the head, but not like this. Toby had been brutalized.

Matthew looked at the man's neck and saw the evidence of strangulation. He leaned in to check for a pulse. There was none, as suspected, but there was something else he noticed about the body after touching it. Something that made the gallons of coffee in his stomach curdle.

"Guys."

"Yeah?"

"This body is still warm."

"Fuck!" Logan yelled, kicking at the grass.

"Wait. Do you think he's still here? Watching?" Millie asked.

Matthew looked around. The woods felt abandoned, but were they really? Could someone be hiding behind these trees? And then it hit him.

"He lives in one of these houses."

"What?" Thomas asked.

"He lives in one of these houses," Matthew repeated, louder. "It makes sense. How he's able to get the bodies here with no one seeing. And quickly enough, the fucking bodies don't even have time to cool down. And I would bet he's in his house, watching us right now."

The team looked around. There were over two dozen houses on either side of the woods up to and beyond this point. The theory didn't really narrow anything down.

"You're probably right," Thomas agreed. "But that's not enough to get a warrant. We need more. We can't just go door to door and ask if the person living there has killed anyone."

"I mean, it would save us a lot of time if we could. Getting a confession would be amazing," Logan said.

Matthew turned back to the body. "He's escalated. Not just strangulation and some blunt force trauma to the head anymore. Officer Lee has been brutalized nearly beyond recognition."

"This one feels almost personal. Like Toby wronged the UN-SUB in some way," Logan observed.

"He was our prime suspect," Thomas said. "He fit the profile."

"So, we're back to square one," Millie said.

"We have a profile, so we're not clear back to square one," Logan pointed out.

"But we don't have a suspect," Millie said.

"Which means we'll need to work extra hard," Logan countered.

"The cooling down period is almost non-existent," Matthew added.

"He's become a spree killer," Thomas agreed. "Which means we need to work fast. He will look to satisfy his craving to kill again soon."

"We're out of people who are close to Rebecca," Millie pointed out.

"If that even is the connection between these men," Logan said. "We kind of made that leap after the fourth victim."

"I think the fact that Toby was stalking Rebecca and then turned up dead, nearly unrecognizable, confirms that we are looking for someone who is acting out of protection or jealousy around Rebecca," Matthew said.

"He's right. The UNSUB has a connection to Rebecca, and he probably lives in one of these houses, but that's all we have for now," Thomas said.

Trevor spoke up for the first time. "We're not out of people tied to Rebecca, who could become potential victims."

"We're not?" Logan asked.

Trevor shook his head. He pointed to Matthew. "We have him."

Chapter Twenty

REBECCA

Saturday, May 23

Rebecca scrolled through the Netflix menu and glanced at the clock again. It was after midnight. She had told herself she wasn't going to stay up and wait for Matthew, especially since it was likely he wasn't going to be sleeping, with Toby missing. But she also couldn't sleep. Not with Toby on the loose. Not with what she had read online about what could happen.

Yeah. She wasn't sleeping until she talked to Matty.

Of course, not sleeping would be aided by watching something, but she couldn't get her brain to focus on anything. She couldn't choose what to put on in the background as she sat and worried.

Rebecca looked over at Benji's room again.

Thank God he didn't know what was going on. She hoped it stayed that way. Forever. He never needed to know that someone in a position that he would look to in order to keep him safe was a danger to him. That when he was innocently playing at school, a man who wanted to do their family harm was documenting him for his own perverse reasons.

She shuddered.

Rebecca didn't even want to think of what would have happened if the serial killer never started killing people in their city. If the FBI hadn't come in. What would Toby have done left unchecked?

Looking at the clock again, she sighed. It had only been three minutes since she last looked at the clock. The night was dragging.

She stood up and paced the room, picking up clutter as she went. The house was kept pretty clutter free, since it was only the two of them, but she did have a kid, and sometimes toys found their way places they shouldn't be.

There was a sound of a key in a lock, and she looked up as the door opened slowly, letting in a bedraggled Matty.

"Is everything okay?"

He shook his head. "Everything is not okay. It's my shift to get a couple hours of sleep. I hope it's okay that I'm here. If not, I'll go up to my room."

She grimaced while gesturing for him to come closer. "Sleeping in shifts is not a good sign."

"Yeah, the shit has really hit the fan in the case, and we're trying to prevent the next killing, and our window is extremely short."

"You still haven't found Toby?"

The look Matthew gave her spoke volumes, and it said, 'Oh My Sweet Summer Child.'

"That's the shit that hit the fan, isn't it?"

Matthew walked over to her and took her by her elbow, leading her to the couch before gently instructing her to sit down. He sat down next to her. "We found Toby. He is now victim number five."

Rebecca's hands flew to her mouth. Her eyes filled with tears. "But I thought he was the killer? We thought he was the killer?"

"We had reason to suspect he was the UNSUB, but apparently he wasn't."

"Was he killed the same way as all the rest?"

Matthew nodded. "He was."

"And now…"

"And now we are starting over, looking over the profile. We gave a press conference earlier, gave the profile, and asked for tips. Now we sort through the tips and see if we can find anything relevant."

"Have you been getting a lot of tips?"

"Yes, but a lot of them are pranks, or are completely irrelevant."

"So, you have to weed through all the tips to find ones that may actually be tips. That sounds tedious."

"It is, which is why we put Trevor on it. He is great at weeding stuff, while also doing techy things."

"So, now you're really splitting up the tasks?"

"Yeah, we have to. Or else we won't get anything done. Millie and Logan are canvassing the neighborhood. Trying to see which house may have the best vantage point to watch the crime scene. Thomas and I are back on victimology. Going over Andy and Toby and seeing if there is something we missed."

Rebecca lowered her hands. "Tell me, are you still working on the notion that the killer is acting out of jealousy over me?"

Matthew frowned. "Yes. But we're wondering if maybe we were wrong about that. Hence, we're going back to victimology.

That's the process. We get to the profile, and then sometimes it may need some more work."

"Fuck, I don't like this. I don't like that another person I know has been killed. I don't like that it seems to be happening more often. I don't like that it all may be tied to me."

"The situation is shitty. Very shitty. This afternoon, Trevor pointed out that the next person who is close to you is me."

Rebecca felt her stomach drop. "No."

"Yes."

"No. No. You have to catch him before he kills you."

"He's not going to kill me. We don't know for a fact that he's killing the people close to you. That may be part of the profile we're deleting. Please don't worry about me."

"So, what's his motive?"

Matthew shrugged. "That's what victimology is for. There is a reason he's only targeting men in their mid-thirties. And it may have to do more with the UNSUB's self-worth than anything. A lot of motives boil down to the UNSUB's view of themselves. They're usually trying to overcompensate for something that they are lacking."

Rebecca closed the gap between them, wrapping her arms around Matthew as he pulled her in tight against him. "I don't want anything bad to happen to you. I hope the UNSUB had a really unhappy childhood and now he's just taking everything out on people he wishes he were like. And it's just a coincidence that every victim knew me, because it's a small town, and we were all the same age, so of course we all knew each other."

"Honestly, that is probably right on the money. Can you think of any kids who were bullied by the other boys throughout high school?"

She nodded against his chest. "Of course. There were a handful that were bullied relentlessly."

"Can you remember their names?"

"Yeah, let me get my yearbook, and I can show you, so you can get accurate spellings."

Rebecca stood from the couch and walked into her bedroom, first peaking in on Benji to make sure he was sleeping. Just as every night, he was sleeping soundly, clutching both his bear and his lucky coin from Matthew. He took him incredibly seriously when he said not to let it out of his sight.

Once she was in her room, she went to her closet and opened it. She reached up on the shelf at the top and pulled down a cardboard box. She carried the box to the bed and set it down. Opening it, she felt her heart break. Sitting right on top of everything was a prom photo of her and Toby. She was wearing a navy-blue dress, and he had a tux that matched. They were in the typical prom couple pose in front of a background. And they were smiling widely. They hadn't yet broken up. They were still young and in love.

That's the boy she would mourn tonight. The boy who made her laugh. Who walked her to class every day. The one she shared an infinite number of inside jokes with. Her first love. She would try to forget about the man he became. The one who was so obsessed with her, he stalked her and her child.

Taking a deep breath, Rebecca set the photo aside and dug in the box for her senior year yearbook. Luckily, she didn't have to dig far. She was pretty organized when she wanted to be.

Before putting it back in the box, she looked at her prom photo one more time.

"I hope you're at peace, Toby. I always cared for you. I wish you could have accepted how our relationship was." She touched Toby's face as a single tear rolled down her cheek. Looking at the picture for just a little longer, she placed a small kiss on her first love's face, and put it back in the box, closing the lid.

Rebecca stood up from the bed, carrying the yearbook with her. Matthew was where she had left him. He was typing something on his phone, and he looked absolutely exhausted.

She approached the couch, clutching the yearbook to her chest, her arms wrapped completely around it. "Maybe we should look through this later. After you've had your rest. Isn't that what you're supposed to be doing? Sleeping?"

Matthew set his phone aside and shrugged. "Yeah. Technically. But this won't take long." He held out his hand for the yearbook.

Rebecca took a step back. "Nope, you're here to sleep, so that's what we're going to do. Sleep. We'll set an alarm to wake up earlier than you need to and I can show you the yearbook then. It's after midnight and you look fucking exhausted."

Matthew gave her a lopsided smile. "Or we could..."

"Sleep," Rebecca said sternly. "Sleeping tonight. When people are tired, they make mistakes. I don't need you making any mistakes."

Matthew frowned playfully. "Fine. Sleep. But if we wake up early enough..." he waggled his eyebrows.

"Funny. You think we're going to not only wake up earlier than the kid, that we'll wake up with enough time to have sex before he wakes up? You have a lot to learn, my friend."

"It's Saturday. Don't kids like to sleep in on Saturdays because they have no school?"

"Not eight-year-olds. Eight-year-olds wake up with the sun because they need to maximize the minutes they have at home in order to play all the video games."

"Being a kid sounds exhausting. Doesn't he know how lucky he is to be able to sleep for however long he wants?"

"Nope, because he's a kid. He'll grow up to be an adult who laments *his* kid not appreciating the finer things in life, like infinite nap times."

"Infinite naps. Now that sounds lovely."

"Too bad we're adults and we don't get infinite naps."

"Kids these days don't know how lucky they have it."

"They're so lucky."

The two shared a smile.

"C'mon sleepy, let's go to bed." She held her hand out to him, and he took it.

He stood from the couch, and using the hand he was holding, pulled her into his body. He leaned forward and kissed her slowly.

She melted into him.

The more they were together, the more comfortable and bolder Matthew grew, and she was reaping the benefits.

Rebecca would never tire of the way kissing him made her feel. The butterflies that formed in her stomach, the way her heart soared.

She hoped it always felt like this when she kissed him. For the rest of their lives.

Matthew pulled back and rested his forehead against hers. She felt him take a breath like he was going to say something but stopped himself.

Rebecca smiled to herself. "I feel the same way." She said it so quietly; he would have been the only one to hear it.

"How do you know what I was going to say?"

"I don't know. A gut feeling? A vibe you're projecting? The way the air felt when you opened your mouth to speak, as if everything were waiting in anticipation for you to say what you didn't say."

"It's too soon to want to say it, isn't it? We've only known each other a week."

"Who's to say what is and isn't too soon? Life can change in a single instant. We may have only known each other for a week, but tomorrow is never promised. If anything, this year has taught me we need to seize every opportunity to hold close the ones you care about. To never leave things unsaid between people. To always say what you mean. You don't know if you'll never have a chance to talk to them again."

Her monologue hung heavy between them in the silent room. They remained standing together, foreheads touching, breathing each other's breaths.

Finally, Matthew took another deep breath, and then, instead of leaving things unsaid, because who knew what tomorrow would bring, he said the thing. "I love you."

Rebecca smiled so widely her cheeks ached, her heart sung, she felt as if she were living in a dream. Hearing the words was every bit as amazing as she knew they would be. And then, because she took her own advice, she also said the thing. "I love you too."

Chapter Twenty-One

MATTHEW

Saturday, May 23

Matthew's alarm went off way too early in the morning. He felt as if he hadn't slept at all. His head felt groggy. Maybe he was dreaming? Right? He had to be dreaming.

"Matty," Rebecca muttered next to him as she pushed him with her hand.

Matthew groaned and rolled over.

He heard Rebecca sigh as she pushed him again. "Matty, your alarm is going off."

He rolled over closer to the night table and grabbed at his phone, stopping the alarm. "Do you think I can get away with being late?"

"Well, if you want to keep sleeping, we can forget about going through the yearbook."

"I'm up." Matthew sprung up in the bed, rubbing his face with his hands.

Rebecca rubbed his shoulder. "Maybe you should sleep more, and I can bring the yearbook to the dining room—"

"No, I don't want Benji coming in the dining room anymore. The pictures on the board...he doesn't need to see it."

"Okay, then let's get up and I'll show you the yearbook."

They stood from the bed and dressed quickly, Matthew in a different suit, and her in some sweats and a t-shirt. He looked at his clothes and frowned. He really needed to do laundry.

"While you're at work, I'll take the suits you're not wearing in to be laundered," Rebecca said, as if reading his mind. "You can leave them by my door, and I'll take them in. I don't know how many times you've worn the same ones, but you're probably starting to smell."

Matthew's immediate urge was to tell her she didn't need to, he was capable of doing it himself. However, he wanted to try out this whole needing others thing, so instead, he smiled at her.

"Thank you. I really appreciate it. I'll have to repay the favor by doing one of your chores when the case is over and before I fly home."

"You really don't need to."

"I insist. I never get clean clothes when I travel for a case. I never have time, so to have something clean to wear will be amazing. I will be so happy. And smell better than everyone else on the team."

Rebecca picked up the yearbook and led them to the kitchen table. She placed the book on the able and opened it.

She pulled out a piece of paper. "These are the people who were bullied relentlessly throughout high school."

She wrote four names. "All four of them still live here in town."

Rebecca pointed to the first name. "This is Reid Davenport. He works in the library." She pointed to the second name. "This is Henry Butler. He is an accountant. This is Billy Vanderplaat." She pointed to the third name. "He is the pharmacy tech at the Hy-Vee in town." And finally, she pointed to the last name. "This is Frank Harwell. He's an insurance agent."

Matthew recognized Frank's name from his interview with David's mother. He was one of the people David hung out with on occasion.

"How relentlessly were these men bullied?"

"Every single day, they were picked on by the more popular boys. Taunted, made fun of. Things like that."

Matthew pointed at Frank's name. "This insurance agent, David's mom mentioned he used to hang out with David. Seems they managed to bury the hatchet?"

"Frank? Yeah, he and David were bowling partners. I think they bowled once a month? Honestly, I don't remember. I kind of tuned David out when he talked about bowling. They were able to put high school behind them."

Matthew nodded, holding his hand out for the paper. "I'll take this to the team and see what our next steps are."

Rebecca put the paper in his hand, and he quickly tucked it into his pocket. He reached out for her, pulling her in close.

Matthew brought a hand up to her face and caressed it. Bending down, he placed a soft kiss on her lips. "You should go back to bed and try to get some more sleep before Benji wakes up."

Rebecca shook her head. "I don't know if I'll get any sleep knowing you're out there looking for the killer."

"I'll be fine. I have my team. We have each other's backs."

"I know. But I'll worry. It's my job as your..."

"Girlfriend?"

She wrinkled her nose. "That feels so juvenile. Like we're back in high school."

"Partner?"

"I like that. Partner."

"Okay, partner. I'll text you throughout the day to update you on whether to expect me. I might try to duck in and say hi to Benji at some point. Spend like a half hour with him or something."

Rebecca smiled up at him. "He would like that. Did you know he has taken you very seriously about that coin? He has been sleeping with it every night."

Matthew's whole body sighed with relief with the knowledge the boy kept the tracking device with him at all times. While he wasn't worried about him going missing, it ticked one thing off of his worry list, knowing he could track him if he needed to. "You don't know how happy I am to know that."

"He really looks up to you and wants to please you."

"I'll try to live up to his expectations."

He bent down and gave her another kiss. "I need to get going."

Rebecca pressed her face against his chest. "I wish you could stay."

"Me too. But I need to catch this killer. Once he's caught, we can spend as much time together as we want."

"Until you need to leave."

"Yes, but I may be able to stay a few days after the case is closed."

Rebecca's eyes lit up. "Really?"

Matthew nodded. "Yeah. I have a lot of vacation days saved up. I can stay here and we can just hang out. The three of us."

"I like that. The three of us." Rebecca looked up at him, and he could see the gears turning in her head. "And, maybe, later in the summer, Benji and I could come and visit you in DC? We have some money saved up, and school's out for the summer…"

"I love it," Matthew cut in. "I think it's a great idea. We can go to the Smithsonian and the zoo. There are so many places I want to show you two."

Rebecca laughed. "When the case is over, let's pick some dates."

"And look at flights."

Matthew captured her lips in a passionate kiss, pulling her closer to him, running his hands down her back until they cupped her ass. Rebecca moaned into the kiss and reacted just as enthusiastically. She ran her hands up his back, pulling his shirt from his slacks, running her hands up his bare back. It was Matthew's turn to moan.

He pressed his erection into her hips, holding her tightly against him. *Fuck, she felt so good*.

Rebecca tore herself away from the kiss. "You need to go to work."

Matthew growled in disappointment.

"I know, me too," Rebecca laughed airily.

Matthew pushed her away from his body and began reciting all the steps to proper victimology analysis. He felt his erection deflate at about the fourth step. "We are going to catch this asshole and then we're going to have all the sex."

"So much sex."

Matthew didn't trust himself to go in for another kiss, so he gave her a smile. "I love you, and I will keep you updated."

"I love you, too. And I will look forward to said updates."

Matthew moved to the door, slipped his shoes on, and walked out the door without looking back. Because if he did, he would talk himself into staying just a little bit longer.

He made his way down to the dining room, reluctantly. He'd never been so reluctant to go to work before. Matthew loved his job. But this was his first time he had something other than work he liked equally as much.

It was a weird feeling.

Very weird.

Thomas was already in the room when he got in.

"Hey, boss, did you sleep?"

Thomas nodded. "A little. You?"

"A little. The alarm sounded way too early."

"After we catch this bastard, we'll have all the sleep in the world."

"After we catch this bastard, I'm taking some vacation."

Thomas smiled at him, his brown eyes twinkling. "Good. It's about time."

Matthew sat down in the chair across from Thomas, picking up the files on Andy. "I told her I loved her last night. Or this morning. Honestly, I can't even tell anymore." He didn't look up from the paper in front of him, even though he wasn't absorbing any of the information.

"Hey, Matty. Look at me."

Matthew looked up at his mentor and father figure.

Thomas' face shone with pride. "And did she say it back?"

Matthew nodded.

Thomas tipped his head forward, his wide smile firmly in place. "Good." He turned his attention back to the file he had been reading before Matthew had walked in.

Matthew turned back to the file on Andy.

He was reading about his childhood and his estranged relationship with his mother when Thomas spoke up again.

"I'm really proud of you, Matty."

Matthew startled. "For what?"

"For opening yourself up. I know it was very hard for you. To let her in. To let anyone in. And to have opened up so much in the last week, that's real progress. Your mom would be proud."

Tears stung Matthew's eyes. He blinked them away. "Thank you, sir. You don't know how much that means to me."

"You know, I think of you as my son. I've known you for over a decade, and I've watched you grow and mature. I'm really proud of the man you've become. You're going to be a great dad to that little boy."

Matthew shook his head. "Don't you think you're taking things a little too far? We've only known each other for a week. I'm not even sure I'm going to have the chance to be a father to him."

Thomas shook his head. "You already *are* being a father to him. What was the first thing you did when you found out the serial killer was targeting people surrounding Rebecca?"

"Asked Logan to make a tracking device to give to Benji, just in case the killer targeted him."

"What made you feel like punching Toby the most? The pictures you found of Rebecca, or the ones of Benji."

"Benji," he answered, not even pausing to think. "The fact that that man was parked outside his *school* where he should be *safe*? He's lucky I could control myself in there."

"And why do you get antsy around six o'clock every night we've been here?"

"Because that's when Rebecca and Benji eat dinner, and I am missing it. And I know Benji is going to be disappointed I'm not there."

"See? Already being a father figure for the kid."

Matthew frowned. "But I'm not there? I have only seen him maybe an hour and a half over the last several days."

"You don't need to be physically with him to be a father to him. You're worried about his safety, you want to protect him, you want to spend time with him. Your heart has already decided that little boy is yours. It's time for your head to join in."

Matthew looked at his boss and knew he was right. That boy was already his. And he was already that little boy's. He belonged to Benji. That night they played Minecraft together on the couch, cemented their places in each other's lives. He would do anything for that kid. And he would give his own life protecting his.

It was funny how fast that that could happen. How quickly he could fall so deeply for a person. But it happened to parents every day, didn't it? After their baby is born and put into their arms, that moment they fall in love. That tiny human they had only known for seconds.

Everyone always talks about the negatives of falling in love so quickly. But no one talks about the positives. How these relationships *can* last forever.

Matthew used to be one of those cynics.

Not anymore.

"Listen," Matthew held up the yearbook Rebecca had given him. "Rebecca told me about some men in town who were bullied by the victims in high school." He opened the book to the pictures. "I think we should start here." He tapped the picture of Frank.

Thomas looked at the pictures and nodded his head. "It is certainly a lead we didn't have before. I'll call in the rest of the team. We'll get an early start. Let's see how many of these men we can talk to today."

Chapter Twenty-Two

REBECCA

Saturday, May 23

Rebecca sat cross-legged on the couch folding laundry while watching the movie Benji had turned on for them. She hadn't intended to get sucked into the Pixar movie, but man, she was a sucker for Disney.

Not taking her eyes off of the little girl as a giant red panda, she reached into the basket to pull out yet another piece of Benji's clothing. It had only been a week since she last did laundry, but the kid had twice as many clothes as she did.

"Hey, how many times a day do you change your clothes?"

"Hmm?" Benji never took his eyes off the TV.

"I said, how many times a day do you change your clothes?"

This time, he turned his head to look at her. He shrugged. "I have my school clothes, my home clothes and my sleeping clothes."

"Do you ever wear your sleeping clothes more than once?"

He shook his head. "I wear different sleeping clothes every night." With that, he turned his head back toward the television, ending the interrogation.

Rebecca shook her head and pulled yet another pair of pajama pants out of the basket. "I need to teach you how to do your own laundry," she muttered under her breath.

She glanced at the clock. It was barely eleven. Time had been moving at glacial speed, and it was beginning to get to her. Trying to keep her mind off of Toby and the fact a murderer who seemed to have ties to her was on the loose in town, she had started doing chores as soon as Matthew had left this morning. Now, she was running out of things to do in the apartment.

Outside, her parents were working on the weekly chores for the bed-and-breakfast. She could hear her mother vacuuming the halls and the distant clanging that meant her father was in the kitchen. However, she didn't think she was bored enough to go out and help in the hotel. It was technically her day off. Besides, she and her dad were in an okay spot right now. She didn't want to rock any boats by washing a pan the wrong way.

No, it was probably best she simply stayed here and watched movies with her kid.

"Is Agent Matty going to come by today?"

Benji's voice startled her from her daze. "Maybe. He said he's going to try. I mean, I need to get his suits laundered, so he'll need to come and get them, or else..."

"He's going to smell terrible," Benji finished.

"Yes."

"Can I try to stay up until he comes? Please? It's not a school night."

"You're right, it's not a school night, but we do have Mass in the morning…"

"Please, mom, please. I promise I'll wake up in time for church, and I will try not to take a church nap."

Rebecca sighed. Benji was gazing up at her, his eyes wide, and she could almost swear he was fluttering his eyelashes at her. *Fuck. He was good. Knew how to play her like a violin.*

"Fine," she acquiesced. "You can try to stay up. But if you fall asleep before he comes, I won't be waking you until morning."

Benji's face split into the largest smile she'd seen on him in a long time. "Yay! You're the best!"

Rebecca smiled down at him, touching his cheek. "We'll see how you feel about me being the best after you're exhausted during church tomorrow."

Benji shook his head back and forth, his smile never leaving his face. "I don't even care about being tired. I'll take a nap!"

Rebecca brought her hand up, pressing the back of it against her forehead. "Who are you and what have you done with my son?"

"Mooom," Benji giggled.

"I'm serious. A nap? You don't take naps."

"I will tomorrow!"

"I'll believe it when I see it." Rebecca glanced at the clock. "Let's go. If we get Matty's suits to the dry cleaner, we can grab some lunch on the way back."

"Picnic at the playground?"

Rebecca pretended to think about it. "Okay. Picnic at the playground."

Benji cheered and ran off to get ready to leave, and Rebecca picked up the basket of folded laundry and carried it to her room. She would take care of putting it all away when she got back.

She gathered the suits Matthew had left for her and carried them to the front room, folding them over the back of the couch. Walking back into her room, she changed out of her house clothes of yoga pants and an oversized t-shirt into what she deemed "hard pants" also known as jeans and a nice blouse.

Returning to the living room, she noticed it was still empty. "Benji! Hurry up and finish getting ready so we can go."

"Almost ready!" he called from his room.

Rebecca went to her purse and set it with Matthew's suits. If she didn't set everything together, she was bound to forget something.

Someone knocked on her door, so she moved to answer it. Standing on the other side of the door was her father.

"*Mija,* I saw that man leaving your room again this morning."

Rebecca folded her arms across her chest. "I thought we'd already agreed. I'm an adult. And I can make my own choices."

"*Si*, we agreed on that, but I still don't like having him around my grandson."

"He's my son, and I get final say on who he does and does not get to socialize with. Did you need something?"

Her father opened his mouth like he wanted to continue the conversation, but stopped, choosing to shake his head instead. "No."

Rebecca nodded. "Okay then. Well, if you don't need anything, Benji and I were going to go out and run a few errands and get lunch. Would you like us to bring anything back for you?"

He shook his head. "No, your mother has made sandwiches for the guests in case they work in the dining room all day again."

Benji came walking into the room. He stopped short when he saw who was in the room. "*Abuelo.*"

"Benji, my boy!" Guillermo held his arms out for a hug. Benji stood his ground. Guillermo set his arms back down at his side and cleared his throat. "What are your plans for today?"

"We're going on a picnic."

Guillermo nodded. "It's a beautiful day for a picnic. I'm jealous. I wish I didn't have to work and could go with you instead."

"You can come with us next time, *Abuelo*." Benji's tone indicated that his invitation was reluctant.

"Yes, *mijo*, next time."

Benji's eyes widened as he gasped. "I almost forgot my lucky coin!" He turned and ran back into his room.

"Lucky coin?"

"Yeah, it's new. Benji was feeling anxious about the killer loose in our town, so Matthew gave him a coin and told him it was magical and could protect him."

Guillermo shook his head. "I do not like that my grandson is afraid to go out, but my opinion of this new man has grown a little. Did you hear about Toby?"

Rebecca nodded. "Yes. It's getting bad, *papi*. Andy, now Toby? Did you know Toby had been stalking me and Benji?"

Her father's face darkened. "What do you mean, stalking you?"

"The FBI found a house with pictures of me and Benji all over town. They thought he was the killer. But now..."

Her father cursed in Spanish. "I'm glad he's dead."

"*Papi*!"

"No, what right did he think he had to follow you and my grandson around taking your picture? Just because he was a police officer?" He cursed again in Spanish. "Maybe he was the killer, and he felt guilty and killed himself after he was caught."

Rebecca shook her head. "Matthew said he was killed with the same MO as the other two."

Her father smiled at her. "Already using the jargon."

She shrugged. "I just listen when he talks."

"Well, I hope they catch the *cabron* soon. Not because I want them to leave town, but because I want Benji to feel safe."

Benji came running back into the room with a smile on his face. "Got it," he patted his pocket.

"I'll let you two get to your picnic. Enjoy your afternoon. We'll see you in Mass tomorrow?"

"We'll be there," Rebecca responded.

Guillermo gave them one more smile and a little wave before turning around and walking away.

Rebecca stood and watched him as he disappeared around the corner, an unease growing in her belly, but she didn't know why. Something about the interaction with her father felt off, but what it was she didn't know.

"Mom, can we go now?" Benji pulled her out of her thoughts.

She looked down at him and smiled. "Of course, let's go."

Rebecca spread out the blanket under the large tree in the park, watching as Benji ran toward the swings. They had been working all spring on teaching him how to swing himself, and he was excited to try out his skills. No mommy help at all. And Rebecca couldn't say she was sad about this newfound independence. Having to sit under a tree on a blanket reading a book while her child is off somewhere else playing? Is this heaven?

She settled on the blanket and pulled out her book, the latest JR Ward, taking one quick glance of her son trying valiantly to get himself started the swing, she delved into the beginning of her book, knowing it wouldn't be long before Benji gave up trying to swing himself and called her over to help.

Quickly, Rebecca found herself completely engrossed in her book and having changed her position from sitting up to completely lounging on the blanket on her stomach, feet kicked up behind her. Every few minutes, she would glance up and check on Benji. He had given up swinging and had made a new best friend, and the two of them were currently playing an elaborate game of tag on the playground equipment. Eventually she would need to call him over to actually eat the lunch they bought, but for now she would let him have some fun, run around. And probably for the first time in years, do it while not being secretly observed by her high school ex.

Rebecca pushed thoughts of Toby from her mind. They simultaneously made her angry and sad. Lots of complicated emotions surrounding her first love. She truly thought their breakup had been amicable all those years ago. And to learn he had been stalking her and her child? Admittedly, she was angry someone had killed him before she had a chance to confront him. Everything would now be sort of murky and unresolved.

"Rebecca?"

She looked up from her book to see Millie and Trevor standing over her, their arms full of paper boxes.

"Hi, what are you doing here?"

"We just picked up some files from the police department. It took us forever. They're icing us out even worse than when Toby was a suspect," Trevor replied.

"We're on our way back to the hotel. What are you guys up to?" Millie asked.

Rebecca gestured to Benji. "He asked for a picnic in the park for lunch." She gestured to the food. "However, I feel like he's forgotten about the actual picnic part."

Millie and Trevor laughed.

"Seems pretty typical for kids in my experience," Millie said.

"Do you have kids?"

Millie shook her head. "No, but I have several nieces and nephews. I'm the favorite aunt."

"Because they view you as fun?"

"Because I have all the creepy stories."

It was Rebecca's turn to laugh. "I can definitely see that."

"What'd you get for lunch?" Trevor gestured toward the bags.

"Nothing special, Jimmy Johns. Can't beat sandwiches at a picnic."

"I'm surprised you didn't just pack up some of your dad's food and bring it with you. He made a literal buffet of food for us," Trevor said.

"Yeah, you see, the food they make is for the guests, not for Benji and I. He doesn't let us take any of it with us. We tried once, and..." she trailed off.

Millie frowned. "Is everything okay?"

Rebecca shook her head, clearing it. "Yeah, sorry. Just memories, you know?"

Millie set the box she was carrying down and kneeled, so she was down at Rebecca's level. "Rebecca, I know what I saw the other day, you sort of brushed it off, but are things with your dad worse than you've been letting on?"

Trevor glanced between the two women, realization dawning on his face as he figured out what they were talking around. "Is your dad abusive to you and Benji?"

Rebecca's stomach clenched, and her palms began to sweat. "What? No. I mean, what do you mean by abusive?"

"Has he ever physically harmed either of you?"

"No," she answered quickly. "I mean, other than the other day when he—"

"He is," Millie interrupted. "I saw the aftermath in the dining room a couple days ago."

"It's not like that. He's just, you know, my dad. He grew up in a different country, a different culture, a different time."

"You don't need to defend him. Make excuses." Millie's tone was friendly, but firm.

"I'm not!" Rebecca yelled before pulling her emotions back in. "I'm not. You're twisting things to seem worse than they really are. Putting words in my mouth, making assumptions about my life when you have only seen a snapshot. I love my dad."

Millie shook her head. "I never said you didn't. And I didn't mean to upset you, but—"

"But nothing. Now please, can you leave me alone? I was having such a lovely afternoon."

Millie didn't say anything. She simply nodded before standing back up to her full height. She picked the box back up from the ground, and Rebecca watched as she and Trevor exchanged a look she couldn't interpret.

"We'll get out of your way," Trevor said.

"I really didn't mean to upset you," Millie apologized. "I'll tell Matthew you said hi when we get back to the hotel. I truly am sorry. Please don't let this get in the way of our friendship."

Rebecca didn't respond. She just watched the two agents walk away as she tried to get her emotions back under control.

How dare they say those things about her dad?

But they weren't wrong, a small voice said in the back of her head.

However, like all the times the voice piped up in the past, she shook her head, silencing it. Instead, she picked her book back up and tried to concentrate on reading again, thankful Benji didn't hear anything that had been said between her and the agents.

He was already leery of his *abuelo*. As much as she had wanted to protect him from his grandfather's darker side, it wasn't working. But she would do her best to shield her from the worst, even if she had to make sacrifices of her own.

Chapter Twenty-Three

MATTHEW

Saturday, May 23

Matthew sat at his laptop, scrolling through social media posts of one of the men Rebecca had circled in the yearbook.

The four men lived pretty normal existences, and most of them didn't seem like they crossed paths with any of the victims. Except Frank, who had several pictures of him and David in their matching bowling shirts on his public facing Facebook page.

"Thomas?" The man looked up at Matthew's words. "Talk something out with me?"

Thomas closed his laptop, giving Matthew his full attention. "Go ahead."

"These murders, they're obviously targeted."

"Yes."

"Our UNSUB obviously is choosing victims he knows, and while the attacks may happen at unplanned times, the method in which he kills and dumps the bodies is very much planned."

"Correct. We are looking at a UNSUB exhibiting anger retaliatory behavior. The attacks have been sporadic over time, but he knows the victims, and the killings are becoming more frequent, indicating his anger is building up more frequently and needing to be let out," Thomas said.

"Our UNSUB is organized, which is clear in his ability to kill his victim in a primary location and move the body to a secondary location without detection. Since he's organized, we are looking for someone with above average intelligence, who is socially competent, and who works in a skilled position."

"Typically, the UNSUB will also have some sort of token from the crime. Something to look at and try to relive the high of committing the murder, but we haven't seen any evidence of that with ours," Thomas said.

Matthew looked back at the yearbook on the table. "Knowing all of this, do we think any of these men who were formerly bullied by the victims could be the UNSUB? Are we wasting our time going down this avenue?"

Thomas shook his head. "At this point, with the cooling down period between kills being almost nonexistent, we can't turn away any possibilities. If all the victims were bullies in high school, it is a plausible lead."

"It is until you factor in Andy."

Thomas groaned. "That is correct. Andy doesn't fit the victim profile."

"Not when you're only looking at the victims who were high school bullies. He fits it in all the other ways."

"Mid-thirties male."

"Who knew Rebecca."

"Are we still considering Rebecca as a contributing factor to motive?"

"I don't know. I just know it's really fucking coincidental that all five of our victims had a personal relationship with Rebecca. If anything, it makes me worried about Rebecca's safety."

"You shouldn't. She doesn't fit the victim profile."

"Yeah, her not being a male in his mid-thirties is the only comfort I have right now."

"Our previous profile states the UNSUB views the victims as romantic rivals. That the UNSUB has constructed a fantasy life around him and Rebecca. These men in the yearbook, they've known Rebecca for years. What if we weren't completely off on this profile? We were just too narrowed down on Toby."

Matthew nodded. "I've thought about that, so I've been scouring social media. Out of the men Rebecca circled all but one are married with families."

Thomas stood from his chair and moved to the table Matthew was sitting, pulling on the chair next to him so he could look at his screen. "Which one?"

Matthew turned his computer so Thomas could look at it. "Frank Harwell."

"Frank Harwell, thirty-six. Single. Graduated with Rebecca from Cove Creek High School. And David Crandall's bowling partner," Thomas read out.

"Still lives in town, and looking at his social media, he seems to be friends with Rebecca still. They were on a trivia team together a couple of years ago."

Thomas leaned back in his chair, crossing his arms across his chest. "Do you think that's strong enough evidence linking the two together?"

Matthew shook his head. "It's the weakest link that we can still even call a link. It's basically nothing."

"I was hoping you would see it the way I do."

"Which is?"

"Which is, while the profile seemed to fit when we had Toby as our suspect, it doesn't seem to fit without him."

"It's time to come up with a new profile."

Thomas nodded in agreement. "It's definitely time to come up with a new profile."

Matthew ran his hands through his hair, letting out a groan. "Fuck. This fucking case."

"I feel you."

"It's like one step forward, five hundred steps back. I can't remember the last time we had to completely throw out a profile. How did we get it so wrong?"

Thomas set his hand on Matthew's shoulder. "I never said we had to completely throw out the profile. We simply need to tweak it a little. Maybe we get rid of the jealousy aspect."

"You're thinking our killer isn't killing because of Rebecca?"

"Correct. What if all our victims having a connection to Rebecca is merely a coincidence? She's not really a motivation in the killing."

"So, we have an organized killer, killing men in their mid-thirties. But why?"

"We're missing something, and it's killing me not knowing what it is."

Matthew picked up his notebook he used to keep his notes on the case. Five victims with a shortening cooling down period. The men were all the same age. All but one had grown up in town. Andy, being a victim, was what was throwing off everything.

"What if Andy wasn't an intended victim?" Matthew thought aloud.

"What is that?"

"What if Andy wasn't one of the intended victims? He is the only one who veers from the victim profile. Four out of five of our victims were local, having grown up here. Andy was a transplant. Four out of five were straight, or straight presenting, men. Andy was gay. What if the reason Andy doesn't quite fit in the victim profile is he was never intended to *be* a victim?"

Thomas leaned forward in his seat. "I never thought of that. Very unlike an organized killer to spontaneously kill like this, but..."

"But if Andy were in the wrong place at the wrong time. Saw or heard something he shouldn't have."

"There's such a small window between Andy and Toby. What if our UNSUB was deep in his surveillance of Toby and Andy caught him?"

"Toby was hanging out around Rebecca's right before he died, and so was Andy," Matthew pointed out. "I was there when both were at her apartment."

"If Andy left her apartment and our killer was around and thought Andy had seen him, he would want to eliminate him."

The door to the hotel opened and closed, the sound of footsteps echoed through the building as whoever had opened the door came closer. Matthew looked as Millie and Trevor walked in, carrying boxes.

"We come bearing all the files the police department deemed us worthy of taking." Millie set her boxes on the table and leaned against them. "They are not our fans."

Trevor set his boxes next to Millie's. "Saying they are not our fans is putting it mildly."

Thomas sighed, shaking his head. "You would think they would be more cooperative now that we're not investigating one of their own."

Trevor pulled out a chair, sitting down. "You would think that, but you would be wrong. It's like they're holding a grudge. They're mourning and pissed off, and they're taking it out on us."

"We're not the enemy here," Matthew pointed out. "I wish the local law enforcement wouldn't treat us as such."

"They don't like it when we come in and step on toes. Add in interrogating one of their own, and we can pretty much expect them to be non-cooperative for the rest of the time we're here," Thomas explained.

"You would think they would want to catch the asshole killing the people in this town," Matthew said.

Millie took a chair next to Matthew and collapsed into it. "I overheard some of them talking about how they're going to just go ahead and conduct their own investigation and, I quote, 'arrest the fucker,' before we do."

Matthew ran his hands down his face. "This fucking case," he said for the second time in an hour.

"You can say that again, Matty," Trevor agreed.

"Oh, Matty, you'll never guess who we ran into on our walk back from the police station?" Millie turned, so she was facing Matthew.

Matthew quirked his head. "Who?"

"Rebecca and Benji! Well, mostly Rebecca. Benji was playing on the playground. But we had a nice chat with Rebecca."

Matthew could feel his stomach turn into knots. "What exactly did you talk to Rebecca about?"

Millie and Trevor shared a look across the table, and it did nothing to ease Matthew's nerves.

"Well, it all started off innocently enough. We were talking about what she and Benji were doing there, and what they were eating. But when I brought up the food her parents made here, she mentioned that she and Benji aren't allowed to eat the food here. It's for guests only. And then she sort of clammed up. And you know how we are, right?"

Matthew nodded. He knew exactly what Millie meant. She had read into Rebecca's mannerisms. The curse of being a profiler.

"So, I asked her if she was okay. And she answered she was fine. But again…"

"The curse of the profiler," Matthew supplied.

"She got really angry when Trevor asked if her dad was abusing them," Millie practically whispered.

"Well, her dad is a fucking asshole. I've had extensive experience with him," Matthew supplied. "He hit her a couple days ago when she disagreed with him."

"Yeah, I know. I was there. In the limited interactions I've had with him, he's seemed okay, but I backtracked because I had forgotten something and witnessed the aftermath of an argument, and it was not good."

"He's a classic narcissist," Matthew explained. "He's been nice and cordial to us because he needs to put on a public face. There's this inherent need to be seen as the best, so he turns it on for us. But in private, he's a harsh critic to those close to him." Matthew remembered his interaction with Rebecca's father a few days ago. The man was completely different from the one he had previously interacted with.

"Poor Rebecca," Millie said.

"Poor Benji," Trevor added.

"Not the ideal situation, especially since they live here," Thomas agreed.

"Have they always lived here?" Millie asked.

Matthew shook his head. "No, they've only lived here for about a year. They moved in after Rebecca's husband died."

"Remind me, how did the husband die?" Trevor asked.

"Car accident."

Trevor pulled out his tablet and booted it up.

"What are you doing?" Matthew asked.

"Looking up the report on her husband's death. What was his name?"

"Jaime Clarke. J-A-I-M-E," Matthew spelled.

Trevor typed some stuff into his tablet, and the rest sat there in rapt silence. Matthew wondered where Logan was. It was probably his turn to get some sleep.

"Well, fuck," Trevor muttered.

"What?" Matthew leaned forward in his seat.

"I'm reading the ME report. It says that Jaime's cause of death was asphyxiation due to a crushed trachea. Not conducive to a car crash. All his injuries sustained in the crash appeared to be postmortem."

"What does that even mean?" Matthew's brain was working overtime to make sense of the new information. And then it hit him. "Wait, the crash didn't kill Rebecca's husband?"

Trevor shook his head. "No. Someone killed him and put him in the car and made it look like he died in the car crash."

Matthew slumped back in his chair. Someone had killed Rebecca's husband. This whole time she and Benji believed he had died in an accident, except that wasn't true. Someone had stolen him from them. If they were in a cartoon, a lightbulb would have popped up over his head.

"Wait. Died from asphyxiation due to a crushed trachea? That's the same MO as our UNSUB."

"Hold on," it was Millie's turn to lean forward in her seat, "are you saying what I think you're saying?"

Matthew wore a grim expression. "What if Jaime Clarke was our UNSUB's first victim?"

"That would put an entire year between victim one and two," Trevor pointed out.

"A normal range for a cooling down period between kills. He killed Jaime, and then a year later, that itch came back. The need to kill again. He had a taste, and he needed more. So that's when he killed Mark Lovett," Matthew explained.

"Jaime fits the victim profile, but the dumping of the body doesn't fit with the MO," Millie pointed out.

"What if Jaime's death wasn't quite as planned out as the others? Crime of passion, which would still fit in with our organized killer. He and Jaime get in an argument, he kills Jaime, dumps his body in a way that makes it look like an accident. But then, he has a full year to ruminate on the job. Think about what he did wrong, what he could do better. When he gets around to killing Mark, he has a plan," Matthew continued. "What do you think?"

"I think it makes sense," Millie said slowly.

"It's definitely worth looking into more," Trevor agreed.

"If we're going to look into this, I don't want to tell Rebecca," Matthew said. "She has a lot on her plate, and she's finally healing. I don't want to reopen wounds if this turns out to be nothing."

"We're going to eventually have to tell her," Millie said.

"I know. But let's wait. At least until we have something more concrete, okay?"

The other three agents nodded in agreement.

They turned back to their respective files to dig with this new piece of the puzzle added to the pile. Matthew only wished they could hurry and see the completed picture.

Matthew stood in front of Rebecca's door, smoothing his hair. It had been a long day of going over all the evidence again, this time with fresh eyes. They were working the case as if Jaime had been the first unintended victim and Andy had been an accident. He still felt like they were going in circles. That nothing was getting accomplished.

The case was frustrating him to no end. And he didn't know if it was because the case was frustrating, or if it was because of his relationship with Rebecca. Never had he formed a personal tie with someone related to a case. Hell, he barely formed personal ties with his coworkers.

Until now.

Opening up to Thomas and Logan felt good, and he didn't know why he held back all these years. Maybe having friends wasn't the end of the world.

Maybe.

Logan had come in and relieved him of duty. It was his turn to have a little time off. And even better, it was dinner time. He had thought about texting Rebecca to tell her the good news, but in the end, surprising her and Benji seemed like the better idea. However, now that he was here, he was starting to second guess himself. Maybe he should have warned her.

Pushing away the urge to run, he lifted his hand and knocked on the door.

Rebecca opened the door, her face lighting up with a smile as soon as she caught sight of him.

"You're here! How are you here?"

"Logan took most of the day to sleep and catch up with his husband. When he came back down, he relieved me so I could have dinner with you and Benji. Something about work/life balance."

"Well, remind me to thank Logan later! Come in. Dinner is almost ready."

Matthew followed Rebecca into the apartment, removing his shoes at the door before continuing through the apartment to the dining room.

"Agent Matty!" Benji exclaimed as soon as he came into view.

"Agent Benji!" Matthew returned.

"I can't believe you're here so early! I asked Mom if I could stay up super late in order to see you, and now I don't have to!"

"I'm glad I could get here early enough so your bedtime can remain intact."

"Especially since we have church in the morning," Benji added. "I promised Mom I wouldn't take a church nap, so she was going to let me stay up."

Matthew turned toward Rebecca. "Church nap?"

"It's when he sleeps during church because he didn't get enough sleep the night before," Rebecca explained.

Matthew nodded his head in understanding. "Makes sense. Yeah, probably not a good idea to be sleeping through church."

"Do you go to church, Agent Matty?"

Matthew froze, unsure of how to answer the question truthfully without causing problems. Rebecca already knew how he felt about religion, but Benji didn't. Would his lack of religious faith be the death knell of whatever this was blossoming between the three of them?

"It's okay to answer truthfully," Rebecca spoke up. "I always try to be honest with him."

"I don't attend church," Matthew explained. "I'm not really sure I believe in God."

Benji's mouth dropped open. "You don't believe in God?!"

Matthew shrugged. "In my line of work, it's kind of hard to see what I see and believe in God."

Benji looked across the table at him, a pensive look on his face. "I think you can work in your job and believe in God. Because you and your friends exist. God created you to do your job and be who you are to put the bad people away. Without God creating you, the people who sin and do the bad things wouldn't have anyone good to stop them."

Matthew stared at the eight-year-old boy in front of him. If he hadn't been sitting right there listening to Benji speak, he would never believe that sort of philosophical realization had come from a child. "You're right, Benj. I'm going to need to sit with what you just said and see if it changes anything. It gives a new perspective on what I've come to believe."

Benji sat up a little straighter in his seat, his chest puffing out just a little, a smile beaming from his face. Man, it's only been a week since the first time he met him, and he was already in love with this kid.

Rebecca brought out dinner, homemade macaroni and cheese and green beans, setting it on the table before taking her seat. She and Benji said grace, and then they took turns serving dinner onto the plates in front of them.

"Are you sure you're going to eat *all* of that?" Rebecca quirked an eyebrow at Benji scooping a mountain of mac and cheese onto his plate.

"I'm starving," Benji said by way of an explanation.

"Uh huh, skipping lunch in favor of playing at the park will do that."

"You skipped lunch?" Matthew asked.

"Too busy playing," Rebecca explained.

"My man, you need to make sure you're eating. Taking five minutes to eat whatever your mom got you for lunch wouldn't hurt."

"Okay, Agent Matty. I'll eat lunch next time."

As they ate, they talked about Rebecca and Benji's trip to the park and how Benji still couldn't quite swing himself, but he was getting there. He'll have it down by the time summer started.

Conversation flowed so naturally, and Matthew quickly forgot about his frustration with the case and all the dead ends. Was this what it was like to have someone to come home to at the end of the day?

As dinner ended, Matthew checked his watch. "I better get back. I have a lot of work to do." He stood from the table and pushed his chair in.

"Thank you for taking the time to eat dinner with us. It was lovely." Rebecca stood from the table with him.

"Yes, thank you. I really liked seeing you." Benji stood from his seat and walked around the table. He threw his arms around Matthew, embracing him in a hug, pressing his face against Matthew's stomach.

Matthew immediately wrapped his arms around Benji, holding him tight against him. "I really liked seeing you as well."

Benji pulled back, turning his gaze to Matthew's. "What's going to happen when the case is over?"

Matthew immediately tore his gaze from Benji to Rebecca's. "Um..."

"Well, Benji, we've talked about this," Rebecca picked up, "Matty would have to go home, to Washington, DC."

Matthew brought his gaze back to Benji in time to watch his expression fall.

"Hey," he said, rubbing Benji's back. "Don't look so blue. Remember, we'll play Minecraft together. And we can always do video calls."

"Phone calls," Rebecca added.

"Maybe a visit?" Matthew said it slowly, hoping he wasn't crossing a line. They had briefly talked about visiting, but they hadn't talked about whether they would keep that a secret from Benji.

"Really? We can visit you?" The way the boy's eyes lit up made any consequences for sharing the possibility of a visit worth it in Matthew's mind.

"Absolutely. I would love to show you around the city, show you where I work."

Benji's head whipped around to look at Rebecca. "Can we go this summer? After school is out?"

Rebecca shrugged. "Sure. If we can find a good deal on plane tickets. I don't see why we couldn't. We don't have anything else planned."

Benji gave Matthew another happy squeeze before he went bouncing off, saying something about getting his book about Washington, DC, and making a list of things they should do.

Rebecca and Matthew were left alone, and Rebecca made her way to him, wrapping her arms around him.

"Thank you," she said, smiling up at him.

"For what?"

"For making our visit to you something I can't easily back out of. Now that Benji is looped in, there's no getting out of it now."

"Hmm," Matthew hummed. "Well, then, I'm glad we looped the kid in. Can't think of anything better than you two in my home."

Rebecca's smile widened, her face lighting up. "You're amazing Agent Grant. I don't know what I did to deserve to have you in my life."

"Funny, I was just thinking the same thing about you."

Matthew bent his head, capturing Rebecca's lips in a chaste kiss.

He pulled away and took a step back from her, knowing if he didn't create physical distance, he wouldn't want to leave. "I'll try to be back later to sleep here, but don't wait up."

Rebecca nodded, following him to the door. He put his shoes back on, and turned to give her one last kiss before opening the door and stepping out, determined to figure out this case so they could move on and start their future together.

Chapter Twenty-Four

REBECCA

Friday, May 29

Rebecca threw her door open and walked in, dragging her collapsible wagon behind her. School ended for the summer at noon for the kids and she had spent the rest of her afternoon cleaning up her classroom and packing up a lot of her personal effects. While she was going to be there in the fall, she didn't enjoy leaving her stuff there all summer.

Her parents had picked Benji up when the students were released at noon, and she planned to go over there for a celebration for the beginning of summer later. Right now, she needed to rest.

And mourn.

The funeral home had called her yesterday to tell her Andy's ashes were ready to pick up. Glancing over to the wagon, her eyes filled with tears looking at the white box that held the remains of her friend.

Picking up the box made everything feel that much more real. He was really gone.

Rebecca swiped at the tears that made their way down her cheek. It was so unfair. Everything.

The BAU had been in town for two weeks now and they were no closer to closing the case as they were when they arrived.

While Matthew had moved into her apartment and slept here most nights, he stopped updating her on the case. Which she didn't know if that was a good thing or a bad thing. She was leaning toward a bad thing. If there was good news to tell, he would probably have told her.

Ever since this past Saturday, Matthew had made it to family dinner nightly. Rebecca was certain his boss had something to do with that. From what Matthew had confided in her, he was not a naturally social person, so his team was probably trying to encourage him.

Rebecca wasn't going to argue. The more time she had with him, the better. Benji also loved the extra time with Matthew. On Monday, which was Memorial Day, Benji spent all day at home working on a surprise for Matthew. When he showed up for dinner, they ate quickly so Benji could show Matthew the house he built for him in Minecraft. She couldn't be certain, but there might have been tears in that man's eyes.

Every once in a while, Rebecca would have to sit back and think about what the last two weeks have brought into her life and wonder if things maybe were moving too quickly. Was it possible to fall completely in love with someone in two weeks?

Then she would remember when she met Jaime, and she would have her answer.

Of course, it was possible.

Of course.

She glanced back at the box of ashes. It completely sucked that this moment of absolute happiness in her life was marred with tragedy. She would always associate her beginning with Matthew as the time she lost her best friend.

Jaime. Andy. David. Toby.

All the important men in her life. Gone within a year. Andy and David targeted by the same psychopath.

Would Matthew be next? Would his association with her be the thing that brought upon his death?

Rebecca closed her eyes and said a silent prayer that he wouldn't. That whoever this was would be caught before he could take the life of someone else.

While Matthew has reassured her multiple times, she and Benji were safe, she was so glad every morning when she watched Benji put the tracker in his pocket. Knowing he had that on him eased her mind a little. Because if Matthew were wrong, and the killer snatched her child, they could find him quickly.

If only she could convince Matthew to carry something around to track him. She could stop worrying about the two most important men in her life.

She opened her eyes and looked at the box again. Sighing, she reached into her pocket to pull out her phone. Andy's mom, no matter how terrible she was, deserved to know Rebecca had received her son's remains. The woman probably also deserved an invite to the memorial service and burial. Andy had left pretty explicit instructions in his will about what to do, and Rebecca planned to honor all of them.

First, there was to be a glorious celebration of his life, no sadness allowed, there in Cove Creek. And then he was to be buried in the plot he had purchased next to Jaime's. It was to make it easier for the three of them to party together when they came back on *Dia de Los Muertos*. Because if Andy loved anything, it was a fabulous party.

The one thing he didn't mention was who to invite and who to exclude. So, it was Rebecca's call, apparently.

Her thumb hovered over Andy's mother's number before she finally gave in and dialed.

As the phone rang, she leaned back against the couch and put her feet up on her coffee table. She was going to be here for a while.

An hour later, Rebecca, thankfully, could hang up the phone with Andy's mom. She was not happy about having no say in her son's final arrangements and she let Rebecca hear all of her grievances. By the end of the conversation, it was decided Andy's mom would come out for the celebration of life and the burial.

While Rebecca was happy his mom could have that closure, she was not looking forward to the chance to meet Andy's mom in person. She had gone all these years not having to spend time with the woman who practically disowned her son for being who he was, and she wasn't sure if she could hold her tongue if the woman said something or caused any sort of drama during the celebration of life. Or during any part of her stay, for that matter. Chances were, she would stay at the Noble Hill Hotel and Rebecca would have to play nice.

Rebecca stood from the couch and pulled her wagon with her. She needed to put all this stuff away before she headed over to her parents' house. Wheeling it to her room, she opened up her closet and paused. Hanging in half of the closet were

Matthew's extra suits. She'd forgotten he had hung them in there after he picked them up from the dry cleaner the previous weekend.

Under the suits, he had stored his suitcase, which had been emptied of its contents into the empty drawer in her dresser. The one Jaime had used.

Somehow, without even intending to, Matthew had basically moved in with her.

Rebecca looked back at her wagon full of stuff from her classroom. Maybe she should have left it in her classroom after all.

When she and Jaime had lived in their house, they had the basement storage for her to keep things in. Here, she was relying on her mostly empty closet to store her things for the summer. But her closet wasn't half empty anymore.

After staring at the closet for another minute, she got to work. Picking up the box holding Andy, she carried it over to her dresser. Pressing a kiss to the box, she set her friend down on the smooth surface of the dresser. He wouldn't have to stay there long, but it felt right to keep him in there.

Her phone pinged, and she reached into her pocket to check the message.

Millie – We have a lot of case stuff to do tonight, but think you can kick Matty out to his own room and we can have a girls' night later?

Rebecca smiled down at her phone. Millie had confided in her earlier in the week that being the only woman on the team was rough at times, and it was nice to have another female around. Rebecca really liked Millie, and she was happy to give and receive that female companionship.

Rebecca – Absolutely. I don't think we'll have to kick out Matty, if you're both not working at the same time, I'm pretty sure the case would be closed.

Millie – Touche. I'll text you when I'm on break?

Rebecca – Sounds good! I think I have a bottle of wine in the fridge, wanna partake?

Millie – With the way this case is going? Absolutely. I think I have some chocolate. I'll bring it.

Rebecca – Wine, Chocolate and Chick Flicks. Perfect.

Rebecca tucked her phone back into her pocket and moved back to her closet and pulled out all the stuff she had stored on the floor of her closet. She had been meaning to reorganize all of this but had meant to do it during the summer. No time like the present.

She had just settled herself on the floor of her room when she heard the front door open and close.

"I'm back here!" she shouted out, knowing the only person it should be was Matthew.

Sure enough, Matthew walked into the room and took a seat on the floor next to her. He leaned over and gave her a kiss. "What's going on here? Your closet seems to have exploded."

Rebecca laughed and gestured to the wagon. "I brought stuff home and now I need to store it. I'm not used to not having a basement to keep it all in, so I get to play Jenga with the closet."

"Oh yeah, today was the last day of school. How's that saying go? No more papers, no more books, no more teacher's dirty looks?"

Rebecca shook her head, giving Matthew a playful shove. "That is how it goes."

"Kids everywhere must be celebrating in the streets. Freedom."

"Kids? How about teachers?"

"Them too," Matthew smiled at her. "Should be a national holiday, the last day of school."

"Really? I'm surprised to hear that coming from you. From what I know about you, I'm guessing you were the kid lamenting the end of the school year."

"Guilty as charged. I fucking loved school."

"Thought so."

Matthew reached over and wrapped his arm around Rebecca's shoulders, pulling her closer to him. He leaned down, capturing her lips with his.

Unlike the kiss when he arrived, this one was deeper and more charged. Rebecca shifted her body, climbing into his lap, wrapping her legs around his hips, her center connecting with his growing erection.

Matthew shifted until his hands were between them, working the buttons of her blouse out of their holes. He pulled back from her mouth slightly. "Benji is at your parents, right?"

She nodded, incapable of talking as they moved together.

"Thank fuck." He gave her another searing kiss, gripping her hips and he ground her into him, causing pleasure to shoot up her body, before pulling back again. "C'mon, teacher. Let's see some of those dirty looks."

Rebecca laid her head on Matthew's chest, pulling the covers up to cover their bodies. Matthew ran a hand lazily up and down her back. She smiled contentedly to herself. She could get used to this.

"Not that I'm going to argue. Since this afternoon has been absolutely delightful, you're not usually here this early."

"I know. I needed to ask you something, and I saw your car out front. But then I got happily distracted before I could ask you what I needed to."

"What did you need to ask me? Does it have to do with the case?"

"Sort of. I wanted to ask you about Jaime."

Rebecca stiffened. "What does Jaime have to do with the case? He's been dead for over a year."

"I know."

"Then what could he possibly have to do with the case?" Rebecca sat up, pulling the sheet with her.

Matthew sat up and leaned against the headboard of the bed. He ran a hand through his already messy hair. "What do you know about the report the coroner made following Jaime's death?"

"Not much. I was grieving, and honestly didn't think I needed to know much about it. I didn't need to know the details about how my husband died. I just know he wasn't incapacitated in any way. He must have swerved for a deer or something on the road."

"So, you didn't read the report at all?"

"No, I didn't see a need."

Matthew sighed. "I was hoping you had, so this wouldn't be such a shock."

"Okay, so I need you to stop being so fucking vague right now and tell me what the fuck you're trying to dance around."

Matthew leaned forward, placing his hands on her shoulders. "I will, but first I need you to take a breath and calm down."

Rebecca shrugged his hands off of her body. "Don't tell me to calm down." She stood from the bed and started getting dressed.

Matthew got up and pulled on his boxers. "I'm going about this wrong."

"Yes, you are," Rebecca pulled a t-shirt over her head. "And now you're stalling."

Matthew scrubbed his hands over his face. "We were following up on the theory the suspect is killing people tied to you. Millie asked how Jaime died. Trevor pulled up the coroner's report, and we discovered that the cause of death didn't match up with what you were told about his death."

Rebecca froze, one leg in her pants. "What do you mean cause of death doesn't match up? He died from his injuries from the car crash."

Matthew shook his head. "No. He didn't. Not according to the coroner's report."

Rebecca's chest tightened, and she felt dizzy. "What did the coroner's report say?"

"It said Jaime died from asphyxiation due to a crushed trachea. All other injuries related to the crash appeared to have been caused postmortem."

Time seemed to slow down as Rebecca took in the information. Jaime died from asphyxiation, not the car crash. Jaime's injuries were caused postmortem. Jaime was strangled. Just like—

"You think whoever is killing these men now killed Jaime?"

Matthew nodded. "Yes."

"But he wasn't dumped in the woods. All the others were dumped in the woods."

Matthew moved around the bed until he was next to her. "We think maybe Jaime was not as planned out as the others. That something happened, things became heated, and it was more of an accident. And that's why the UNSUB covered his tracks by making it look like an accident."

Rebecca sank to the bed, her pants forgotten, pooled at the ankle of the one leg she shoved in before the bombshell was dropped. "Who would want to kill Jaime?"

"That's what we're hoping you can shine a light on. What can you tell me about your lives right before Jaime died?"

"Um." Rebecca tried to focus on the past, not what Matthew had just revealed. "Life was great. Jaime had just accepted a new position within his insurance company that was going to move us up to Minneapolis. It was a huge pay raise, and the company was going to pay for our move. Andy and I were both looking for jobs up there. Everyone was excited. We had just put the house for sale."

"Was there anyone who wasn't excited?"

Rebecca shook her head. "No. I mean, my parents were a little sad, but they were already planning their trips to visit on the calendar."

"Did he mention anyone he was having a disagreement with? At work?"

"I can't remember. I wish I could, but I can't. Nothing is sticking out. If he was, he didn't tell me."

Matthew sat down on the bed next to her, wrapping his arm around her shoulder pulling her close to him. He was still in his boxers. She rested her head against his bare shoulder, and he placed a kiss on the crown of her head. That simple act was her undoing. She sobbed.

"It's okay. You're okay."

"Someone killed my husband."

"I know. And we're going to catch the bastard before he can kill again."

Chapter Twenty-Five

MATTHEW

Friday, May 29

Matthew let himself out of Rebecca's apartment, locking the door behind him. It had taken the better part of an hour to calm her down after his revelation. It made him feel terrible. He probably could have told her about Jaime with a little more tact than he had, but he didn't even know where to start. How do you tell the woman you love her husband had been murdered? Pretty sure even Logan didn't have advice on how to make that a more palatable revelation.

Now, she had to go have dinner at her parents' with Benji and put on a brave face, not revealing anything to anyone. Not for the first time in the last week and a half he wished Andy had not been killed. Rebecca needed someone to talk to about everything who wasn't him. Matthew hoped she had someone to open up to. Talking with him couldn't be her only release. Especially when he was the one giving her the bad news.

Matthew made his way down the corridor to the dining room. He couldn't hear a lot of talking, which meant the room was empty, everyone having gone out to get some food. His stomach took the moment to remind him he had skipped lunch, and he was more than likely going to miss dinner. He had been spoiled the last few days eating dinner every night with Rebecca and Benji.

It was a great preview of what life could be like. Not that he was getting ahead of himself or anything. They were going to come and visit him in DC this summer for a bit. He was thinking of it as a trial run in his mind. Sometimes he would feel guilty thinking about them having to uproot their lives and move across the country to join him, but that's where his job was. Rebecca had mentioned she was willing to teach anywhere. His job wasn't one he could do from anywhere. And he loved his job. Hopefully, moving wouldn't be their downfall.

Shaking his head, Matthew banished those thoughts. There he goes again, getting ahead of himself. For someone who was against having a relationship for so long, he was sure jumping into this one with two feet. Full throttle. No holds barred.

Is this what being in love was like? It was such a novel feeling.

He entered the dining room and stopped short. It wasn't empty like he thought it would be. Thomas was sitting in the corner, staring down at his phone. His eyebrows were drawn together and he was frowning.

"Everything okay, boss?"

Thomas looked up, startled. "Matty, I didn't hear you come in."

"Sorry, sir. I didn't think anyone was in here. It's so quiet."

"Everyone else went to dinner."

Matthew gestured toward the phone in Thomas's hand. "Is that Carla?"

"What?"

"The message. Is it from Carla?"

Thomas looked down at the phone and back up at Matthew. "Oh. No. I haven't heard from her in a couple of days."

Matthew walked toward Thomas, taking an empty seat across from him. "Everything okay?"

Thomas shrugged. "Oh, you know. Just going through a rough patch. Nothing you should worry about. It happens when you've been together as long as we have. And when the kids grow up and move out, it takes a lot of adjusting to having an empty nest."

Matthew nodded along like he understood, but honestly, he didn't, not really. It sounded like something several veteran agents had told him about. Rough patches, usually having to do with the job. Too violent. Gone too long. The inability to have a work/life balance.

How long until the job claimed his relationship with Rebecca?

"Was that about the case, then? More bad news?"

Thomas shook his head again. "No. Not about the case. Honestly, it's nothing."

"Sir, it's been a lot of nothing texts since we've gotten here that have had you looking very concerned at your phone. It really doesn't seem like nothing at this point."

Thomas looked long and hard at Matthew, and Matthew could swear he could see the man debating internally about whether to tell him what was going on.

"Okay," Thomas finally said, leaning forward. "Shortly before we arrived here, I started getting some strange text messages."

"Strange how?"

"They started off vague enough to make me think they were wrong numbers or phishing texts. But then when we got here, they got more specific."

"Specific how?"

"He knew what city we were in and details about the case."

Matthew felt his blood run cold. "Do you think it's our UNSUB, taunting us?"

Thomas shook his head. "No. I already thought of that. He hasn't been bragging about the case, or taunting me about how we haven't solved it. It was more of a, 'I know this very specific thing about what you're doing right now'."

"Have you tried tracing the number?"

"He uses a different number each time, and when I trace the number, it goes to random businesses around the country. He's spoofing numbers."

"So, you don't even know where this guy is, or how he knows what he knows?"

Thomas touched a finger to the tip of his nose. "Exactly"

"Is he up to date with the details of the case?"

Thomas shook his head. "I don't know. He's stopped talking about our case and has moved on."

"Moved on? To what?"

Thomas's face took on an expression that made him look his age. "He's started bragging about the kills he was going to do."

Matthew sat up straighter in his chair. "Future crimes?"

Thomas nodded.

"What the fuck?"

Thomas handed his phone over to Matthew, who looked at the screen. The most recent message was pulled up. On the screen was a wall of text. Matthew scrolled up to the beginning of the message and began reading.

The texter had greeted Thomas by name. What followed was the ramblings of a textbook narcissistic predator. "Pay attention while I do as I please" seemed to be the message this person was trying to convey. The bravado, the certainty he would never get caught. The *detail* in which he went into describing his potential crime. It was grotesque.

"Do you think this man is going to actually kill someone?" Matthew took his gaze off the message and brought it to Thomas, who shrugged.

"Truthfully? I don't know. This could be the work of a deeply troubled man who enjoys the fantasy. Or..."

"He could be someone who has a history of concerning behavior who is bound to escalate to murder."

"If he hasn't already committed one."

Matthew handed the phone back to Thomas. "What are you going to do?"

Thomas slipped the phone back into his pocket. "What else can I do? I'll monitor the situation, keep tracing the number as it changes. But technically, no crime has been committed."

"So, we wait until one is committed."

"Or until he gets bored and stops with the messages."

"Do you really think this person is going to get bored?"

Thomas shrugged. "I mean, not really. But what else can I do? Look, Matty, I don't want you worrying about this. We have other, more pressing things to worry about. Did you talk to Rebecca?"

"I did."

"And what did you find out?"

Matthew sighed, sitting back in his chair. "Other than the fact that I have all the tact of a bull in a china shop, that prior to his death, the Clarke family was planning on relocating out of state. Apparently, Jaime had a promotion, and they were moving up to Minneapolis. Rebecca said she couldn't remember if he had any trouble with anyone during that time. She also mentioned she never even looked at the coroner's report. Just took everyone's word."

Thomas nodded. "Makes sense. A grieving widow wouldn't think to look at the coroner's report. Moving away because of a promotion. That is definitely an angle worth looking into. Let's cross check employees at his old job to our list of people who were bullied."

"Jaime wasn't from here. He moved here after he and Rebecca were married. He wouldn't have bullied any of those men in high school."

"Correct. But if we're building off the idea that Jaime was victim number one, and everyone else who came after was a catalyst to the UNSUB getting a taste for killing after accidentally killing Jaime..."

"Then the list would be something worth looking into," Matthew finished.

"Exactly. So, if you aren't doing anything else, why don't you get started with gathering a list of employees who worked at Jaime's company, and once you have it in hand, start cross referencing it to the people on the list Rebecca gave us last week. We're going to find a connection."

Matthew nodded, pulling out his tablet. Getting the list of employees should be pretty easy. It was only a year and some change since Jaime died. The list of employees shouldn't be too different now than it was then.

"Are you going to Rebecca's for dinner?"

Matthew shook his head. "No, she's going over to her parents' house for dinner. Benji is already there. School ended this afternoon."

Thomas smiled, but said nothing.

"What?"

Thomas shook his head. "I didn't say anything."

"You didn't need to. You have a look."

"What look?"

"Like you want to say something."

"Have you guys talked about what you're going to do when we wrap the case?"

"Yes."

"That's it? Yes?"

Matthew set his tablet aside. "She and Benji are going to come out and visit sometime this summer."

Thomas's smile widened. "And?"

"And what? That's it. They're going to come and visit. We're taking things slow. We've only been together for two weeks, barely."

"Two weeks, and you're not self-sabotaging?"

"I'm trying really hard not to."

"I'm proud of you."

"Thanks. That means a lot coming from you. I know you probably don't want to hear this, but I've always thought of you as a bit of a father figure. I've always looked up to you and respected your opinion."

Thomas leaned forward and placed a hand on Matthew's shoulder. "Matty, other than the fact you calling me a father figure makes me feel old as hell, I feel honored that you feel that way. But, Matty, I wish you could open up about what you thought of me sooner. I love you, kid, but holding us at arm's length all these years has been hard."

"I'm sorry. My mom was killed when I was young, and ever since, I just couldn't let anyone in. I grew up having nobody. People leave. I didn't think I could handle losing anyone else. I'm trying, though. I don't want to be that way anymore."

Thomas squeezed his shoulder. "I knew about your mom, and I figured your issues were related to unresolved trauma. Which is why I made myself available to be here for you whenever you were ready to open up. As fucked up as this case is,

I'm kind of glad we're here, because if we never came, you never would have met your person, and you would still be moving through life as a shell of a person."

Matthew could feel his eyes welling up with unshed tears, his chest tight. "I have a lot of wasted time to make up."

Thomas shook his head. "Don't worry about making up for wasted time. Worry about not wasting time moving forward."

Matthew nodded, lifting a hand to swipe away at the tears.

Thomas gave his shoulder another squeeze before sitting back in his seat, picking up his tablet, signaling an end to their conversation.

Taking his queue, Matthew also picked up his tablet, returning to his task. He pulled up the company's website and went to the employee page. The second he opened the page, his heart rate increased.

"Holy shit."

Thomas shifted. "What?"

"You will never guess who is currently working in the position Jaime was working in when he was killed."

"Please tell me it's someone from the yearbook list."

Matthew turned his table around so Thomas could see the smiling faces of the employees. "Frank Harwell."

Thomas let out a low whistle. "Shit. I think we finally have a new lead."

"And a new suspect."

Chapter Twenty-Six

REBECCA

Friday, May 29

Rebecca pulled into her parents' driveway, putting her car into park and shutting it off. Before getting out, she took a moment to gather her thoughts. It had only been an hour since Matthew had dropped his bombshell on her, and she hadn't recovered.

She wasn't sure if she would ever recover.

Her husband had been killed, probably by the same man who was killing everyone close to her, or at least in her orbit. And no matter how much she wracked her brain; she could not come up with anyone who would have wanted to kill Jaime. Other than Toby, who was also a victim of this person.

Jaime was beloved in the town, and everyone was so happy for them when he got his promotion. There was going to be a party to celebrate. Everything was great! To think someone had killed him was unfathomable.

She pulled down her visor and gave herself a quick once over in the mirror. She didn't want to look as if she had been crying. Benji would think something was wrong, and she didn't want to worry him. He didn't need something to stress about. Well, something *else* to stress about.

Satisfied no one could tell she had been crying, she pushed the visor back up and smoothed her black hair, taking care of any stray fly aways. School was over, summer was beginning, and she and Benji had a trip to look forward to. The future was right there. No amount of crying would be able to change the past.

The BAU would take care of this. They would figure out who was killing everyone and stop him from killing anymore people. Millie and Matthew would solve it.

Taking a deep breath, Rebecca grabbed her purse from the passenger seat of the car and swung open the door. Her sandaled feet hit the sun warmed pavement, and she immediately felt grounded.

Summer. Benji. Matthew. Washington, DC.

Those were the things she needed to keep in the front of her brain. Happy thoughts. Just like in *Peter Pan*, happy thoughts would get her through the night. She could fall apart again once she was safe at home and in bed after Benji was asleep.

Locking her car, she made her way up the small walkway to her parents' front door. Rebecca took one more calming breath before opening the door, letting herself in. The second she entered the house, she was assaulted by the delicious smells of dinner.

Her mom, Charlotte, was a born and bred Iowan. Her father, Guillermo, had immigrated into the state when he was a young boy. His dad had gotten a job at the meat packing plant in a nearby city. When her parents met, it was love at first sight. They married young and her *abuela* started teaching her mom all the traditional recipes. And that's how she grew up. The best of Mexican and American food.

Tonight, it smelled like they were making tamales. Her parents and Benji had probably been working most of the afternoon on dinner.

When they were planning their move to Minneapolis, her biggest hesitation was to move Benji away from his grandparents. Rebecca knew she could continue to pass on traditions herself, but there was something about her parents passing them on that made it so much more special. She knew they weren't moving too far away and could visit often, but it wasn't down the street, or in the same building, like they had been for the last eight years.

Washington, DC, was even further away than Minneapolis.

Shaking her head, Rebecca banished those thoughts. Focusing on the here and now.

"Hello?" Rebecca made herself known as she moved through the house toward the kitchen.

"In here, Becks!" her mom called out.

Rebecca made it to the kitchen and laughed. "You guys have been busy today."

"Mom!" Benji ran over and gave her a hug, careful to not touch her with his hands.

The kitchen was covered in pots, pans, and bowls. Her parents and Benji were wearing aprons and had obviously been working in a sort of assembly line.

"*Mija*," her dad greeted with a smile, "you're just in time. The little one needs some help with the tying. We're backing up a little here."

Rebecca pulled the fourth apron off the hook in the kitchen and pulled it over her head. Tying it around her waist, she followed Benji over to his station at the counter. Sure enough, there were a lot of tamales piled up.

"Have you had a good afternoon?"

"Yes!" Benji exclaimed. "*Abuelo* and Grandma took me to McDonald's for lunch, and then we came back here and started making dinner. Grandma let me put everything in the pot, and then we went into the garden while the meat cooked. Things are already sprouting!"

Rebecca tied the ends of a tamale closed and set it to the side. "That's so exciting! Sounds like a fantastic afternoon."

"It was. Did you have a good afternoon?"

"I did. I was able to clean out my classroom for the summer, and I was able to check out, so I shouldn't have to go back in."

"Yay!"

"*Bueno*. Now you can work full time at Noble Hill."

"Well, dad, I was thinking I would work the same amount of time at Noble Hill and enjoy my summer with Benji."

Silence filled the kitchen as Rebecca's answer hung in the air. Rebecca looked down at Benji, and he was dutifully tying tamales, unaware of the tension that had filled the kitchen.

Her father stopped what he was doing and turned to face her. "We agreed that if you were going to live in the Noble Hill, you were going to work there. And there would be increased hours when you were done with school. You even had us write it all up in that silly little contract. You cannot go back on your word."

Fuck, the contract. Rebecca had completely forgotten about the contract she had an attorney draw up that described the terms of her working with her parents. She had insisted on it after they had offered her the staff apartment in the hotel in exchange for working the overnight shift. She knew they would try to push for her to work more. They had always wanted her to be more involved with the B&B, but she didn't want them to take advantage of her.

The only concession she had made was she would work more in the summers. Which, with everything going on, she had completely forgotten about it.

Rebecca threw her hands up. "You're right, I agreed to increase my hours during the summer, but I never agreed to full time. I still want time to spend with Benji, and we're going to be taking a vacation in July."

"Vacation? What vacation? I don't remember you asking permission to plan a vacation."

"That's because I'm thirty-six years old, dad, and I don't need your permission to plan a vacation. Per my contract, I will work increased hours but will have time to go on a vacation. We're going mid-July. There's nothing in the contract that I need your permission to take one."

"She's right, Guillermo. It's all in the contract."

Rebecca shot her mom a thankful look before focusing back on her father, whose face was turning redder by the minute. "Where are you going on this vacation of yours? Somewhere close?"

"We're going to Washington DC to visit Agent Matty!"

Rebecca's eyes widened at her son's helpful information. Sometimes she wished she were a child. So innocent and unaware of the vibe of the room, along with the inability to know when to keep certain information to themselves.

"What? Is that true?"

Rebecca squared her shoulders. "Yes. It is. We're in the beginning stages of the plan right now, but we are thinking about spending about a week in July visiting Matthew and seeing the sites."

"Did you know about this?" Guillermo gestured at Charlotte, who shook her head.

"This is the first I'm hearing about it. Becky, are you sure this is the best idea? You've only known the man for two weeks. Should you be making these sorts of plans?"

"These sorts of plans? You mean a vacation? Yeah, Mom, I think it's safe for me to be making plans for a vacation."

"What if he leaves and things don't work out between you two, and now you have tickets to Washington, DC?"

"Then Benji and I go to Washington, DC. We can still have a vacation to our nation's capital."

"Mom and Matty won't break up. They're soulmates," Benji piped up from where he was still dutifully tying tamales.

"Soulmates??" Her father was angry now, practically growling out the words. "How would you know they are soulmates, Benji? They tell you this?"

Benji shook his head. "No, I can see it. The way they look at each other. It's how Mom and Dad used to look at each other."

Rebecca felt her heart swell with Benji's admission. She didn't know he had noticed.

"Two weeks," her father growled out. "You have known this man for two weeks, and now you're making plans to uproot your family and move all the way across the country."

Rebecca brought her hands up and ran them through her hair, tucking the stray ends in. Her face grew warm, and her heart sped up. She wanted to blurt and yell, but that wouldn't do anything other than escalate the situation. Instead, she took a calming breath before she spoke, clearly and concisely.

"You're interpreting things how you want to. I never said we were moving. We are going on a vacation. We are visiting. Which I think is a very reasonable plan to make after knowing someone for two weeks. Taking a trip to get to know someone better. Isn't that a good thing?"

"How is the prospect of you moving away, abandoning your family, a good thing?"

"I wouldn't be abandoning my family," Rebecca could feel her blood pressure rising. "If I were to move, Benji would come with me."

Her father slammed his hand down on the counter, causing everyone in the room to jump. "That's not what I meant, and you know it. You are purposefully misconstruing my words."

"You mean like you're doing to me?" Rebecca matched her dad's tone and volume. "Benji and I aren't moving, but if we were, you can't stop us. I thought you would be happy that I'm happy. That I've found someone to love again."

"Of course," her mother spoke up. "Becks, of course we're happy. But even you have to admit, this is all very hasty."

"What is? That I met someone new? It's been a year, mom. A year. Am I supposed to be in mourning forever?"

"No, you're allowed to be happy, and I'm thrilled that you met someone new, but like your father said, it's only been two weeks. Maybe you can slow down? He's the first guy you've felt anything for since Jaime. Maybe don't put all your eggs in one basket."

"I love him!" Rebecca shouted. "I. Love. Him."

"You just *think* you love him. When the case is over, and he goes back home, and he's no longer in your orbit, you'll see that this was just a case of heightened emotions. And you'll feel silly for thinking it was the real thing."

"You should wait to buy the plane tickets to visit him. It will be a waste of money. Stay here all summer. And if you're still together, visit him next summer. Give it a year," her father said in a calmer voice.

Rebecca untied the apron from her body and threw it on the counter. "I am thirty-six years old. Why are you treating me like I'm some teenager in the throes of puppy love? I am an adult, and I am fully aware of my feelings. I'm not going to sit here and listen to you criticize either of us. I don't need your permission to be in a relationship, or to go visit my boyfriend. I thought it would be nice for you to know."

She moved over to Benji and helped him untie his apron and threw it on the counter next to hers. "I have been saving a lot of money this last year, thanks to living at the Noble Hill. Consider this my notice. By the end of the summer, Benji and I will live elsewhere. You better start looking for a new night manager, because I'm done."

Rebecca reached her hand out, which Benji took immediately, and she led them out of the house and to her car, never looking back.

Chapter Twenty-Seven

MATTHEW

Friday, May 29

Matthew looked up as he heard the door to the Noble Hill slam open and shut again. He glanced at the time. It was barely five. All the agents were in the dining room looking up everything about Frank Harwell and trying to finish getting the warrant to search his home while he and Thomas went to question him. Which meant the person coming into the hotel was Rebecca, who wasn't supposed to be there.

He heard two sets of footsteps stomp past the dining room and back toward the apartment.

Everyone's heads swiveled to look at him.

"What?"

"Didn't you say she was having dinner with her parents tonight to celebrate the end of the school year?" Thomas asked.

"I did."

"I don't think they ate dinner," Logan said.

"Yeah, I guess they didn't."

Silence filled the room as four pairs of eyes locked their gaze on him, unrelenting.

"She sounded upset," Millie hedged.

"You could tell that from her walking?"

"Matthew, my man, go check on your girl," Trevor said bluntly.

"And listen to her when she vents, but don't try to give her the BAU treatment. Don't analyze her. It will make everything worse. Trust me," Logan advised.

"Yeah, that," Millie piped in. "Don't analyze her. Listen to her, console her, but don't try to solve the problem like a behavioral analyst. That would just make everything worse, and she'll move her anger to you."

"Listen, don't analyze, got it." Matthew stood from his seat and smoothed out his suit. He looked back at Thomas and opened his mouth to ask a question but was cut off.

"I'll text you when we're ready to leave to question Harwell. I know you want to go with."

Matthew nodded and headed out of the dining room and toward Rebecca's apartment. He pulled out his key and entered it into the door, but the door swung open before he could turn it. A frazzled-looking Rebecca greeted him.

"Oh! I heard someone outside the door and thought it was going to be my dad."

"Is everything okay? I heard you come in, and I was really surprised, since you were supposed to be eating dinner with your parents."

Rebecca sighed and stepped back, allowing him access to the apartment. "You better come in. It's a bit of a long story."

Matthew moved into the apartment, removing his shoes. He glanced over at the couch to see Benji playing Minecraft, his feet propped up on the coffee table. He didn't even glance at him.

"Is everything okay?"

"*Abuelo* yelled at Mom about you. We have to move," Benji piped up from the couch, never once taking his eyes off the screen.

Matthew's jaw dropped. "What?"

Rebecca rubbed her face with her hands. "Well, that's the CliffsNotes version of the evening. Would you like some context for Benji's interpretation of events?"

"Um, yeah. Context would be good. Because I'm a little concerned about the whole you have to move part of that bombshell."

Rebecca took him by the hand and led him to the couch. They sat down near Benji.

"You don't want to have this conversation in private?" Matthew asked.

Rebecca shook her head. "Benji was there for the argument. It's probably good for him to be here for the rest of it. So he can have a little more context to what he was witness to."

"Wait, so your dad yelled at you in front of Benji?" Matthew could feel an urge to run out and deck the man rising.

"He did. It was bad."

"What happened?"

"While making dinner, we told my parents we were going to come visit you this summer."

"That's it? You told your parents you were going to take a vacation, and they kicked you out?"

"We kicked ourselves out."

"I think I need more gaps filled in."

"They were so angry, Matty. So angry. It was like I was a teenager living at home again. The judgment for moving on. Like a year was not long enough to mourn."

"I think mourning is different for every person. There's no right or wrong way to do it."

Rebecca smiled at him. "I think so, too."

"It's taken me a lot of years and a lot of therapy to come to terms with that. To not feel guilty when I'm not being sad about my mom. When I'm happy living my life."

"The guilt. I can relate to that exactly. Even before I met you, I would feel *so* guilty if I went a day and I didn't think about Jaime. And right before I met you, I was finally at a place where I felt okay moving on. Then I met you, and everything just fell into place, and I'm happy. For my parents to minimize this progress, and to trivialize my feelings? They're acting like I'm not even an adult."

"So, that's the part where your dad yelled at you about me."

"Yep."

"So, what's the part where you have to move?"

"That was me being fed up with being infantilized and making a rash decision in the moment. I told my parents by the end of the summer I'll be out of here in our own place. I've saved up enough this last year that I can afford to move us. The only problem is, I haven't even started to look for somewhere."

"I can help you. When the case is over. That's something we can do long distance easily."

Rebecca leaned forward and placed a kiss on his cheek. "You're amazing, and we're so lucky to have you in our lives."

Matthew felt his cheeks redden. He wasn't used to having those words said to him. He wasn't usually told by someone they were lucky to have him.

"I can probably even take some time off to help you pack. Whatever you need, I'm here for you."

Matthew's phone chose that moment to vibrate, alerting him to a text message. He reached into his pocket and pulled out his phone. It was Thomas telling him they had the warrant, and they were getting ready to leave to search Frank's home and go question him.

"The case?" Rebecca asked.

He nodded. "Yeah. We have a suspect."

"What?"

"Yeah, a really good one. We have some pretty solid leads and he fits the profile."

"Wow," she breathed out.

"Yeah, that message was to tell me we have the green light to search his home and question him."

"Are you searching the home, or are you questioning him?"

"Questioning."

Rebecca sucked in a breath.

"It's okay," he reassured. "We question at the police station. I'll be absolutely safe. I also won't be alone. Thomas will be questioning him with me. We do everything in pairs to make sure we stay safe."

"Logically, I know this is a low-risk activity. However, I can't help the niggling feeling I have that something is going to go wrong. Maybe it's because every man who has been in my orbit in the last year has been murdered."

Matthew rested his hand on her shoulder, giving it a small squeeze. "I'll be fine."

"You don't know that."

"I do. I've done this job for ten years. I have always been safe, and today will be no different. Believe me."

"I know. It's illogical for me to worry like I am, but I really have a bad feeling about this. Can you trade? Or stay back?"

Matthew shook his head. "I can't stay back, and I'm always in the interrogation room. I promise you, I'll be fine, and I will be back here later tonight to sleep."

Rebecca brought her hand up to grip his wrist. "Promise?"

"Promise."

Matthew stood from the couch and went to move toward the door but was stopped by Benji running over and throwing his arms around his waist.

"Please be safe, Agent Matty," Benji mumbled into his stomach.

Matthew wrapped his arms around the boy and gave him a firm hug before unwrapping the boy from him. He took a step back so he could look Benji in the eye. "You don't have anything to worry about. I'll be safe. You and your mom go about your night like normal. Maybe this won't take very long, and I'll be back before you go to bed."

Benji's eyes lit up. "Is it okay if I stay up and wait for you? It's not a school night, or a church night."

"Well, that's up to your mom. I don't think I can decide whether we can forget about bed time or not."

Benji turned his head expectantly at his mom, who gave him a small smile. "I think we can come to a compromise as to how long you can stay up. Since it's not a guarantee Matty will be coming over, I don't want to keep you up all night."

"Yay! Thank you, mom! I can't wait to see you later." Benji threw his arms around Matthew's waist one more time before retreating back to his spot on the couch.

Matthew watched him play his video game for a minute before glancing back at Rebecca, who gave him a smile. He returned the smile and then headed toward the door. Slipping on his shoes before bending down to tie them, he said a silent prayer that Frank Harwell would be their guy. He needed a win on this case. Not just for the city to be a safer place, but for the people he loved. He didn't like seeing Benji worried about his safety.

He stood back up and took one last glance at Rebecca and Benji. They were sitting side by side on the couch, Rebecca watching as Benji played. Matthew smiled to himself before opening the door and letting himself out.

He pulled out his key and locked the deadbolt. He knew Rebecca felt better when the door was locked while she was home. Turning around, he started on his way back to the dining room before stopping suddenly.

The hairs on the back of his neck stood up, and it felt as if someone were watching him.

His heart rate increased as he slowly turned around.

Nothing.

Just the door to Rebecca's apartment a few feet behind him.

Turning back around, he tried to slow his heart, but something in his gut wouldn't let this go.

Something was wrong, but he didn't know what.

He started back toward the dining room, determined to report to Thomas that something wasn't right, and maybe someone should stay back to keep an eye on things here, but he never made it.

The first thing he registered was the sharp pain of something colliding with the back of his head. The next thing he knew was nothing but black.

Matthew groaned as he slowly regained consciousness.

The last thing he remembered was leaving Rebecca's apartment and then getting the feeling someone was watching him.

Apparently, the feeling was correct. Someone had been watching him, and that someone had gotten the jump on him.

It was very out of character for him to get caught unawares. In the ten years he had been at the BAU, he had been so careful, taking every safety precaution. Never did he think he would be pummeled from behind.

He squeezed his eyes shut against the pounding of his head.

He had been certain when he looked behind him, there was no one there. The hall had been empty. No one was there, despite the feeling of being watched. Where did the person come from?

He didn't know what he was hit with, but he was sure he probably had a concussion.

Matthew tried to bring his hands up to his face, but found he couldn't move them. In fact, he couldn't move his arms at all.

Slowly, he opened his eyes, bracing himself to be blinded by a light, but as he peeled his eyelids open, he was greeted by a mostly dark room, the only light coming in from the egress window across from him.

Looking around, he noticed he was in a basement of some kind. It wasn't a finished basement, but it wasn't a dank dungeon, either. The walls were exposed cinder blocks and concrete, and the floor was uncarpeted. The air was heavy with moisture and cool.

The other thing Matthew noticed was he had been tied to a chair. He tried to work the ropes loose by working his arms in and out, but whoever tied the knots must have known about that trick and tied a more complicated not because the ropes were not budging.

Matthew started to panic. He was well and truly fucked.

No one knew where he was.

He was supposed to be with the team, but would they notice he was missing, or would they think he was staying with Rebecca and Benji?

Rebecca and Benji.

They were right to worry about his safety, apparently. And they currently thought he was with the team at the police station.

No one would be looking for him.

At least not for a while.

He tried to think about the timeline for the killings. How long between the kidnapping and the body turning up?

That's one thing they were not completely certain of, but it was less than twenty-four hours. Possibly less than twelve. He had less than twelve hours before he was strangled and dumped in the woods.

He had to work quickly.

"You're awake."

Matthew stiffened at the voice coming from behind him.

He knew that voice.

The sound of the footsteps grew closer as the man walked toward him. He moved around Matthew until he stopped in front of him.

In the dim light of the basement, Matthew recognized who his abductor was. The man who had been terrorizing Cove Creek for the last several months, the person who killed Rebecca's husband.

It was Guillermo Hernandez.

Rebecca's father.

Chapter Twenty-Eight

REBECCA

Friday, May 29

Rebecca bopped along to the song blasting on the TV while she washed the last of the dinner dishes. Benji was watching one of his favorite Disney movies, and the songs were catchy. She had bought the soundtrack for them to enjoy on their drives in the car, inspiring many a sing along. Everyone always talked about the hard parts of parenting. No one ever talked about the parts that brought so much joy. Like singing about a man named Bruno at the top of her lungs with her son as they drove to school.

Luckily, despite their failed dinner with her parents, she had some tamales from the last time they made them in her freezer. They defrosted the tamales and ate in front of the TV, watching a movie. It wasn't the same, but that was okay. They were together, and that was all that mattered.

Rebecca regretted the falling out with her parents happened in front of Benji. She tried so hard to shield him from the worst of his grandfather. But this time it couldn't be helped. So far, he seemed fine. He took it all in stride. But she needed to prepare herself for the inevitable questions. She knew her son. He needed some time to process things before asking questions about it.

She looked around the kitchen and sighed. Maybe she shouldn't have rashly stated they were going to move by the end of the summer. That was probably the most impulsive thing she has ever committed herself to. She was a planner, type A sort. She made lists and then more lists whenever she needed to make a big decision. Never had she just *blurted* it out. But she refused to go back on her decision.

Her parents were treating her like she was a child. They had been ever since Jaime died last year. When she needed to rely heavily on them through her grief and getting back on her feet. And now that she was better and flourishing, it was like they were resistant to her growth. Denying she didn't need them anymore.

Rebecca had let it go on for too long. It was time to reassert herself, draw a line in the sand.

Too bad the line she drew involved uprooting her family.

Grabbing a notebook from the kitchen counter, she took a pen from her cup and walked to the couch, plopping herself next to Benji on the couch.

"What are you doing?" he asked, leaning over to see what she was writing on the paper.

"Making a plan."

"For where we're going to move?"

"Yep."

"Are we going to move far away?"

Rebecca shook her head. "No, we're probably going to just find somewhere new in Cove Creek to live. Things will still be the same. We just won't be living in the Noble Hill."

"If we're not living here anymore, will you still have to work here?"

"No. I will not."

"So, after school, we can just hang out? Like we have been for the last two weeks? Like before dad died?"

Ever since the BAU had taken over the hotel, Rebecca didn't have to spend the evenings at the front desk. She had set up an automated messaging system telling callers they were fully booked until further notice. Not having to be at the desk freed her up in the evenings, and she and Benji could go back to the way things used to be, before she was working two jobs.

"Yes."

A wide smile spread across Benji's face. "I'm sad that we have to move again, but I'm really happy that I get you back. I missed you."

"I missed you, too."

"Are we getting a house?"

Rebecca shrugged. "I don't know. We can certainly look at houses, see what is available. What we can afford."

"Are we going to buy one?"

"No, I know for sure we can't afford to buy one. We're just going to rent for now."

"Too bad we can't just move to Washington, DC, now."

"Why is it too bad?"

"Because then we would only have to move one time instead of two times."

"Hmm, you have a good point. Moving is kind of terrible. But I don't think we're quite ready to move to be closer to Agent Matty yet."

"No, not yet. I'm not ready to say goodbye to Grandma. Or my friends. But maybe I will eventually."

Rebecca smiled down at her son. "We'll cross that bridge when we get to it. Let's focus on things we need to take care of now."

She put her pen on the paper and wrote 'HOUSE VS APARTMENT' on the top line.

"So, Benj, let's talk about what would be the good things and the bad things about living in a house versus living in another apartment."

Before Benji could answer her, a knock sounded on the door.

They both turned to look at the door before Rebecca set the pad of paper and pen down. She stood up and made her way to the door. Opening it, she frowned.

"Millie! You're earlier than I thought you would be."

Millie gave her a tight smile. "Rebecca, I was wondering if I could have a word with Matty?"

Rebecca frowned. "Matty? He's not here. He left a couple of hours ago after Thomas texted him."

The smile slipped from Millie's face. "He never showed. We assumed he stayed here to comfort you after whatever happened that caused you to come home early from your parents' house. I was coming here to pass on that Thomas was super pissed at him."

A pit grew in Rebecca's stomach. If he wasn't here, and he wasn't with the BAU, then where was he?

"Have you tried his phone?"

"It keeps going to voicemail. We assumed he was ignoring us."

Panic clenched at her heart, and the pit in her stomach soured, causing nausea to rise in her. "Where is he?"

"Your guess is as good as mine at this point. What time did you say Matty left here?"

"It was immediately after he got Thomas's message. He told us he was going to go question the suspect. I asked if he could stay behind. I was really worried about him. But he told me there was nothing to worry about. He put his shoes on and he left."

Millie pulled out his phone and checked it. "That was a group text. Thomas sent the message around five thirty. That was two hours ago."

"Do you think the suspect he was supposed to question took him before he could get there?"

Millie shook her head. "Thomas and Logan questioned him. He was with them the entire time. There was no way he could have abducted Matty. His alibi would be airtight. Besides, we're pretty sure he's not our guy."

"And Matty disappearing is more evidence toward letting him off the hook."

"Exactly."

Millie stared off into the distance for a second before bringing her gaze back to Rebecca.

"Now that I think about it, I don't think he made it past the dining room. I don't remember hearing any footsteps. If he left, it wasn't through the front door."

"Can you trace his phone?"

Millie turned back to her phone, typing out a message. "Trevor will be able to trace his phone. It shouldn't take long."

Silence fell between them, the only sound in the room being Benji's movie, which seemed to be tonally out-of-place now.

Millie's phone chimed, and she glanced back down at it. "His phone's last geolocation was here in this hotel. It's been shut off since then."

Rebecca brought her hands up and ran them through her hair. Her breathing increased, and she was pretty sure she was going to hyperventilate. "You're going to find him, right?"

"Yes."

"He took him, didn't he?"

"Who?"

"Him. The killer. The person who has been targeting all the men in my life and killing them."

"It's a possibility. It's also a possibility that he's sleeping in his room upstairs because he's exhausted from this job."

Rebecca shook her head rapidly. "No. No. I told him. I told him he was going to be targeted, and he brushed me off. He told me everything would be fine, and you were going to catch the guy before anyone else was killed. And he was wrong. He was wrong."

She was sobbing by the time her rant was over, and Millie closed the gap between them, wrapping her in a tight hug.

"We will do everything we can to find him. We have time. What I need you to do is take some deep breaths for me."

Rebecca took in a deep, shuddering breath.

"Good. Now do that again."

She did it again. And again. Slowly, her breathing returned to normal.

Millie pulled back, placing his hands on her shoulders. "Losing your shit isn't going to help get Matty back. We all need level heads. We aren't one hundred percent sure about the current timeline, but we do know it's not huge."

"Agent Matty will be fine," Benji contributed from his spot on the couch.

Millie gestured toward the couch. "See, Benji has the optimism that we need."

"Nothing and no one can hurt him. I made sure before he left."

Rebecca turned slowly around until she was facing the couch. "What are you talking about, Benj?"

"You were so worried about him getting hurt. So, before he left, I sneaked my lucky coin into his back pocket. That way, he will be protected. I was very sneaky, so he doesn't know I don't have it. I don't want him to get angry with me, since he told me to always carry it with me."

Rebecca's mouth fell open. "Agent Matty has your lucky coin?"

"Yes. Please don't be upset, Mom. I wanted him to be safe, and he told me that whoever was carrying it would be safe."

She brought her hands up and covered her mouth.

"What lucky coin?" Millie asked from behind her.

"Agent Matty gave me a coin when he first got here because I was scared of the dangerous man. He told me to always carry it with me and it would protect me. Nothing bad would happen. So, I gave it to him last night before he left. Nothing can hurt him now."

Rebecca removed her hands from her mouth. "It's a tracker."

"What?"

She whirled around to face Millie again. "It's a tracker. Matthew had a tracker made just in case Benji was taken. He told Benji it was a lucky coin."

Millie waved her hand dismissively. "I know about the tracker. But you're telling me Matty currently has the tracker on him?"

"Yes."

"One that Trevor made for Benji."

"Yes."

Millie said nothing else. She turned and walked back out the door. Rebecca didn't hesitate. She followed her out. Behind her, she could hear Benji following along as well. She almost told him to go back and wait, but she would feel better if he were there with her. One person disappearing was enough for one night.

"Trevor, I need you to turn on that tracker you gave to little Mr. Clarke."

"Fuck, is he missing?" Trevor leaped up from the chair he was lounging in.

"No, but Matty is. And the young man had the forethought to plant his tracker on Matty before he left their apartment."

Trevor immediately grabbed his tablet and began tapping away.

Rebecca felt Benji wrap his arms around her waist and rest his head on her. She lifted her arm and wrapped it around his shoulders, bringing him in closer.

Everyone in the room waited with bated breath as Trevor worked on his tablet. The only sounds in the room were the tapping on the tablet and everyone breathing.

"I have him."

Rebecca felt her heart catch and her stomach clench in anticipation. *Please let him be okay*, she prayed.

"Where is he?" Thomas asked.

Trevor frowned and then looked up, his gaze seeking Rebecca's. "I'm so sorry."

"What do you mean? Why are you sorry?"

Trevor turned his tablet around so everyone could see the blinking dot on the map. "He's at your parents' house."

Rebecca shook her head. "What?"

The agents were already moving around, gathering what they needed, but she was still trying to understand. Why would he be at her parents' house?

Thomas came over and stopped in front of her. "Stay here with Benji. We're going to go rescue Matty."

As the agents rushed out of the door of the Noble Hill, that's when it finally hit her.

Matthew was at her parents', which meant her dad must be the killer.

Rebecca tightened her arms around Benji and let out an anguished cry.

Her dad was the killer, and he had killed Jaime.

And Andy.

And now he had Matthew.

Chapter Twenty-Nine

MATTHEW

Friday, May 29

Matthew stared at the man in front of him. Never would he have thought Guillermo Hernandez would be the man who they were looking for.

But then, when he thought about it, the man fit the profile.

He was a narcissist who needed everyone to like him.

He had a close relationship with Rebecca.

He had incredibly easy access to the trail in which the bodies were dumped, and a view of the dumping site from his window.

Matthew thought back to all the interactions he had previously had with the man. None of them were positive. The man treated Rebecca like shit. Like his property. He obviously emotionally abused his family, but Rebecca told him physical abuse was rare.

"Why?"

Guillermo laughed. "Why do you think? You're supposed to be smart. Brilliant. I've heard them talk about you. Your boss has gone out of his way the last two weeks to brag about your supposed genius. I think it was his way of trying to convince me you were good enough for my daughter. So, *genius*, why do *you* think I've done what I've done?"

Matthew stared at the man in front of him. The arrogance oozing from him. He was a man who knew he wouldn't be caught. That anything said in this room right now would not be leaving it. A man with nothing to lose was a dangerous thing.

"Well, I know your actions have something to do with Rebecca."

Guillermo laughed. "It doesn't take a fucking genius to figure that out, *gilipollas*. I've been around your room. I know you have that part figured out, at least. You've had it figured out for weeks."

Matthew's head was killing him, and it was preventing him from thinking clearly. Guillermo had access to their entire investigation. He had listened in on theories, to see how close they were to closing in on him. The fact that he was never on their list of suspects more than likely emboldened him, giving him the confidence to kill twice more since they had arrived in town.

In fact, the week since Toby's death had been the longest cooling down period since John Davies was killed on April 30. The working theory had been the killer had been spooked by the BAU gaining on him. But the truth was, he was just biding his time.

"We thought the UNSUB was killing because he wanted Rebecca for himself to form a romantic relationship. That he fantasized about him, Rebecca and Benji all being a family."

"Ah yes, but I'm her father and his *abuelo*. They are already part of my family. I already have what I want."

Matthew's brain worked its way through the evidence. What every victim had in common. They were all tied to Rebecca, but not romantically. Then he remembered what Rebecca had told him about what life was like before Jaime died.

"You killed Jaime because of his promotion."

"I didn't mean to kill him. It was happenstance that we ran into each other at the grocery store. We were just going to talk, say hi. But I had always planned to convince him to turn down the promotion and keep my family here. And if he wouldn't do that, maybe leave Rebecca and Benji here and move himself. I lured him away to talk in private. And when I broached the subject, he refused. He talked about love and how this job would improve their lives. He didn't give any thought about what her mother and I wanted. Our feelings."

"He shouldn't have to. Rebecca decided with him. She's an adult."

"She's my little girl!" Spit flew out of Guillermo's mouth with the force with which he screamed the words.

"And she will always be your little girl, but you have to let her go."

"No, I don't. And I told Jaime as much. We argued, and the next thing I knew, he was on the ground at my feet. Dead. I panicked. I was certain someone had seen us arguing. So, I made it look like he had a car crash. No one was the wiser, and my daughter and grandson didn't move away."

"What a fucking selfish thing to do."

"I did what I needed to do to preserve my family. When Rebecca went away for college, her mother was heartbroken. But at least she would come home for holidays, and we knew once she graduated, she would be home. But she brought *him* home with her. And they got married, and he took her away from us, but at least they still lived in town. But how dare he try to take her away permanently to another state?"

"You realize that not only is your daughter an adult, she is also not your property?"

Guillermo laughed. "Of course she's my property. She is my daughter."

Matthew shook his head and instantly regretted it as pain flashed through it. "So, you killed her husband because he was going to move her away. Why kill Mark Lovett and John Davies? They were married, and they had no romantic interest in Rebecca. You robbed other children of their fathers."

"They visited Rebecca in her apartment. With no chaperone. They were causing her to be a sinful whore."

Matthew was taken aback. "Wait, so your daughter can't be married to a man, nor can she be friends with one?"

"*Si*. Now you're understanding."

"No, I truly am not."

"That's because you're a godless heathen who is causing my daughter to sin. You wouldn't understand."

Matthew felt whiplash. "Wait, so if Rebecca is sinning by being with men alone in her apartment, aren't you also sinning by killing these men? Isn't one of the commandments, 'Thou Shall Not Kill'?"

"There is nuance to it. When the military goes to war, their kills are not sin because they are necessary. That's what I did. I have cleansed the world of men who wished to corrupt it."

"That's not your job. You don't get to decide who gets to live and who dies. God, who you profess to believe in, does. Based on your beliefs, everything you've said should be considered heretical."

"Fuck you. You're an atheist with no faith in God whatsoever because of your job, so you don't get to judge me and my actions. You don't know what you're talking about."

"How do you know that?"

"What?"

"That I'm an atheist because of my job? When we talked, I only told you I don't have any real religion. I've only talked about the specifics with Rebecca and Benji, and that doesn't seem like something she would share with you."

Matthew paused, and the answer came to him, and the realization made him feel sick to his stomach.

"Video or just sound?"

"What?"

"You monitoring in Rebecca and Benji's apartment, are you watching video or just listening in?"

Guillermo visibly recoiled.

Gotcha, Matthew perked up. He finally found something that caught the man off guard.

"So, which is it?"

Guillermo schooled his expression back to one of indifference, but Matthew got the first ounce of hope since waking up. He needed to keep finding ways to throw him off his guard. Then, he would make mistakes and give Matthew a chance to escape.

"I'm not watching my daughter's apartment. That would be a violation of her privacy."

So, we were going to straight up denial then. Got it.

Matthew tried to move his hands back and forth to loosen the knots on the rope that was holding him, but they still wouldn't budge. He tried not to fixate on that. He needed to call out Guillermo on his lie. But he needed to be delicate with the way he broached it. What needed to happen was for Guillermo to reveal himself in his lie.

"What about Andy?"

Guillermo narrowed his eyes. "What about him?"

"Did you kill him to rid the world of his sin?"

He barked out a laugh. "No, that was a convenient secondary result."

"Then what was the primary reason? Andy was gay, so he wasn't sleeping with your daughter or even had any romantic feelings toward her. What reason could you have possibly had other than his sexuality?"

"The same reason I had to kill that other outsider. He was going to take my Becks away from me. They were planning to leave together. I had to stop it."

It was Matthew's turn to be caught off guard. This was the first he was hearing about Andy and Rebecca's plans to leave Cove Creek. She never told him about that. If she hadn't told him, there's no way she would have told her father. They weren't close.

"Where were they planning to move?"

Guillermo shrugged. "No concrete plans. But they talked about it. The man also had the audacity to imply that my grandson was afraid of me. Just because he came at me with a Nerf bat once doesn't mean he was afraid of me. He loved me."

"He can love you and be afraid of you at the same time. Both things can be true."

"There is *no reason* for Benji to be afraid of me!"

"I don't know. The bruise on his mom's face a couple weeks ago is an excellent reason for him to be afraid of you, in my opinion."

"You speak of matters you don't understand."

"Oh, I think I understand perfectly well."

"Okay, genius, let's hear it."

Matthew sat himself up straighter in his chair. This was either going to be a power move or the stupidest fucking thing he's ever done. "You're a narcissist who gets off on being the most powerful man in the room. While you may have not physically abused your wife and daughter, you have certainly abused them emotionally. You are in the service industry because you love the attention it gives you, and running your own business gives you the power you crave.

"I don't think your reasons for killing all these men rest solely on the fact they were sinners in pursuit of your precious daughter. No, I think killing those men gave you the power you craved. You killed Jaime, and it gave you a high you never knew you needed, and you wanted more. Then, when you found a perceived slight against these other men, you took it. You needed to kill again, needed to get that feeling again. That high. And if my *genius* brain is correct, after you finished killing those men and dumping their bodies, you would come home and wake your wife up to fuck her because killing those men gave you the biggest—"

Pain shot through Matthew's jaw as Guillermo's fist contacted it.

"Shut your fucking mouth!"

Matthew's stomach dropped. The situation was escalating much quicker than he expected. He knew the man would have a short fuse, but he didn't realize how short the fuse would be. He had taken his share of punches over the years, but he had never taken the full force of one to the jaw while being unable to move or try to defend himself. That was definitely going to leave a mark.

"Did I say something you didn't like?"

"I've never liked you."

"Really? Never? Is it because you knew I would see right through you and you would be caught?"

"You come into *my* town, into *my* business, and you make eyes at *my* daughter. Thinking you can poison her mind against her family and convince her to move across the country. I thought you were a whim, a rebound, helping her realize what is really important. That you would leave here, and she would forget you. But tonight, she came into *my* house and told my wife and I that she was abandoning her family to follow a stranger to his home, and I knew I had to put a stop to it. I was going to just let you leave, but now I know I cannot."

Matthew frowned, at once regretting that decision when pain shot through his face. He had just seen Rebecca before Guillermo had abducted him. Her version sounded nothing like what he just told him. "I don't think that's what happened."

"Are you calling me a liar? You weren't even there!"

"I wasn't, but I talked to Rebecca, and I know the plans. They aren't planning to move with me, they're just planning to have a vacation to visit. Your daughter isn't even allowed to have a vacation?"

"It's not a vacation!" Guillermo screamed, spittle flying out of his mouth in Matthew's direction.

"It is. We've only been dating for two weeks. Don't you think that's a little fast for us to be moving in together?"

"You kids are always moving so fast. Rebecca and Jaime were married so young. I couldn't take the chance that she would make a mistake a second time."

"So, what's your plan? Any time your daughter becomes remotely interested in a man; you're going to kill him?"

Guillermo shrugged. "Yes."

"That doesn't sound sustainable."

"Eventually, Rebecca will simply stop bringing men around. She will have learned her lesson."

Something came over Matthew and, in that moment, all his training in negotiating with suspects went out of the window. That was the only way to explain why he said what he did next. "Good to know you're not only a fucking terrible human being...you're an even worse father."

Just like the earlier blow, Matthew didn't even see it coming before the fist contacted his face. In the same spot it had before. Except this time, Guillermo didn't stop after the first blow. He kept hitting him. Matthew felt when one blow broke his nose, the warm trickle of blood flowing down his face.

Even through the pain, the analytical part of his brain kicked in. The escalation of the beatings made sense now. Toby was beaten so severely because of the level of his threat to Rebecca.

When Guillermo stopped hitting him, Matthew didn't allow himself to relax. He was in so much pain. All he wanted to do was cry, but he knew that wouldn't be any help. Because he knew what came next. It was the same fate that befell all the other victims.

He just hoped some day in the future, Rebecca could forgive him for abandoning her.

Chapter Thirty

REBECCA

Friday, May 29

The second the BAU started running out the door, Rebecca had already decided she was going to follow them. Damn them and their demands. She couldn't sit here and wait, wonder.

Her father.

Her *father* was the man who killed all those people.

Killed Jaime.

Captured Matthew.

And would more than likely kill Matthew if they don't get there quick enough.

No. She couldn't sit here and wait. She needed to be there. See for herself the second they bring Matthew safely out of her parents' home.

She began moving toward the door, intent on following them.

"Mom?"

She stopped short.

Fuck.

Benji.

"Come on," she pulled her phone out of her pocket and dialed the number of someone who was on her way to her parents.

"Hello?"

"Julie?"

"Becks?"

"Can I drop Benji off at your place? Can you watch him for a while?"

"Of course. Is everything okay?"

Rebecca tried to swallow the sob working its way up her throat, but failed. "No. The shit has hit the fan, and I really need someone I trust watching Benji right now."

"Shit. When are you bringing him?"

"Right now."

"I'll be outside ready to meet him."

"Thank you, Julie. I owe you one."

She hung up the phone and gestured for Benji to climb into the backseat of the car.

"Where are we going?"

"I'm taking you to Ms. Boyle. She's going to watch you for a couple hours."

"Where are you going?"

Silence filled the car as Rebecca tried to think of something to tell Benji. She didn't want to tell him the truth. He would worry. But she also didn't want to lie to him.

"I need to make sure—"

"You're going to go save Agent Matty, aren't you?"

Rebecca sighed. "I am."

"Please don't go."

"I can't just sit around and wait. I need to do something."

"You would be doing something. You would be taking care of me."

He was right. She knew he was right, but even then, she knew she couldn't simply sit on the sidelines.

"You will be safe with Ms. Boyle."

"What about you? Will you be safe?"

"Yes."

"How do you know?"

"I just know. I know I will be safe."

A small sob echoed through the car from the backseat. "What if you don't come home? Where will I live?"

Rebecca moved her gaze to the rear-view mirror, looking for Benji's. She caught his and held it in the mirror. "I will come home." She enunciated each word, making it clear to him. Making sure he understood what she was saying. No room for misinterpretation.

Benji's sobs subsided into sniffles. "I will pray the rosary the whole time you're gone. And I will ask Dad to watch over you and make sure you come home."

"Do you talk to Dad a lot?"

She caught him nodding in the mirror. "All the time. I asked him if it was okay for me to like Agent Matty. If it was okay for me to want him to be my step-dad."

"Benji—"

"He told me it was okay."

"What?"

"He told me it was okay."

"He talks back?"

"He came to me in my dream. He told me he already let you know it was okay to move on. That he wanted us to be happy, and he knew that I still loved him. He didn't think Agent Matty was replacing him, but he knew he would take care of us. He was what we needed."

Tears sprung to Rebecca's eyes, and she didn't even bother to hold them back. "I'm so happy you could have that conversation with your father."

"Did he visit you in your dream?"

Rebecca shook her head. "No, but he communicates with me in different ways. You're *so* lucky you got to see him and talk to him. So. Lucky."

She took the turn into Julie's driveway. As promised, she was standing out in the driveway, waiting for them. Rebecca put the car into park but left the car running. She unbelted herself and turned to look at Benji.

"I love you. So much. And I will see you soon."

Benji launched himself at her through the center console of the car. He wrapped his arms around her neck, squeezing her tight. "I love you, too."

They held each other for a minute longer before they pulled away from each other. Benji opened the door and hopped out. He moved quickly to Julie, who wrapped her arms around him, holding him close to her body.

Rebecca was frozen in place. Maybe Benji was right. Maybe this is where she should be. She should stay here with Benji and wait for the BAU to contact her and tell her that everything was fine. There was no reason she should go to her parents' house. What good would it do? She would just be stuck outside. And what if they were too late and Matthew was dead? Did she really want to see that?

She brought her gaze up to meet Julie's. Keeping her arm around Benji, Julie nodded her head at her and mouthed the word, "Go."

Rebecca took a deep breath and threw the car into reverse, backing out of Julie's driveway. As she drove off, she kept her eyes on Julie and Benji until she couldn't see them anymore.

As she drove the short distance to her parents' house, she could feel her heart beating so fast it was quite possible it was going to beat its way out of her chest.

This was so reckless.

It wasn't a very long drive to the house, and as she neared, she could see the barricade already set up. They created a wide perimeter, blocking off access to the entire street. Local police and the BAU were set up at the beginning of the barricade and they were all suited up in Kevlar vests and sidearms.

She pulled over onto a side street and parked her car. Taking a deep breath, she pushed open the door of her car and stepped out into the muggy air.

The sun was setting, casting everything in shadows. Rebecca approached the barricade, squaring her shoulders. She needed to give the appearance of being confident, even though everything in her body was telling her to turn around and go the other way.

"Rebecca?" Millie walked over to her, concern etched on her face. "What the hell are you doing here? Where's Benji?"

"He's with a friend. What's going on?"

"You need to go home. Or to your friend's home. Anywhere but here."

She shook her head. "I can't simply walk away. I need to be here."

Millie sighed. "I know anything I saw won't sway you, so you can stay, but you *need* to stay here."

"Where's my mom?"

"As far as we are concerned, she is in the house. We are treating her as a possible hostage until we know otherwise. We have everything under control. You're a civilian, and we really need you to stay out of the way, so we don't have to worry about you, too. Please."

Giving Rebecca one more sympathetic look, Millie turned around and walked back to the rest of the group, leaving Rebecca standing on the wrong side of the barricade and too far to do anything.

Looking around, Rebecca tried to decide what she should do. She didn't come over here and leave her child to stand here and be useless.

She had told herself that just being here was enough, but now that she was here, it really wasn't. Standing here and watching the chaos that had flocked to her parents' quiet neighborhood, the neighborhood she had lived in with Jaime and Benji.

Her dad did this. Brought this nightmare into their town.

She squared her shoulders and turned from the barricade. Having lived in this neighborhood, she knew it like the back of her hand. Leaving her car where it was parked, Rebecca moved swiftly toward the entrance to Murphy's Woods. She knew exactly where she could enter from the trail that would lead her directly into her parents' yard.

The sun was quickly setting, and Rebecca was losing light. She needed to move quickly unless she wanted to be doing this in the dark. As soon as she was out of sight from the barricade, she broke into a run. She was in a race against the sun, and she would not let the sun win.

Rebecca jogged the short distance to the entrance to the woods. She bared left and made her way up the paved pathway. She was honestly surprised no one was out here trying to come in from behind. Maybe they didn't know?

Matthew would have known. He knew everything, and he was very familiar with the makeup of Murphy's Woods, since that was the site where all the bodies had been dumped. It was about five hundred feet from the entrance of the woods to where her parents' house was. As soon as she saw the trees she knew marked the back of her parents' property, she bared left again, wading into the tall grasses. Briefly she regretted wearing shorts, but she would happily deal with the poison ivy rash later. What mattered was getting to Matthew before her dad killed him.

As she neared the property line, she was thankful her parents had never fenced in the backyard, relying on the natural boundary of trees to keep people off their property. She dashed behind one of the trees, pressing her back against the rough bark of the tree. She took a minute to catch her breath. Once her heart rate slowed close to normal, she turned herself, so her front was pressed against the tree. Quickly, she glanced around making sure her instincts were correct. There were no BAU agents or police officers back here. They were all focused on the front.

Rebecca took a deep breath, focusing herself. She locked her gaze on the back door of her house. The door led into the back part of the kitchen where the door to the basement was located. It was a straight shot, and her parents never locked it. Well, usually her parents never locked it. She made the sign of the cross and said a quick prayer that was still the case before dashing across the yard to the house.

It took her seconds to reach the house, her hand coming in contact with the handle of the door and turning it. It was unlocked and she let out a quiet thanks as she let herself in.

Inside the house, she heard the sound of the television being blasted from the family room. Her mother watching some program on HGTV, completely oblivious to what was happening in her house and her neighborhood.

As quietly as she could, she walked across the floor to the door of the basement. Her hand touched the knob, and she paused.

"Please let him be alive," she whispered.

Bracing herself for the worst, she pushed down on the door handle and pulled the door open. The basement was illuminated by a light, signaling someone was down there.

Was she making a mistake? This was a terrible idea. She should really turn around and go back out and wait by the barricade like the BAU told her to do.

"Argh." The scream came after the sound of something making contact. She couldn't tell if it was a weapon or a fist.

Without stopping to think, Rebecca allowed her feet to carry her down the stairs into the basement. She rounded the corner and stopped short.

Her father was standing with his back to her. He was facing Matthew, who was tied to a chair. Her father's hands were wrapped around a baseball bat, which he held in front of him as if he had just completed a swing. He was panting.

Matthew's head was hanging loosely by the neck, blood dripping down onto his white shirt. The low groaning emanating from him the only sign he was still conscious, but just barely.

Guillermo swung the bat back up into position as if he was going to make contact with Matthew again.

"Stop!" her scream echoed through the basement, causing her father to swing around.

"Rebecca?"

"Dad. Stop."

"What are you doing here?"

Rebecca kept her gaze on Matthew, who was trying to raise his head to look at her but was failing. "I came to stop you."

"How did you even know?"

"The BAU figured it out after you took Matthew."

"You need to leave. I don't want you to see this."

"You think I'm just going to walk out of here knowing that you're going to kill my boyfriend?"

"Yes."

Rebecca let out a bitter laugh. "What on earth makes you believe that?"

"Because I am your father, and you will obey me."

Rebecca shook her head and pulled out her phone. She opened up the recording app and pressed it to start.

"What are you doing?"

"Calling the police to tell them where to find you."

"You would betray your father?"

"You killed my husband!"

"He was going to take you away from me. I had to stop him."

"And the rest of them? What is your excuse for them?"

"They were corrupting you. They didn't deserve to live."

Rebecca didn't even bother to stop her tears. Her father needed to see her emotions. "And Matthew?"

"Same as Jaime."

She shook her head. "You're a monster."

Guillermo raised his lips into a smirk. "I'm your father."

Rebecca took her gaze off of her father and moved it to Matthew. He had lifted his head and looked at her, and the sight of him took her breath away. His face had been so abused, one of his eyes was swollen completely and the other was barely holding open. His mouth was trying to move, but he was failing.

Rebecca swung her gaze back to her father. "Let. Him. Go."

Guillermo laughed. "Go home. Go back to your son. This is none of your concern."

"Let. Him. Go," she ground out through clenched teeth.

"*Mija*, I don't want to hurt you. Go. Home."

"You would hurt your own daughter?"

"If it meant not getting caught."

"Does mom know?"

"What?"

"Does mom know you're the killer?"

He shook his head. "She does not."

"Did you kill them all here?"

This time, he nodded.

"And she still doesn't know?"

"She listens to her television loudly."

Rebecca shook her head. "I don't understand how you could take the lives of all these people."

"It was easy. They were wronging me, so I put a stop to it."

"Daddy, please let Matthew go. I love him."

"That's exactly why I won't be letting him go."

Guillermo turned around, putting his back toward Rebeca. He put his bat back into position, ready to swing it at Matthew again, completely ignoring her.

What was taking the BAU and the police so long? They should have come in here by now. They were wasting so much time in the street.

Right as Guillermo brought his arms back to swing the bat, Rebecca made a run for it. She grabbed onto her father's arm, stopping him from completing the swing.

"Fuck!" he screamed, trying to shake her off, but failing. She had wrapped her arms around his, hugging it to her body, trying to get him to drop the bat.

He shook his arm, trying to free himself, and she held on tighter. She was feeling a little smug about her success until the blow came to her head, causing her to loosen her grip on his arm. While her head still spun from her dad hitting her with his spare arm, he took advantage of the situation and peeled her off his arm and threw her to the floor.

Rebecca hit the concrete floor hard, pain shooting up her right hip from where she hit the ground. She quickly flipped over onto her back, pushing through the pain. Pressing her arms to the ground, she tried to push her body up. Lifting her head, she saw her father looming over her, the bat raised.

"Dad?"

"I'm sorry."

Rebecca brought her arms up, bracing herself for the impact. Instead, a loud bang echoed through the basement.

Above her, her father's face was frozen in shock, before he slumped over, collapsing on the floor, a spot of red blooming on the front of his shirt.

Rebecca screamed.

She felt arms wrap around her, pulling her into a tight hug. Only then did she realize she was shaking.

"You're okay," Millie murmured into her ear as she held her tight. "You're safe. Matty is safe."

Rebecca never removed her gaze from her father, who was lying still on the ground, staring blankly at her.

She knew people were flowing into the room, but all she could focus on was her dad and the mixed feelings she felt at his demise.

Chapter Thirty-One

MATTHEW

Sunday, May 31

Matthew stood outside the door of an unfamiliar house. It was the home of one of Rebecca's coworkers and friends. She had been staying with her since the incident with her father two nights ago.

He hadn't had a chance to see her since the BAU had stormed the basement and rescued them. Between his stint in the hospital and giving his statement, he had been busy wrapping up the case. He had never been part of the wrapping up of a case from the victim's side before, and he hoped he never would again.

Luckily, Guillermo hadn't seriously injured him. Matthew had a minor concussion, and he didn't look pretty, but he was lucky. They credited Rebecca arriving when she did with saving his life.

Rebecca.

She had been reprimanded for going against orders and sneaking in the back of the house before the BAU could get in there. At the same time, they were hailing her as a hero, risking everything, confronting her dad, and ultimately saving him.

Matthew was eager to see her and ask her how she was holding up. He knew firsthand how horrible it was to watch your parent die in front of you. However, his mom wasn't killing his spouse and friends when she died. She also wasn't an abusive narcissist. He could only imagine the mix of feelings whirling inside her right now.

Finally, he reached forward and pushed the doorbell. The door opened immediately, as if Rebecca had been waiting right by it, anticipating his arrival.

She was sporting a black eye but looked otherwise healthy. She flung herself into his arms.

He brought his arms around her, holding her tightly against him. Her body trembled with her sobs, and he ran his hands along her back in soothing circles.

"I've been wanting to do this since Friday, but they wouldn't let me see you," she whispered into his chest.

"Same. I'm sorry it took so long to get over here. The doctors wanted to monitor me to see how serious my concussion was."

"I'm so sorry."

Matthew took a step back, bringing his hand to her face, running his thumb on her cheek. "Why are you sorry?"

"Because my dad did this to you. He kidnapped you and tried to kill you because of me."

"Not because of you. I don't want you to think you're responsible for your father's actions. He did this on his own. He is the only one to blame. You are just as much a victim as I am. Never forget that. Never."

Rebecca sucked her lips into her mouth, and Matthew knew that whatever he said now wouldn't fix everything. They were going to have to work through a lot of stuff. And he hoped they would work through those things together.

"Do you want to come inside?"

Matthew nodded.

Rebecca took a step back, turning toward the interior of the house. She took his hand and led him into her friend's house. The house was quiet but for the soft sound of the television coming from somewhere in the back.

Rebecca led him to the couch and sat him down. She moved in front of him, stepping in between his legs. Matthew rested his hands on her waist as she slid her hands, so she was cupping his face, lifting it up to inspect it. Leaning forward, she placed a soft kiss on his forehead.

"How are you feeling?" she asked as she pulled back.

"Very sore, but rotating ibuprofen and acetaminophen really helps dull the pain. Mild concussion, so I'm lucky."

Rebecca brushed her thumb along his jawline. "I'm so happy I didn't listen to your boss and stay put. I don't even want to think about what would have happened if I didn't."

"You came in at the right time. Your father had just picked up the bat and had done a practice swing against the chair to scare me. My injuries would have been much worse if he had actually contacted my body."

"Who shot him?"

"Millie."

Rebecca nodded. "I had a feeling it was her. She was the first person I saw. She comforted me."

"She saw you on the floor with your dad lifting the bat above your head, and she acted."

Rebecca gave him a small smile. "She already came by to check on me, while you were still in the hospital. She never came out and said she was the one who shot him, but she did apologize. I told her no apology was needed. My feelings about the situation are...mixed."

Matthew nodded gravely. "As expected."

"And I want to talk to you about it, and have you use your mind magic on me, but I don't think I'm ready right now."

"I'm here for whenever you are. I love you."

"I love you, too."

Matthew wrapped his arms around Rebecca's waist, pulling her closer to him so he could rest his head against her stomach. Rebecca wrapped her arms around him, holding him close. Closing his eyes, he breathed in her scent and was immediately calm. A lot of his pent-up anxiety about coming here melting away knowing she still loved him, still wanted to be with him, after everything.

"Agent Matty!"

Benji came running into the room before flying onto the couch next to him. He wrapped his arms around his neck and pulled him into a hug.

"Benji, careful."

Benji immediately backed off, scooting back to move away from him, but Matthew reached out and pulled him back, wrapping his left arm around him, pulling him into his chest. Benji rested his head on his chest and wrapped his arms around his torso.

"I heard I have you to thank for my rescue."

Benji nodded against his chest. "Please don't be mad that I gave you my lucky coin and didn't keep it with me at all times. But I thought it would keep you safe."

"I'm not mad. I'm so, *so* thankful. I'm alive right now, because of you. You did good, Benji."

"I love you, Matty," Benji whispered against his chest.

Tears sprung to his eyes. Benji had never told him that before. His heart swelled. "I love you, too. So much."

Rebecca moved around and settled on his other side on the couch. Matthew took her hand in his and she rested her head on his shoulder.

If you had asked him before he left for this case two weeks ago if he saw himself having a family someday, he would have laughed. There's no way he would have dreamed he could let someone into his life like this.

What a fool he had been. His life was so much fuller now that he had Rebecca and Benji in it. And he knew things would only get better as he continued to let his coworkers into his life and actually allowed them to be his friends.

Matthew leaned his head against the back of the couch, tilting it so his cheek rested against Rebecca's head. He flinched as Benji arranged himself on his chest, but the pain was a minor thing to bear.

He was so happy.

Who knew what the future would bring, but that wasn't something for him to think about now. He would happily live in the moment, with his family.

Epilogue

MATTHEW

THREE MONTHS LATER

"This is the room where you'll hang out on the days I have to pick you up from school," Matthew pointed into a rarely used conference room.

Benji was standing right next to him and nodding his head.

"My office is right across the hall, so if you need anything, you won't have to go very far."

"And it'll only be once a week, probably. When I have other duties," Rebecca was standing at his other side, peering into the office.

The two of them had come down mid-June to visit, and it was during that trip Rebecca and Benji agreed that maybe a change of scenery was necessary. They both loved the city. It was completely different than where they were from, and the best thing was there were no reminders of everything that they had gone through and lost.

It didn't take a lot of conversations between Rebecca and Matthew to finalize the decision to move. They had only been long distance for about two weeks, but it was the longest two weeks of his life. It just wasn't the same, and he missed them. They missed him, too.

It didn't take long for Rebecca to find a new job and enroll Benji into a new school, and the three of them were living together by the end of August.

"And I would just do my homework?"

"Yeah."

"What if I don't have any homework?"

"I can put a TV in here and a Switch dock?" Matthew looked over at Rebecca for approval. She was trying to encourage him to take a more active role in parenting, but he was still nervous about making the wrong choices. Rebecca gave him a subtle nod.

"Really?"

"Sure. But I'll keep the Switch in my office, and you'll only get it if you're finished with your homework."

"Of course," Benji agreed easily. He leaned around Matthew to speak to his mother. "Mom, can Matty pick me up from school a lot?"

Rebecca laughed. "We'll see. Remember, he travels for his job."

He had traveled once since closing the case in Iowa, and that was for a short consultation trip. He was hoping he would stay put in town through the first part of the school year to help Rebecca and Benji adjust.

"I know he does, but when he's not?"

"I don't know..."

"Let's try once a week, and we can go from there." Matthew put his arm around Benji's shoulders and pulled him close.

Matthew thought about the ring he had at home in his office drawer. He had confided in Jorge, his Uber driver, on the way back home after his last trip that he was anxious to take the next step and make his little family official. Jorge was the only person he knew who wouldn't blab to Rebecca. A neutral third party, if it were.

He and Rebecca had already had a few conversations about marriage and the possibility of adopting Benji, but he wanted to formally ask them both.

He hoped they would say yes.

"Motherfucker!"

The exclamation down the hall had Matthew throwing earmuffs on Benji and looking apologetically at Rebecca.

She gestured with her head toward the outburst. "Go. See what's wrong. I'll take him down to see where the cafeteria is."

"There's a cafeteria?!" Benji looked up at his mother with wide eyes.

"Yes, and you'll have a special allowance to spend there. We'll talk about it on the way there."

Rebecca leaned up and gave Matthew a quick kiss before taking his hand and leading him away toward the cafeteria.

Matthew watched them walk away before turning around and walking in the direction he heard the outburst.

He got to Thomas's office at the same time as the rest of the team.

"What happened?" he asked.

Everyone sort of shrugged.

Thomas was staring down at his phone, his eyes wide, his mouth slightly open. Whatever he was looking at was making him shake his head.

"Thomas?" Matthew asked.

"Matthew, remember what we talked about in Iowa?"

Matthew shook his head. They had talked about a lot of things in Iowa, but he didn't know what Thomas could be referring to. And then it hit him.

"Fuck. Did it escalate?"

"Did what escalate?" Logan piped up from across the room.

"Yeah, fill the rest of us in," Trevor said.

Thomas looked up from his phone and cleared his throat. "For the last couple months, I've been getting text messages from burner phones and spoofed numbers. They're all from someone taunting me. Telling me they will be the next great serial killer and we will never be able to catch them. The texts have been harmless descriptions of crimes they could commit."

"Until now," Matthew interrupted.

"Until now," Thomas confirmed.

He turned on the screen in his room and messed with his phone. Soon, projected on the screen, was the picture of a woman. She had been stabbed multiple times, and it appeared she had also been strangled. She was placed haphazardly on the ground near a dumpster. Leaning against her body was a single rhododendron. Scrawled on the dumpster in her blood were the words, *Catch me if you can.*

CHECK OUT THESE OTHER AMAZING TITLES FROM ROWAN PROSE:

Stephanie R. Caffrey is a romantic suspense author who lives with her family in the Midwest. When she's not working on her books, she's a substitute teacher, and loves to write fanfiction. She is a proud marginalized voice in the Mexican-American community. Besides writing, she enjoys sewing, knitting, and cross stitching.

www.srcaffrey.com